CREATING

CHANCE

by

Valerie Knupp

OTHER BOOKS BY VALERIE KNUPP

Restoring Hope – The Jack Tyler Series Vol. 1
Finding Faith – The Jack Tyler Series Vol. 2

Available on Amazon.com for Kindle or in paperback

www.thrillersbyknupp.com

Dedication

Fam-i-ly

Noun - a group consisting of parents and children living together in a household.

       Lorea, Maima, and Akins, we are so much more than what is described in this definition. I dedicate this third and final book in the Jack Tyler series to each of you, because without your support I could never have gotten through this incredible journey.

       We are family, and to me the real definition means that we stand strong in the face of anything and everything. We protect our home like a fortress that holds our love, and we trust in each other even in the face of fear, anger, or hurt.

Trust

Noun – firm belief in the reliability, truth, ability, or strength of someone or something.

       To me the above better describes our very special family. I love you all very much!

ISBN-10:0-9899029-2-7
ISBN 13: 978-0-9899029-2-2

Printed in the United States of America

Prologue

He stood looking at himself in the mirror. A smile crept up at the corners of his mouth. The doctor had done a fine job. A fine job indeed! The past three months had been spent healing. He had driven straight through from Springfield, IL to Scottsdale, AZ only stopping for gas, food, and ice.

It hadn't taken him too long to decide where to go. Scottsdale was certainly the perfect place to recover. Facial scars were not all that uncommon to elite residents and starlets undercover. Those who were so vain they felt compelled to stretch, nip, tuck, and pull at sagging skin. Skin drooping from age and sun, offended by close up cameras. Vanity had nothing to do with his reason for the change. Oh no, vanity was the last thing that drove him. Protecting his family was his only concern. He had to protect them. Keeping them together was his only motivation.

After arriving in Scottsdale he arranged for a three month lease in a house common for those seeking refuge during recovery. The accommodations included everything one could want. He arranged for groceries to be delivered as frequently as desired. At first the only thing he was lacking was a freezer. He made arrangements for one to be delivered, nothing elaborate this time. He couldn't risk it, just a simple deep freezer that could be stored in the garage. He didn't like it, but he quickly and frequently reminded himself that it was temporary and that the only thing that mattered was that he remained with his family.

For the three months he stayed mostly inside, except for spending time on the private patio. He spent many days next to the pool while sipping cold tea, wine, or the occasional Coke Zero.

Now looking in the mirror he knew it was time to move on. The scars were healed, and his new look was complete. He was pleased that the work, though extensive, was good. The raised cheekbones, widened forehead, and cleft chin had not taken away from the natural good looks that had always aided him. More importantly, with his new look he was not recognizable. The man that had gained unfortunate notoriety no longer existed.

In recent days he'd reached out to his contact in Los Angeles and gained access to another new identity. Additionally, he'd requested two new spares, just in case he needed them later. He knew one can never be too careful.

"So sorry to disappoint you, Agent Maxine Nichols," he said out loud as he continued to admire his new look in the mirror. Laughter exploded out of his perfectly re-shaped mouth.

Chapter One

Special Agent Maxine Nichols returned to Virginia after, once again, being unsuccessful in apprehending Dr. Jack Tyler. Since her return she had been assigned to a cargo theft case. There were millions of dollars in pharmaceuticals being stolen, and following each robbery the thieves seemingly vaporized into the night. They were highly efficient and capable of taking a tractor trailer rig in just seconds from a truck stop parking lot or distribution center. The operation was big and growing. The money from the drugs was then used to fund other activities like buying weapons.

The assignment was interesting and certainly something different from anything Max had worked on before, but in the back of her mind there was always the nagging feeling that she had missed something that could be the single piece of evidence that would lead her directly to Dr. Jack Tyler. An absolute professional, Max always worked her cases with purpose and drive. But her own time was dedicated to finding Tyler.

Upon returning from Illinois after finding the body of the cosmetic surgeon, Tyler's most recent victim, her relationship with fellow FBI agent Mark Wells had only deepened. They weren't working the same case right now, and at times their schedules were not in sync. But what time they did have together was intense, yet peaceful. Their love was growing, and Max was beginning to really envision a future with Mark. It was a strange reality for her to allow her mind to picture a future that included more than her career.

***

It was late at night, and Max sat with her feet in Mark's lap as they each respectively read through files and drank wine. Mark's current assignment was a pedophile case, and she knew it was weighing heavily on his mind. Tonight though, they both were scouring over the Jack Tyler files. Mark wanted to apprehend Tyler as much as she did.

It was odd to think that Tyler had actually brought the two together. Max remembered the instant attraction between them when Mark had come to Los Angeles to help provide a profile on a serial murder case she was leading. She was an LAPD detective then, and they spent long hours over a couple of days working through the case files. It was then that she started to fall for him.

Mark had to return to Quantico after delivering the profile. He left after a single night filled with passion. Months passed before they would be reunited when the profile they had developed had actually helped lead them to new murders in Illinois. Despite every effort to avoid getting close to him again, she found herself back in his arms.

Now she looked at him and rubbed her foot down his thigh, garnering a quick smile across his strong face. His deep blue eyes settled on the green of hers, and without saying a word they both chuckled. The comfort she felt in his presence was certain. Pushing a thick, auburn lock of hair back behind her ear, she returned her focus on the file in her lap.

Tyler's case was considered cold thirty days ago, and resources were pulled back. As a FBI most-wanted serial killer in multiple states, Tyler had effectively slipped through their fingers twice. A master of deception and a psychopath with narcissistic characteristics, he had proven to be unstoppable thus far.

Max removed her feet from Mark's legs and swung her feet to the floor to stand and stretch. She could feel Mark's eyes watching her as she left the room. She made her way down the hall and went and pulled a white sheet from the closet. She walked to the office and grabbed a small plastic cup containing pushpins and a roll of tape. She returned to the living room dragging the sheet behind her.

4

Mark looked at her, and she could tell by the look on his face he knew exactly what she was thinking. She pulled the love seat away from the wall then pulled a chair from the dining room table to stand on.

Mark laid to the side the file he'd been looking through and stood up. "Need a hand?" he asked smiling, taking one edge of the sheet.

"Sure," Max smiled. Her eyes connected with his again.

She was not sure what he would think and silently feared he might chastise her for falling into her former habits. Mark had not always supported the unconventional way Max would work a case. On more than one occasion, Max had used her living room wall as what was called a murder board. She lined the room with a white sheet and laid out the facts of the case by the order of events, displaying each detail of the grisly events. Then using the facts she would look for links, trends, and any missing elements that might help lead her to the killer. In this case Jack Tyler.

When Dr. Jack Tyler, a once prominent and well respected surgeon, killed six people in Los Angeles and buried them in shallow graves in the Malibu canyon hills, she used her living room to narrow possible locations where he had potentially relocated. His killing signature resurfaced in a burial site just outside Tulsa in the rural outskirts of a small town called Inola. Tulsa had been one of the top three locations Max had narrowed in on by using her living room wall murder board process.

She wasn't sure what else to do, but she knew she couldn't just keep looking at the files. With Mark's help, and after exchanging a knowing look, a few minutes later they had successfully hung the sheet on the wall to create a canvas for the murder board.

For the next hour, they pasted photos and created a timeline. When they were done they stood arm in arm looking at the morbid reality of the carnage Jack Tyler had left behind in his troubled wake.

The murdered included six in California, six more in Oklahoma, and five in Illinois. The last five slain included three young girls. The lives were all lost in the midst of Tyler trying to reinvent his family. Tyler's wife and daughter were killed in a car accident in California. Tyler began to fragment on that day.

Though they had never seen it, both of the agents believed that Tyler had used parts from his many victims to create replications of his dead wife and daughter. The evidence recovered indicated that he was using some crazy formula of chemicals to preserve the body through a mixture of embalming, taxidermy, and cryonics. Neither one of them knew how long the concoction would last, but Max feared that Jack would start all over if his formula failed.

Max also knew that they needed to find a lead somewhere in the middle of the evidence or from within the case documents accumulated during the investigations. She was certain Tyler no longer looked like Dr. Jack Tyler, given that his last victim had been a cosmetic surgeon who specialized in a wide variety of plastic surgery, and she knew this was going to make apprehending him even more difficult.

Just before leaving the trail cold Tyler contacted Max, taunting her as he'd done on a few other occasions. He told her that he could sit next to her on the bus or plane, and she wouldn't even recognize him. Max believed him and realized that they were going to have to outsmart him if they were going to catch him. And so far outsmarting Jack had proven to be quite difficult.

Chapter Two

       Even though it was only late March it was already getting warm in the desert. Realizing the freezer could not travel with movers for two or three days in the heat. He also knew he couldn't trust the contents with anyone else. Jack decided renting a U-Haul truck for his precious cargo was the only way.

       He needed to get to his destination quickly. He planned to drive straight through. The journey was just over four hundred and fifty miles. It would take over seven hours to make the drive, and that was with minimal stops. Thinking about it he figured it would likely take him eight or nine hours. He wasn't really looking forward to the drive, but the reward at the other end was going to be well worth it.

       Jack took a few minutes to perform a final walk through of the rental home and before leaving placed the keys on the counter as the landlord had asked. Locking the door behind him, he stepped outside and double checked the hitch on the U-Haul to make sure the tow for his van was secure before pulling away.

       He hadn't been out much since coming to Scottsdale, thus allowing his face to heal and ensuring he was not detected. As he navigated his way through the city streets out to the highway he saw the signs for Phoenix. He remembered his in-laws and wondered how they were doing. He knew Hope would love to see her sister Mindy, but well, that just wasn't possible. The thoughts suddenly made him feel melancholy.

       Mindy had tried to come around right after the…accident, but he shut her out. He wanted nothing to do with her. She seemed genuinely concerned for his welfare, but when they were kids he never fully trusted her. She always seemed distant with him, and after the accident he was in no frame of mind to deal with family.

Even with all of his reservations about Mindy he couldn't help wondering how she and her family were doing. As he was passing through Phoenix he saw the exit that he and Hope had taken so many times when they'd gone to visit for the holidays or a long weekend. Hope adored Mindy. They were very close in age and often times were mistaken for twins. The visits to Mindy's house were always pleasant, and Jack found himself trying to remember why he ever distrusted her. Hope always told him he was just imagining things. With Phoenix growing in the distance he considered if she'd always been right.

The time spent driving went quickly despite the somber mood that had filled him as he left the Phoenix area. His feelings were further tormented when he found himself wishing his wife and daughter could ride in the front with him.

Crossing into California, Jack immediately felt his emotions begin to lighten. Jack pulled out of Arizona at just after two o'clock. The sun set before he crossed into California, but he never minded driving in the dark. He could almost feel the ocean breeze and the mountain air and was very excited to return to his home. It'd been far too long, and there were a few things he needed to know.

He imagined driving up into the Malibu Canyon, but immediately realized that was a very bad idea. Besides, there was nothing there anymore. He knew Agent Maxine Nichols had destroyed the site. He shrugged reminding himself that as long as he had his family none of that mattered. All he'd ever needed was Hope. She'd proven that to him so many years ago.

Feeling much better now Jack turned on the radio. He flipped through the presets until he landed on a song that was familiar and hummed along. Soon the city lights were an endless glow as city after city flew past him. He'd chosen to take Highway 134 to avoid any late night traffic on the freeways and finally was pulling through Santa Paula. The orange groves passed by, and Jack lowered his window to enjoy the fragrant air. Ahhh… yes, he was home. Well, he would be in less than an hour.

As he passed through Ventura, he could see the white caps of the ocean waves crashing near the pier. He finally made his way up the mountain road, gliding on the pavement in the dark through Oakview and finally pulling into the small quaint town of Ojai. His heart raced as he stopped at the light on Main Street. He wasn't expecting his feelings to be so conflicted.

He both felt elation and anguish all at the same time as he made the necessary turns along the all too familiar path. Even though it had been years since he had been here the vehicle seemed to know its way without any assistance. He followed the curve of the driveway just past midnight and sat staring through the darkness at the large house.

While in Scottsdale, Jack worked for weeks negotiating the purchase of the home in Ojai…his home. Returning to the place where everything began with Hope somehow made perfect sense.

For years all he'd ever wanted to do was leave this place, and now suddenly it seemed the only place he could possibly be. He could change things. With Hope he could do anything, and raising Faith here could take the demons away. He knew it was true. Certain it was the only way he looked forward to his new life.

Getting out of the vehicle, he approached the porch and inserted the key he'd already put on his key ring. The tumbler turned, and the door clicked open. He took a deep breath and stepped inside.

10

Chapter Three

Any evening that Mark's assignment drove a schedule that did not align to hers, Max spent the time combing through files, creating individual searches, and even working unusual possible scenarios.

Mark was still assigned to a serial pedophile case, and it was certainly taking its toll on him. She didn't know much of his case, but she was aware that a young boy's mother had arranged the sale of her son to a middle man known for selling children to pedophiles. Mark was working nearly twenty-four hours a day trying to find the boy before the pedophile took possession of the child and hurt him or before the boy disappeared for good.

Mark would occasionally wrestle around in his sleep, waking sweaty and out of breath. It wasn't like him. The man she knew was always strong and composed. She was beginning to worry. The case seemed to be getting into his head. He seemed to be falling into the trap he always warned her not to allow happen. "Don't let Jack get into your head, Max," he would say. She knew she was going to need to talk to him soon if he continued to struggle. She hoped they would catch the un-sub quickly. Then his mind could rest again.

Max decided she'd give him just a little more time, trusting him to manage through the case and whatever demons he was fighting. But she planned on keeping a close eye on him and would be there for him when he was ready to talk.

Turning her focus back to Jack Tyler, she realized that she needed some resources, and she didn't have permission to use the FBI databases to work on Tyler's case on her own time. She also had yet to build relationships with people working in data jobs. Being a fairly new graduate still in her first year she had not yet proven herself, or made the tight connections that she could reach out to when she wanted to look into something outside of her existing case.

Oh, sure there was a certain amount of granted respect just from having graduated the FBI Academy, but that alone was not enough to gain access to systems and tools or even people who would be willing to help on what was right now considered an inactive case.

She had an idea. Picking up the phone, she dialed a familiar Los Angeles number and waited half expecting voicemail to pick up. She was pleasantly surprised when she heard a familiar voice.

"Max? Everything okay?" Cortez asked.

"Hey, Lorraine, yes, everything's fine, just hoping to get some help," Max replied to her friend and old LAPD partner.

She and Detective Cortez were partners when Max first started working the Jack Tyler case while she was still a Detective in Los Angeles, California. The two women spent weeks studying the case files in Max's living room. They would sit around on Friday nights when they weren't working, drink wine, and stare at the sheet extended across the wall that contained the photos and case facts. It was on one of those Friday nights they had narrowed the cities that would be likely places for Jack to relocate. Sure enough, several months later one of the top three cities—Tulsa—was where Jack ended up and continued his killing spree.

"Okay, you know I'll help if I can."

"Well, I was thinking about the names Jack has chosen. I think there might be name combinations we could identify based on the names he has chosen so far. We could create a list of the most likely names he might choose. I need to know if there was a history on the names he's used in the past. Did the history start right when he moved to Tulsa for Thomas, for example, or did he buy a name with a history, and if so, where was that history? I don't know what that part will tell me, but the more we know about those identities the more likely we can figure out what new identity he might be using."

"It's not a bad idea, but why are you reaching out to me? Don't you have like a million data analysts and all kinds of FBI toys to do your digging around on?" Cortez teased.

"We do, but it's not my case and I don't have a go to person yet. That takes time. Bobby could do this, I'm sure. I just need him sweet talked."

Cortez gave a hearty laugh. "God, I remember you working him. He would start shaking his head right when he saw you coming, but he could never tell you no."

Max laughed too. "He totally busted my chops all the time," she said agreeing.

"I'm not sure I have the magic to get him to go around the chief, but I'll give it a try."

"Give Bobby my best." Max was still laughing.

The two women talked for quite a while longer, catching up on the latest in each other's lives. They laughed and before hanging up agreed to get together sometime soon.

Max smiled at the phone after they said their goodbyes. She truly missed Cortez. They'd been a good team. She loved Mark, but they seldom got to work together.

For a few minutes she remembered when the chief told her she would be taking Cortez with her on the Tyler case. Her initial reaction was negative. Max was used to working alone, and she liked it that way. Working with Cortez had changed that for her. By later working with Mark, she had learned how to work as a team and had come to realize the advantages of doing so.

Her mind drifted back to Tyler, and she hoped Bobby would come through for her. He'd worked magic for her many times in the past, but she was no longer part of the LAPD and knew she was asking a lot.

14

Chapter Four

As soon as Jack stepped through the door a familiar smell assaulted his senses. It was masked some by a new, pleasant smell. Over the top of the old wood, linseed oil, and furniture polish that was baked in over the years was a new smell of vanilla and cinnamon spice. The new smell was that of pies, cookies, and flavored teas. Jack found himself focusing on the newer smells. The old ones flooded him with memories that he'd spent years trying to forget.

Making his way through the familiar floor plan, he took the stairs two at a time. At the top on the landing he turned to the right towards the master bedroom. He paused outside the door, his fingers wrapped around the cool brass knob. His heart raced, and sweat covered his brow. The palm of his hand made the brass knob feel wet, making it nearly impossible to turn. Tightening his grip, he twisted harder and slowly pushed.

Stepping into the room, his eyes scanned his surroundings. He let out the breath he'd been holding. Things had changed. The bed was on the other side of the room. There was a small lamp on the table next to the bed, illuminating the room slightly. Jack slowly approached the bed and stared down at the frail body under the covers. The woman was asleep, her eyes closed and her frail, twisted hands clung to the blankets near her neck.

Jack clicked off the lamp and retreated back out of the room. No need to disturb her now. He needed to get the rest of the family safe and out of the U-Haul.

He retraced his steps back down the stairs, but instead of going through the front door he turned down the hall then took a left off the kitchen through the laundry room. He opened the door that led into the garage. Reaching inside he felt for the switch, flipped it into the on position, and flooded the garage with light.

He looked around. An older model Mercedes sat parked on the left side. A thin layer of dust covered the gold paint, an obvious indication that it hadn't been driven in a while. Gardening tools filled one corner. The familiar workbench lined the front wall, and miscellaneous items covered the opposite wall.

Assessing the situation, he descended the two steps that dropped him onto the concrete floor. Remembering where the outlets were, he looked between two stacks of boxes and began moving the one that more likely covered the place to plug in his precious cargo. Ten minutes later he had cleared a large enough space along the wall opposite the car for the freezer. This would have to do for the next few days.

Looking up he noticed there was a garage door opener that didn't used to be there. He glanced over to the wall next to the door and saw the activation button mounted next to the light switch. Walking over he pressed the button and waited for the garage door opener to raise the door.

Ducking under the door as it rolled over his head, he retrieved keys from his pocket and began methodically removing the tie downs that secured the van to the trailer. He pulled the stowed away ramps out from the backend of the trailer and verified they were flat on the ground before opening the door of the van. He climbed in behind the steering wheel of the van and slowly backed it off the trailer and onto the driveway.

Next, he removed the tow bar and hitch from the trailer, unwound the support wheel and dropped the trailer onto the driveway off to the side and out of the way. Climbing into the U-Haul, he backed it into the garage opening after properly lining it up, then he slid back out of the truck and walked around to the back.

He retrieved another set of keys from his pocket and pushed the silver one into the padlock that had secured the doors during the trip. He slid the latch open and pulled the doors apart. Grabbing the straps from under the tailgate he backed up, dragging the ramp out, and then he dropped it into place.

Jack climbed his way up the ramp and removed the two four-wheel dollies from the wall of the trailer, then lifted each end of the freezer onto the dollies. He slowly skated it down the ramp and maneuvered it over to the space he'd cleared. With the freezer in place he plugged it into the wall and immediately felt comforted when he heard the low hum of the compressor kick on. He really wanted to open the lid but knew better than do that right now. It was best to let the cold air stay inside until the entire system cooled back down. He slid his fingers along the lid and silently bid the contents good-night.

Reinserting the ramp into the trailer, he pulled the truck forward far enough that the U-Haul was no longer in the garage before rolling the trailer back in place behind the bumper and reconnecting the tow bar and hitch. He then wound the wheel back up into the towing lock.

Tomorrow he would return the U-Haul and trailer to the dealer down in Ventura. For now he needed some rest. Grabbing his suitcase, medical bag, and laptop bag from inside of the van he returned inside, turned off the garage lights, and found himself wandering through the house touching the familiar things. The furnishings had changed, but the fireplace was the same, the crown moldings, and the granite counter tops in the kitchen all the same.

Room by room he walked through the house until he came to his old bedroom. Of course all of his boyhood things were gone, but the light on the ceiling was the same. And when he finally settled down to rest he found himself staring up at the light fixture.

Memories flooded him. He thought of the times his mother would come into his room and wake him up, making him join her in her bed. Other times she would just climb into bed with him, sliding all over him. He lay there rigid, closing his eyes and trying to force those memories away. For a little while he began questioning why he'd come back here.

Then he remembered why he returned. This house would be a home again, and it would be filled with love. After all, this was where it all began. Different memories filled his mind. Memories of Hope, how they'd sat on the edge of his bed when they were fifteen, and he'd finally worked up the nerve to kiss her for the first time. That kiss had been the beginning of a new life for him. He remembered how nervous he'd been and then how shy he felt and how she had touched his hair afterwards. Their eyes met, and then they both giggled.

17

Suddenly, the room seemed happy again. It was with Hope that this would be a great place to live and raise their daughter. His mother could no longer hurt him. With that thought he drifted off to sleep.

Morning came quickly, but he rose with excitement. It was time to start rebuilding his life again. He was finally going to have his family with him, the months of waiting almost immediately faded into the past.

First, he needed to check on Vivian, his house guest. Making his way across the hall, he arrived at the master bedroom. Tapping lightly he turned the knob and entered to find the elderly woman awake leaning back against her pillows. She looked frail.

It had been years since Jack had seen her last. Her daughter, Suzanne, was frequently left to babysit him. He liked her just fine and she was always nice to him, but he was still pleased when she had died at the young age of thirty-three. More satisfying was the fact that there were no other living relatives. Vivian's husband died years earlier, and after having fallen ill she has had a caregiver for the past six months. It seemed she had advanced lymphoma. Jack contacted her lawyer and made arrangements for her health care in her final hours.

Under a different name he bought the house outright under a mocked up business name, citing interest in it from a historical perspective, wanting to make it into a bed and breakfast inn. He'd only been able to seal the deal after agreeing to allow Vivian to live in the home until she died. All of the transactions were untraceable and could not be linked back to him.

Jack was a man of his word. A matter he prided himself in. He would care for Vivian until she passed away. The people in the town of Ojai would think he was her long lost nephew—a son from a deceased brother who had fathered a child he'd given up his paternal rights to at birth. This too could be confirmed. He'd made sure the paper trail was air tight. Just in case…

"Good morning, Vivian," he said as he approached the bed. "I'm Tyler Thomas, your new caregiver and a licensed physician."

"Good morning," she replied in a soft whisper.

He looked down at her and knew she had little time. He felt both pleased and sadden by this realization. His ambivalent feelings were twisted by his history with Vivian. He remembered that she would often offer him cookies and milk as a young boy.

"I trust they told you I was coming?"

She merely nodded in acknowledgement.

"Can I get you some tea and toast this morning, Vivian? I thought our first day together I would spend some time getting to know what you need and want. I don't want to force things on you just because your doctor is saying this is what you should or shouldn't take. I'm a doctor too, and I want to be sure to give you the best care."

Vivian smiled, noticeable only by a slight lift at the corners of her mouth. "Thank you. Tea would be nice."

Jack checked her catheter, IV drip, and medicines that had been left on her night stand. He then walked across the room and opened the door of a small refrigerator and looked at the various medications inside. He administered the appropriate dosage from one of the vials into her IV drip and returned the vial back to the refrigerator.

"I'll be back with your tea in just a few minutes. You rest then we can talk." Jack patted the old woman on the arm before turning to leave the room.

"Have we met before?"

Jack turned back surprised by the question. "No, I don't believe so. Why do you ask?"

Vivian struggled for a moment before gasping out, "Your eyes." She laid back into the pillows, and her eyes closed.

Jack walked down to the kitchen and put the teapot onto the stove. His mind raced about the comment she had made. The old woman despite being on medication had recognized something in him—his eyes. He was sure of it. While he waited for the water to boil, he retrieved his laptop bag from where he had left it the night before and began powering it up.

The teapot began to whistle. He went to the stove, moved the water off the fire, and turned off the gas flame. Retrieving a teacup from the cupboard, he realized Vivian had her cups in a different cabinet than his mother had. He was pleased that she'd moved things

19

around. Already the house was feeling like his. Not hers! Not his mother's.

Jack carried the tea up the stairs, careful to not spill any, and once again approached the large bed Vivian rested in. His footsteps caused her to open her eyes. He could feel her studying him. Smiling he said, "Here's your tea. It's pretty hot. You'll need to be very careful."

The woman continued to study him as she took the cup gingerly in her thin fingers and raised it to her lips. She sucked in a small amount into her mouth and then set the cup aside on the nightstand. "Thank you."

"You're welcome. Are you sure you don't want any food right now? You really should eat. I could bring you some chicken broth, Jell-O, or an Ensure milkshake. We have to keep your strength up."

"You're kind, but nothing now. Maybe later. The tea is lovely."

"I see there's an intercom here on the nightstand, so you can call me any time you need me, even if it's just because you'd like me to come up and read to you. I don't mind," Jack said nodding at the book lying next to the woman in the bed.

"I don't need much these days. Keep the pain away. Visit me occasionally. I think it helps."

"I'm here to care for you, and I'll do just that."

Vivian's eyes wandered over him. He knew there was a familiarity that she was remembering. Memories returned of the days he'd spent with her. She used to talk with him, asking questions and challenging his mind. She'd tell him how smart he was. He was counting on the fact that the meds were potent and her mind was too far gone to make any connections.

"You go. I'm going to drink my tea and then rest for a while." She lifted the tea cup. It was cooler now, and she could handle it a bit better.

"Okay, you rest. I'll be back in a while to check on you. Call me if you need anything." Jack pulled her blankets up for her. He smiled as he leaned over her, their faces very close together. He could sense her eyes on him.

Pulling away, he stared down at her then turned and headed out of the room. He was beginning to wonder if the work he had done was enough. His mind scanned the people over his life that would be able to recognize him. It would only be people who have spent a tremendous amount of time with him. There was no one else in Ojai. Teachers maybe would be the only risk, but many of them would have died, transferred, or retired.

Jack had few friends during school other than Hope, no one he was ever really close to, so he felt comfortable that with Hope's sister nicely tucked away in Phoenix, he should not be running into anyone here in Ojai that would recognize him, especially given the changes he had made. There was just one detail that would seal the deal.

Returning to the kitchen where he left his now fully booted up laptop, he logged onto the Internet and began a quick search. Within minutes he made a purchase for an overnight delivery. Sighing, he closed the computer and decided he needed to see his family. A little reassurance right now was necessary.

He entered the garage through the door off the laundry room. He flipped on the lights and immediately made his way to the freezer. Standing in front of it, he took a deep breath and lifted the lid.

Chapter Five

Mark returned home late and telephoned Max to let her know that he would see her in the morning. They were still living separately, though the only time they weren't together was when either was on a case and their hours didn't match up. They agreed to share time between their respective homes, except lately it seemed they were getting closer to living together.

Max continued to claim residence in a two bedroom apartment that she had rented after moving to the area to be near Mark. She was comfortable in the apartment for now.

After talking on the phone for a while they agreed that Mark would come pick her up around eight. It was Saturday, and they were going to spend the morning together. Max worried even though he'd said all the right things, but the stress was very clear in his voice.

Max went to bed after their call and found herself tossing and turning. Her mind was tormenting her both about Jack Tyler and Mark's obvious anguish. She didn't remember falling asleep but woke in the morning completely tangled in her sheets and with lingering, faint memories of her dreams.

Shaking it off, she untwined her lean, muscular legs and slid off the bed, heading directly to the shower. It was nearly seven o'clock when she got out of the shower. Mark would be there in an hour.

As Max got dressed, fixed her hair and makeup, she considered how she could address her concerns with Mark. This would be new to their relationship. So far they had never had a situation that caused any type of pull between them, at least not since they officially started seeing each other and Max had made the big decision to relocate to Virginia. They had gone months not seeing each other after their first passion encounter in California, but after reconnecting in Oklahoma their relationship had been near perfect.

Max had just finished a cup of coffee when Mark knocked on the door, and then used his key to come in. She grabbed another cup and decided that they needed to talk before they got out in the world where there were too many distractions. Mark came over to where she was standing in the middle of the kitchen and wrapped his arms around her, leaning in to sweetly kiss her.

Max could never resist his touch or his kiss and instantly fell into his embrace. She leaned into his hard body and returned his kiss, teasing him gently. Pulling back she brushed the one curl that always dipped across his brow, pushing it away from his eyes. Their eyes met and Mark pulled back looking down at her.

"Talk to me," she said deciding the direct route would be the best approach, go straight for it.

"It's a rough case."

"I get that, but it's getting to you. You always tell me not to let it get into my head. Mark, it's in your head. Talk to me, what's going on with you?"

After picking up the coffee cup Max set it in front of him. Mark nodded. Taking her hand, he led Max to the dining room table.

"Sit down. It's complicated."

"Okay," she said waiting for him to continue.

"We found the boy."

Max waited, unsure where this was heading. Her mind immediately went through the gambit of possible outcomes. Had the child been found dead? Was he alive but severely abused, tortured or…

"He's alive," Mark offered obviously reading her silence. "The pedophile had just taken possession of him. Needless to say he was terrified. We found two other bodies, both boys, both dead. The boy's fate was certain if we hadn't gotten to him."

"This is great news, Mark. I know you've been struggling with what would happen to him. What about the mother and the middle man?"

"The mother committed suicide. The guy she sold the boy to gave up the pedophile. He also is responsible for the sale of several other children, both boys and girls. We're trying to track down the other kids."

Max sat quietly listening, allowing Mark time to talk. When he seemed to come to a stopping point she inquired, "This case really rocked your world. Can you talk to me about that?"

"It did," Mark admitted nodding his head. "The boy, he was so scared. He held on to me. When we arrived he said, 'I knew the good guys would come.' He's only five."

"Mark, there must be more to this. Not that this isn't enough, but you've been distant and struggling ever since you began this case."

"Max." Mark stopped and seemed to stare off in the distance.

She pulled her chair closer and took his hand. "Talk to me, Mark."

He looked over at her. His eyes connected then looked away. "You've met my brother and sister. What I didn't tell you was I had another brother. His name was Thomas. We called him Tommy.

When I was twelve, Tommy and I rode our bikes down to the store on the corner near our house. We went inside, and I was looking at comic books. Tommy was in the other aisle picking out some candy. I don't really know how long I looked at those comic books. Old man Gus always let us come and hang out."

"All the kids in the neighborhood went there a lot. On hot days we would go and get an ice cream. Anyway, when I finally got done I went into the next aisle to tell Tommy it was time to go, but he wasn't there. I looked in all the aisles then went to get Gus. He was in the back room and came out when I called him. He helped me look for a few minutes. I ran outside and looked for Tommy's bike, thinking maybe he had gone on back to the house. It was parked right there where we left them." Mark stopped, looking into her eyes.

Max could see the torment in Mark's eyes. "What happened to him, Mark?" she prompted, holding his eyes with hers.

"After I couldn't find him, I raced home and told my mother. She called the police. Hours later, they found Tommy's body in a freezer in the back room of the store. Gus, it turned out, was a pedophile. Later, they discovered that he was responsible for several child abductions. Tommy had been raped before being strangled. They figured out that he was dead while I was still in the store.

While I was reading those damn comic books, Gus was torturing and killing my ten year old brother."

Max could see the shame and anguish in Mark's eyes. "Mark, I am so sorry, but you were just a boy."

"I know. I also know that if I had paid more attention Tommy would be alive today. This case just drummed up all of those old feelings...old feelings of inadequacy and failure."

"When we first met you told me your father was a cop. You also told me that it ran in your genes. Were you talking about Tommy? Being in law enforcement, all the way to the FBI, is it about trying to get it right?"

Mark stared at Max then shrugged.

"Mark, this is important. You have to trust me with who you really are and what drives you."

"I guess so. My father kind of fell apart after Tommy's death. He was on his way to detective prior to his death. Afterwards he stayed a beat cop. His spirit was broken. My parents stayed together, but they swirled around each other rather than remain married. I've always felt like it was my fault. Of course they both tell me it's not, but deep down I know I could have prevented it."

"I think I'd feel the same way."

Mark's eyes darted up to hers again, locking in on the green. She could see relief flood over him. "I wasn't sure how to...," his voice trailed off.

"Mark, you have to know you can tell me anything. If we're going to share our lives and make this work, if we're in this for the long haul then you have to trust me, and I have to trust you, even with our deepest secrets, fears, and skeletons."

"My family never speaks of Tommy, and I've never told anyone about him before. Of course Quantico knows, because they know everything."

Max leaned in and kissed him. "I'm glad you trusted me."

"I do trust you, Max." Mark paused, took a deep breath then continued, "There's more."

Max leaned back so she could see his face. "Okay, what is it?"

"The boy," Mark nodded. "In my case, he has no one. He trusts me. I want to spend time with him, maybe even help until they find him a home."

26

Max thought for a few minutes, not sure how to respond. "Mark, I understand the connection to Tommy, but I'm concerned that you're getting too close. We're trained to not get connected to the victims in our cases."

"I know, Max. I really do, and I've thought about that, even questioning myself about why I want to do this. He's nothing like Tommy. He's blonde and small. Tommy was dark and tall for his age. I don't think it's because of Tommy, although I realize I could be just trying to rationalize it. I don't know for sure. I just feel like I left him. I just don't want him to feel alone and afraid forever."

"Can I meet him?"

Mark turned to her, obviously surprised by her sudden question. "Yes, I think you can."

"Let's do it. Let's go see him. Where is he?"

"They were putting him into an emergency foster home last night. I told him I would come see him today. I had to pull some strings to get that approved."

"Okay, so what do we have to do to ensure you can stay connected with him?"

"I'm not sure. I wanted to talk with you first before talking to the social worker about visitation. Once he's settled somewhere it should be better."

"Well, let's not worry about that now. Let's take him to breakfast if they'll let us."

Mark reached for his phone and was already placing a call. Max could see the stress slowly slipping away, and she felt relieved. She knew getting so personally involved was not the best idea, but she also knew she had allowed herself to get deeply involved in the Tyler case, and she didn't even have a personal trauma to justify it.

A few minutes later Mark hung up. "We can take him for two hours. The foster home is willing to let me see him periodically, but it's just a temporary home. They're trying to find him a permanent one. With his mother dead they hope he won't get bounced around too much."

"What's his name?"

"Heath. His name is Heath."

"Well, let's go get him. I'm sure he'll be glad to see you." Suddenly, Max realized the boy may not want to meet her. "How do you think he'll respond to me? Clearly his mother betrayed him. I'm sure he's too young to fully understand that, but there's likely a part of him that does understand it."

"He trusts me. I think it will be okay. I'll just have to talk to him first. Once I tell him that I brought a friend…"

Within a few minutes the couple was on their way to pick up the young boy. Inside the vehicle Max reached over and took Mark's hand. She had mixed emotions about the boy they were about to go meet. She knew supporting Mark right now was important, especially given the background he'd just shared, but she also worried that he was getting into something that might be bad for either him or the child. Deciding that she wouldn't be able to control this, she resigned herself to just being supportive of Mark.

Their ride was quiet, and then Mark pulled the car in front of a small house in an older neighborhood. He turned to Max, his eyes searched hers. As always it seemed he knew what she was thinking. "I know you think this is crazy. I just need to make sure this little guy is okay. Trust me?"

"I do trust you, and I'm here for you. Just let me know what you need and how I can help." Max paused. "Promise me you won't pull away, that you'll stay open with me."

"Deal." Mark kissed her gently. "Okay, let me go talk with him. I'll be back in just a few minutes."

Max waited patiently in the car while Mark entered the home. A few minutes later he came down the walkway with a small blonde haired, blue-eyed, beautiful, little boy. The child seemed to be tugging Mark along the path as he pulled on Mark's hand. In Mark's other hand was a child's safety seat for the car. Smart. She hadn't even thought about car safety.

Max watched as they came closer. The boy was smiling, and she found herself admiring his resilience. She shook her head as she acknowledged the amazing strength in character of a child able to rebound from unconscionable circumstances.

Mark opened the passenger door, leaned over to the child, and looked directly into the boy's eyes. "Heath, this is my very good friend Maxine. You can call her Max. That's what I call her."

Heath laughed. "That is a boy's name."

"I know. Cool, right?"

"Yeah."

"Hi, Heath, nice to meet you."

Heath looked at Max with a small amount of apprehension, taking about a half step behind Mark. "Hi."

"I was hoping, if it was okay with you, to go and have some breakfast with you and Agent Wells. I'm really hungry, and pancakes sound very good to me right now. I think they even have those with the funny face and strawberries on them."

Mark looked at Heath. "What do you think, buddy? She does look pretty hungry."

"Okay, I'm hungry too."

"Well, let's do it then, big guy."

Mark spent the next couple of minutes getting the child's seat appropriately setup in the back behind Max before Heath crawled up into the seat, and Mark buckled him in.

A few minutes later with everyone seat belted in, they headed off to the restaurant. Mark navigated through the streets thinking of a kid friendly restaurant and pulled the car into the IHOP parking lot. They piled out of the car, and with Heath holding onto Mark's hand, they went inside.

After settling into the booth, they ordered, and Max took the kids' menu and began coloring with Heath. After a few minutes he warmed up to her. Max looked up at Mark and saw him smiling at Heath and her chattering away to each other. She had to admit, being with Mark and Heath felt very comfortable. She'd never considered what the future would look like with Mark, but at this moment she could picture a family. She liked the way it felt and the possibility of the future.

The food came and Max set aside the picture they had made. Tearing into the food, and with sticky fingers from syrup and hot cocoa, Heath devoured the entire smiley face on his plate and some of what Max had ordered.

Once the food was gone the boy seemed to turn a little somber. He turned to Mark and asked, "Is my mommy dead?"

Mark looked a little surprised, but obviously elected honesty as the best policy. "Yes, Heath. I'm sorry, but it's true. She is."

Heath looked really sad, but no tears came. "Who will take care of me?"

"For right now the lady you're staying with will take care of you while we work to find a home for you for forever."

"Will I get a new mommy?"

Mark was clearly struggling, so Max jumped in. "Heath, Agent Wells can't answer that right now. But there are a lot of smart people trying to make sure you find a very good family."

"Can you be my new family?" Heath asked.

There was an air of innocence in the question that tore at Max's heart strings. She could see the fear in his eyes caused by the uncertainty. His mother had obviously never treated him well. Any mother who would sell her own child was not going to win mother of the year, but to Heath it was all he knew and as long as he had his mother, he had something. Before he learned of his mother's death, he had a semblance of safety. His five year old mind wasn't capable of realizing the magnitude of the danger his own mother introduced into his little world.

"Heath, it's not as easy as that. A lot of important people are working on making a good decision for you," Mark responded as Max tried to collect herself. Tears had nearly drawn, and she pushed hard to hold them back.

"You are important people, right?"

"We're people who care about you a lot. We aren't going anywhere. We'll be there to be sure this works out okay for you."

Heath nodded, but he remained quiet.

Mark paid the bill, and then the trio headed out to the car. Mark looked at his watch. "Hey, we have a few more minutes. It's a little cool out still, but the sky is clear. How about we go to the park for a little bit?"

For the first time since the conversation at the table, Heath looked up and smiled. "Yeah!" There was excitement back in his voice.

"Let's do it!" Max added as they piled back into the car.

An hour later they loaded back into the car after playing on slides, swings, a merry-go-round, and monkey bars. Mark had helped hold Heath up to the bars and guided him across. They'd both pushed him on the swings, and had taken turns going down the slide

30

with him and catching him at the bottom. They'd all laughed a lot. It had been a good time.

Heath fell quiet again once they were back in the car and began their return trip to the house where he was staying. He stared out the window from his perch on the child safety seat. Max could see Mark checking on him frequently out of the corner of his eye. She knew Mark was worrying about returning him to foster care.

The car idled up to the curb in front of the white-sided house, and Mark killed the ignition and climbed out. Max got out too and waited as Mark got Heath out of the car seat. They stood on the sidewalk for a moment saying good-bye. Max was pleasantly surprised when Heath hugged her tightly. She whispered in his ear, "Stay strong, big guy."

Mark took the boy's small hand and the safety seat in his free hand and headed up the sidewalk.

Chapter Six

The lid swung open, and Jack stared down into the freezer. The body of his daughter, Faith−or at least his reproduced version of her−lay facing up, wrapped carefully in plastic, on top of Hope. He gently lifted the plastic-bound body and lovingly laid it on the floor of the garage. He gingerly unwrapped the plastic and stared at the exposed body, then breathed a sigh of relief after he examined her and found everything as he had expected.

Hugging the body he spoke, "Faith, honey, Daddy's here. I'm sorry you had to stay away so long. Let's get Mommy out here now, so we can all be together."

He gently kissed Faith on the cheek, oblivious to the incisions around her mouth where just a few months earlier he had sewn on the mouth from a little girl in Illinois that had been his patient.

The little girl, Jessie, had reminded him of Faith with her crooked little smile. He'd spared the girl only because he had become quite fond of her. After sedating the child he'd taken her mouth then crudely sewn on another mouth from one of his other victims. Before she had time to wake from the procedure, he left her at the door of the emergency room entrance.

When she was discovered he was called upon to help. He rushed to the hospital where he offered his expert services on a number of occasions.

After explaining to the family that the child's mouth had been removed and apparently sewn back on, he raced into surgery to reapply the mouth in expert fashion, making him, for a brief moment, the town's hero. Except… except for Special Agent Maxine Nichols forcing him to leave town to protect his family.

Pushing the memories from his mind and his focus back to his family, he returned to the freezer to retrieve his wife. Lifting the larger plastic-wrapped body from the bottom of the freezer, he carried it over to the floor next to where the grotesque, pieced together body of his daughter lay.

Demonstrating the same care he had shown just moments before with Faith, he unwrapped the body. He felt his head pounding and his heart racing. He couldn't believe his eyes, and as the reality of what he was seeing set in, rage filled him.

Stumbling backwards, he tripped as his foot tangled in the corner of the plastic from Faith's body. Laying in the middle of the floor was the body that he had spent so much time creating, the exact replica of his wife Hope, carefully preserved, and whom he had lavished with love and care for months, now lay crushed and flattened, beginning to fall apart.

In his rage, Jack grabbed anything in his path and threw it across the garage, slamming his fists against the drywall, driving holes into the wall and exposing the wooden studs. "NOOOOOOO! Hope, I need you. Hope!!!!"

Dropping to his knees next to the body, he scooped it up in his arms and rocked back and forth. Her still slightly frozen head rolled back to clearly show the decay and crushed check bone. His worst fear was coming to life—his beloved wife stolen from him again.

The voice of Maxine Nichols rang in his head, "It can't last forever, Jack, what you've done to those bodies." "Shut up, Shut up!" Jack shouted, placing his hands over his ears. He stared back down at the body. "Hope, darling, I am so sorry. I'll fix this. I promise you." Looking over at the child's body next to his wife, he turned Faith's head away.

He lifted Hope's body and carried it into the house to the kitchen. He laid the body down on the kitchen counter and grabbed his medical bag. "Think, Jack. Think!" he shouted out loud.

He returned to the garage and carefully wrapped Faith again. "Honey, Mommy isn't feeling well. I know we were going to spend some time together, but I need for you to take a little nap while Daddy tries to help Mommy feel better. I promise to spend some

34

time with you a little later." Jack stood back and looked down at the body as he placed it back into the freezer and closed the lid.

Racing back inside he returned to Hope's side. He stood, contemplating what he could do. The body was badly decomposing; he could see that now. He couldn't think of any method to repair the damage that was already done. He considered Botox to re-inflate the areas that had become flattened, but instantly knew it wouldn't work. He thought of a more robust taxidermy approach, but knew it would leave the body hard and not lifelike. That would never do.

Jack knew of another process called Thiel soft-fix embalming. He'd never tried it personally, but his understanding was that the method retains the body's natural look and feel. For a moment he got excited at the thought of it, then realized it was too late. He would have needed to do that when he'd first begun the preservation process.

Suddenly, the gravity of the situation overcame him. He held the body and wept. Despair began to overcome him. He had no idea how he would survive now.

He had no idea how long he'd been standing there with his face buried in the dress Hope was wearing, his tears dry now. He was shocked out of his grief by the sound of the intercom buzzer and a frail voice requesting his assistance.

Pulling away he turned to the kitchen sink and washed his face with cold water then dried it with a paper towel before going to see what Vivian needed.

He tapped on the door before pushing it open. Stepping inside he spoke softly, "Everything okay?"

"Yes, I was just hoping to get some water or ice chips. My mouth is so dry."

"Of course, which do you prefer?"

"Ice."

"Sure. Is there anything else I can bring you?"

Despite his attempts to avoid her, Vivian looked into his eyes. "You look sad."

"Do I? I'm probably just tired. I'll get that ice for you."

"How much longer do you think this will last?"

"This?" Jack was surprised by the question. It certainly wasn't the first time he had a terminally ill patient ask that question, but for some reason it seemed different with Vivian asking.

"Me, just laying here day in and day out, sleeping most of the time away in between the pain, this is no life."

"I suppose that depends on the strength of your body and…mind."

"Or you?" Vivian locked her eyes on his.

"Let me get that ice for you," Jack said pulling his eyes away.

As Jack entered the kitchen his heart wrenched as he saw Hope, or what was left of her, lying on the counter. He averted his eyes, trying to remain focused on getting ice for Vivian. For the moment Vivian was helping him avoid what he knew he was going to have to deal with.

He retrieved a glass from the cupboard and let ice crush into it from the ice machine in the front of the stainless steel refrigerator. The appliances were all new, a much nicer touch than the old white ones his mother had. After getting a spoon out of the drawer and with the ice in hand, he retraced his steps back upstairs.

Tapping lightly on the door again as he entered, he crossed the room to the bed. Vivian had dosed but stirred as he approached. A slight smile crossed her lips as her eyes settled on him. He felt exposed by her and yet comforted all at the same time. He couldn't quite grasp the emotion he felt. There had been far too many already in the few hours he'd been awake.

He scooped some of the crushed ice bits onto the spoon and slid them into the old woman's mouth. She closed her eyes again, appearing soothed as the cool slivers graced her dry palette.

Opening her eyes again, she spoke softly, "You never answered my question."

"I'm sorry? What question was that?" Jack asked truly confused. For a moment he thought perhaps she had dosed deeply enough that she'd entered a dream state for a brief moment.

"Will you help me?"

"Vivian, that's why I'm here, I came here to care for you."

"That isn't what I mean." The woman began to cough.

Jack took a tissue from the side of the bed and swabbed at her mouth. Suddenly Jack understood. "No, it's not time yet, Vivian. Your body is still alive, and your mind, although weary, is still awake."

"When it's time, will you help me? When it's time?" Her eyes misted over, and this time they pleaded with him.

He struggled. He certainly had killed plenty of people, but not like this. Not when he…needed her. He couldn't, not now. He stood there avoiding her eyes then looked at her and nodded. Scooping another spoonful of ice, he looked at his watch as she sucked on the chips. It was time for her pain meds again.

After feeding her a few more ice chips he delivered morphine into her IV, and within a few minutes she dropped back off to sleep. He stood and stared at her. His feelings were all mixed up right now. Hope was dead and Vivian was alive. Nothing was making sense right now. And Faith, what about Faith?

Since Vivian was going to be asleep for a while he returned to the kitchen. He stared at his wife and suddenly knew what he must do. He went to his room and searched through his luggage, finally pulling out a white dress for Hope. He carried it downstairs and slowly removed the clothing she was wearing. He carefully slipped her in the white dress. When he was done he stood back, and his breath caught at the sight of her beauty. Tears ran down his cheeks.

Turning away, he went into the garage and looked around. In the far right corner he saw a shovel. Lifting it he went back inside. From memory he wound his way through the kitchen and out the back door. The door slammed behind him. The sound was so familiar. He couldn't remember how many times as a boy he had bounded down the step with the door slamming behind him as he went out into the woods towards his playhouse.

For a moment he got scared and wondered if his playhouse would even still be there. What if Vivian's husband tore it down? What if over the years it had fallen apart?

Forcing himself to calm down, he made his way through the overgrown brush. It was obvious no one had been down this path for a while now. The path was barely visible, the grass tall and vines wrapped around each other.

He used the shovel to help break through the dense brush, breathing a sigh of relief when he soon came upon the small playhouse, which has been nearly consumed with vines. He noticed that some of the vines appeared to have been removed at one point, and he wondered who'd been inside. Could it have been Vivian's husband before he died? At first he felt violated, but then realized it didn't really matter. He was home and no one would be going in there again.

Laying down the shovel, he began pulling at the vines, ripping them away from the house until finally he uncovered the door and windows. He took the shovel and cut through the vines around the base of the house, and after nearly an hour he was dripping with sweat as he stood back and stared. His childhood sanctuary was fully revealed. The small building showed some signs of age, but it looked just as he remembered.

With the playhouse unveiled, he pulled on the small door, which creaked as he tugged on the handle, until it swung open. Poking his head inside his senses swirled as memories flooded in from the smell. He could picture Hope sitting in the corner, cross-legged on the planked floor, her blonde hair pushed behind her ear on the right, her tank top falling off her shoulder, and her knees dirty from climbing trees and hiking through the woods. His heart tugged, and a lump formed in his throat.

Climbing through the door, swiping away cobwebs and dirt, he had to duck a little since he was unable to fully stand up inside, his height restricting him in the small room. He looked around and poked his head up into the small loft. His old cot was still there, but broken. He went to the other side of the room and bent down. From his childhood memory he tapped his toe against the old boards, then reached down and tugged on the familiar loose board, pulling the plank out. He peered down inside, but it was too dark to see. Reaching in, he felt around and only touched dirt. *Impossible.* Dropping to his knees he reached even further into the opening, feeling all around. Still he found nothing.

Unable to believe his treasures were missing, he quickly got up and began running back to the house. Going inside, he rushed into the garage and looked around until he found a flashlight. Clicking it on, he was pleased when the batteries didn't fail him, and at a near run he returned to the playhouse.

The door creaked, and the hinges whined against the years of no use. Inside he dropped to his knees again, shining the light down into the opening in the floor. Straight down he could see where the box that had contained his treasures had once been. The square imprint in the soil was obvious, but the box was gone!

"You bitch, Agent Maxine Nichols!" He was so angry he spat out the words. Suddenly he knew his sacred spot had been violated. Standing up, he shone the flashlight and peered into the loft.

His magazines were gone too. The magazines Hope had given to him. Their magazines, their future, their plans—gone!

"You'll pay for this! I promise you that!" The rage was climbing in him. "I live here now, Agent. Just try to come back, I dare you. I'll be here protecting my family now."

With that and his adrenaline driving him, he retraced his steps back to the house. Inside he got a blanket from the hall closet and carried it to the kitchen. He laid it out on the floor and gently lifted Hope from the counter, laying her body in the middle of the blanket. He leaned down and kissed her tenderly, ignoring the mushy indention on her head.

"I love you, Hope. I'll always love you. I'll find a way for us to be together forever. Just wait, I need some time to figure it all out, but I promise you I will never give up. Faith needs you, and I need you." He wrapped the decaying, pieced together body in the blanket and then lifted her in his arms. He carried her out the back door towards the playhouse.

Upon arriving at the playhouse, he pulled the door open with his finger as he carefully balanced the bundle in his arms. He laid the wrapped corpse on the floor inside and then returned to the house where he retrieved a hammer, pry bar, plastic sheeting, and some nails from the garage.

With the supplies in his hands, he listened at the bottom of the stairs for a minute, ensuring Vivian was still asleep before once again heading into the woods.

Inside the playhouse he worked the floor boards loose until he had an opening large enough that he could drop through to the dirt below. Taking the shovel he began to dig. Tears rolled down his face. He dug until he had a hole four feet deep and five feet long. He laid the plastic into the hole and then climbed back out to retrieve Hope. He sat down with his feet dangling into the hole as he held her in his arms. He didn't even notice the boards digging deep abrasions in his back as he slid down into the hole until his feet hit the ground. He clung to Hope inside the blanket, protecting her as he tightly cradled her body.

He lowered her into the hole and wrapped the plastic tightly around the blanket, folding the ends around her head and feet to create a cocoon. For a long while, he kneeled next to her and sobbed. His heart was breaking. He wasn't sure he could survive without her.

He also knew he didn't know how to care for Faith without Hope. He could barely acknowledge it, but he knew what to do.

Pulling himself back up onto the floor of the playhouse, he went back to the garage. He walked to the freezer and lifted the lid. He stared down at Faith. Inside he knew what to do, and it was killing him. "Faith honey, Mommy needs you now. I need some time to bring us back together again, but in the meantime you'll need to help take care of your mother. She's not feeling very well and having you will make her feel better."

Lifting his daughter from the bottom of the freezer, he carried her out into the woods and into the playhouse, slid down through the floor again, and laid the small plastic-wrapped body next to Hope. The sobbing that started when he first began digging continued, and there seemed to be no end in sight.

Jack lay down in the hole with the two bodies. He wept until he couldn't cry any more, feeling paralyzed by his grief.

He jumped with a start. Looking around he realized he'd somehow fallen asleep with his wife's and daughter's bodies wrapped in his arms. His fingers were coiled in a grip around the plastic, and as he uncurled them they ached from being so tightly clutched. He knew he couldn't prolong this any longer. He stood up and retrieved the shovel and began to slowly, pensively scoop the dirt onto the bodies.

Once he completed the burial of his family, he pulled himself back onto the floor of the playhouse. Methodically, he reinstalled the planks, nailing them into place, being careful to not crack the brittle boards. With the task complete, he looked around the playhouse and noted that if not for the shiny nail heads everything looked as it always had. His absolute most valued treasures were stored under those boards.

He headed back to the house, trying to ward off the desperation that was building. The darkness was swirling around him. It was everywhere. He knew what it meant, and he knew he wouldn't be able to fight it for long. Not without Hope. Not without his family.

Chapter Seven

After dropping Heath back off at his temporary home, Mark and Max returned to Mark's house and spent the day replaying the time with the boy. Over dinner Max decided to address with Mark the topic of the child's future. She needed to understand what he was thinking. Not really wanting to cook, they ordered in Chinese food from their favorite little delivery spot.

Max plucked vegetables out of the white container with her chopsticks and watched Mark consume an eggroll. She leaned back, dropping her chopsticks into the little tub. "What do you imagine with Heath?" she asked in her usual direct fashion.

Mark looked up from his food, chopsticks in mid-air. He set his food down and leaned back in his chair. "I don't know, Max. All I know is he needs someone in his court. I want that someone to be me…us."

"He's an amazing kid, but I'm not sure what you can do."

Suddenly Mark got up from the table and left the room. He was gone for a few moments and then returned. He walked over to her and took her by the hand, lifting her from the chair.

"When we returned from Illinois I went shopping for your Christmas gift. I bought you that necklace that I gave you, but while I was shopping I bought something else. I knew it wasn't the right time to give it to you, but I knew it would be one day."

Max stood looking at Mark, confused by what he was saying. "I don't understand."

Mark reached into his pocket and slowly knelt down on one knee. "Maxine, I love you. In fact, I have loved you from the moment I saw you get off your motorcycle, well, actually from the moment you removed your helmet and I saw you. The very minute I saw you, I knew my life would never be the same. I know we agreed to wait at least a year, but I don't need a year. I know I love you, and I know I want to spend the rest of my life with you. Maxine Nichols, will you make me the happiest man in the world and be my wife?" Mark opened the small box he'd been holding, exposing a beautiful teardrop diamond ring, the band glistening with smaller diamonds.

Max stood staring down at Mark, her emerald eyes glistening, his words causing her heart to race. She loved this man. There was no doubt in her emotions. She smiled and bent down to kiss him tenderly. "I love you too. Yes, Mark. I say yes." She pulled on his hands to raise him up to her level and settled into his embrace.

After a few moments Mark pulled back and removed the ring from the box. He took her left hand and slowly slid the ring on. "I wasn't sure what size, so I guessed. If it needs to be sized we can do it any time."

"Mark, shut-up and kiss me," Max said leaning into him, pressing her body against his, sliding her hand down his chest and across the front of his jeans, immediately feeling the response of her touch.

A small gasp escaped Mark's lips as Max slowly unzipped his pants and slipped her hand inside. She wrapped her other arm around his neck as he lifted her off the floor and carried her to the bedroom. They sank into the pillows as Mark expertly pulled her jeans away and slid her top over her head.

Her hands ripped at his shirt as the desire rose in her. His fingers played on her flat stomach. She felt like her skin was on fire with every touch. Wrapping her legs around him, she pulled him to her and pushed at his pants with her feet, slowly working them down his legs. He pulled back and slid her to the edge of the bed as his clothes dropped to the floor. Slipping his fingers into her thong he rolled the silky material down her thighs.

She worked her feet out of the material and locked her legs around his hips. His erection was full, and she could feel it against her stomach as she rose off the bed and embraced him, wrapping her fingers in his hair as she teased his lips with her tongue.

His hands explored her body, finger tips gently teasing her nipples and sliding down her waist across the tops of her thighs and between her legs. His thumb circled her wetness, causing her to rock forward. He pushed her shoulders back, kissed her neck and down her shoulders, lowering his mouth onto her breast and flicking her nipple with his tongue, then traced her muscular belly down to where his thumb continued to tease.

Max was starting to lose it. The teasing was driving her crazy, and she found herself nearly begging. "Mark, please I want you inside…." Before she could finish the sentence Mark slid his body on her, pushing inside and thrusting deep within. She arched her back and felt as if she would explode, her ears ringing. Their mouths met, tongues probing with unbridled passion.

Max began to rock, following Mark's rhythm as their bodies pulsed together. It seemed as though there were drums inside her head as they worked each other to total ecstasy.

Hours later and only after having repeated the experience in a tender, slow and purposeful manner they dosed off. Awaking famished and realizing they'd never even finished their dinner, Mark hopped out of the bed naked and disappeared down the hall. A few moments later he returned with the Chinese food on plates. He'd warmed the food in the microwave and returned smiling with chopsticks in hand.

Max sat up in bed, leaned back against the pillows, and pulled the sheet up under her arms. After setting the plates down on the bed, Mark left again for another minute, this time returning with two glasses of wine. Crawling back in bed, he shoved a bite of food into Max's mouth, playfully teasing her.

Max watched Mark devour his food and smiled at the realization of how much she loved this man. The reality of the proposal was setting in. They would be married one day, and this is how life could be. Her mind returned to Heath as she sucked a snow pea into her mouth. Although she didn't want to ruin the moment, she needed to know something. "Mark, why tonight?"

"Why tonight?" Mark seemed genuinely puzzled by her question.

"Proposing, why tonight? I mean, we were discussing Heath and how he fits into your future and then suddenly you proposed? Don't get me wrong, I'm thrilled and I love you. I see a future with you, but why tonight? Why when we were talking about Heath?"

Mark set his plate down on the nightstand next to his side of the bed and turned to her. Leaning in, he kissed her then began explaining, "I wanted to ask you at Christmas, but I knew it was too soon. I knew you weren't ready then. Now with Heath and all, I've seen over the past couple of months, I see you as my future, and I don't want to wait any more. I see kids with you, especially after watching you with Heath today. You were amazing, and I want that for the mother of my children."

"Mark, talk to me about Heath. Something happened with the two of you. What do you see happening with him?"

"I honestly don't know. I wish I could say. I wish I knew what I could do for him."

"I saw you with him today. It's more than you just wanting to help him. You feel responsible for him. You want to be responsible for him. I don't even know if you realize that yet."

"What are you saying, Max?"

"I'm saying he needs someone he can count on, and you imagine being that someone."

"Whoa, I never said that," Mark said holding his hands up and palms facing her in protest.

"You don't have to say that. It's obvious."

Mark stared back at her. He seemed to be absorbing what she was saying. "I don't understand. What are you saying, Max?"

"I'm saying you won't be happy without knowing for certain that Heath is safe. And…there's only one sure way to know he's safe."

Mark shook his head. "I still don't understand, Max."

"I'm saying you should apply for foster status and try to get him placed with you. Honestly, I think that has a lot to do with why today is the day you asked me to marry you. In your heart that's what you want, and you see us together as a family. A single man won't likely be granted custody, but a married couple would."

"Now wait a minute, Max. If you think I only asked you to marry me because I wanted Heath to come live with me, you don't know me very well."

"I didn't say that, but on an unconscious level, I do think it plays a role."

"Max, I'm sorry. I…I don't know what to say."

44

Max set her plate aside. "Mark, don't be sorry. I love that you feel responsible and care so deeply for that little guy." She took his hand and turned towards him, wrapping her foot over his leg and pulling him to face her. "I said yes. I already knew even if you didn't, and I said yes anyway. I love you, and if loving you includes Heath, then I still say yes."

"What do we do?"

"I don't know, but I think tomorrow you should call the social worker and find out what the chances are."

"Is it too fast?"

"Life is fast. Heath's life changed too fast. It's not necessarily the order which I pictured, but I know my life includes you. I love you."

"You, Maxine Nichols, are amazing. I have no idea how or why I got so lucky." Leaning over, he kissed her deeply then handed her plate back to her and fed her another snow pea before picking up his own plate and loading his chopsticks with rice.

Chapter Eight

Jack returned to the house and went in to take a shower. He felt totally spent. Physically, he was covered in dirt and tears. Emotionally, he was riddled with rage, fueled by despair and the feeling of failure. He turned the water on very hot and scrubbed at his skin as if somehow the scalding water could wash away the pain and anger of his loss. The vigorous cleansing left his skin feeling raw and sore. The tingling just made him more aware as if his skin itself was angry.

After toweling off he dressed quickly and then went to check on Vivian. Respectfully he tapped on the door before entering the room. For a moment his heart stopped as the old woman lay in the bed, and he thought that she too was dead. Suddenly he realized she was breathing lightly, and he sighed.

Checking the catheter, he emptied the contents of the bag in the toilet of the adjoining bath. When he flushed the toilet, the noise caused the woman to stir. She opened her eyes slowly and faintly smiled.

"Hello, Vivian. You've been resting for quite some time. Would you like the T.V. turned on?"

She nodded her head, and he picked up the remote control to turn on the flat screen that was mounted on the wall. He flipped through channels until she selected something.

"I'm going to get you something to eat. Ice is just not enough. How does some broth sound?"

Vivian shrugged.

"Is there something else you would prefer? Ensure? I saw that there was strawberry, chocolate, and vanilla in the cupboard."

"No, broth is fine."

"I need to check your catheter site. And can you tell me when you last had a bowel movement?"

"Do what you need to do." She seemed to be considering his question. "I think sometime yesterday. It was when James, my prior caretaker, was here."

"We need to get you onto your side for a while. I don't want you getting bed sores."

Jack pulled back the blanket, trying to allow the old woman as much dignity her plight would afford. Determining that the catheter was looking as it should, he slowly rolled her to the right and then adjusted her pillows so she was more comfortable. With her situated and watching television, he left to make her some broth.

As he entered the kitchen he choked back the pain caused by seeing the bare counter where hours earlier his wife had laid. He forced his eyes away and went to work finding a can of chicken broth and a bowl that he could microwave to warm the liquid. With the broth hot, he collected a spoon and a fresh glass of cold water.

Carrying the items up the stairs, he entered the room and set the bowl and glass on the nightstand then took a chair next to the bed, pulling it up close enough where he could assist in spooning the warm broth into Vivian's mouth.

"It does taste good. Better than I thought it would."

Jack smiled. Seeing the woman eat made him feel better, as if there was hope. Hope, he needed to have Hope.

He could feel Vivian studying him again and tried to distract her by offering her some water.

"Why do you appear sad?" she asked.

"Me? You must be mistaken. I'm just tired from my trip," he lied. He wondered how she could read him so well.

"I see your sadness. It's okay."

Jack looked at her and ignored her comments, continuing to offer her broth as she could take it.

After feeding Vivian, Jack gave her another dose of pain medication, and it wasn't long before she fell asleep. He took the dishes down and put them in the dishwasher—another new appliance, modern conveniences that had not been there during his childhood.

48

The sun set and darkness blanketed the outside and filled him inside. He knew Vivian would likely sleep through the night. He decided to go for a drive. Grabbing his medical bag after pulling on a sweatshirt, he walked outside and realized that in his grief he'd failed to return the U-Haul and frowned at the inconvenience. Shrugging at the realization that it was only one more day, he decided he could return it in the morning.

He climbed into the driver seat of the van and navigated it past the U-Haul down the driveway and headed towards the beach. He watched as the mountains grew smaller in the rearview mirror and the city lights of Ventura came into view.

As he entered Highway 101 he could see the Ventura Pier and chose his location. He exited at Seaward and headed west towards the beach. Turning left on Pierpont he went to the end, entering Marina Park. It was getting late now, and there were few cars. Jack pulled into a space, rolled down the window. The fresh, salty ocean breeze wrapped itself around him. He waited and watched.

The sound of the waves crashing and then ebbing could be heard in the distance. He'd been here many times as a child and knew there was a jetty just over the small slope and past the ship that sat on the sand and served as a playground for the local children.

Within the hour the parking lot emptied out, and Jack reached into his medical bag, pulling out a rag, gloves, and a syringe that he always had prepared. He shoved the rag into his pocket as he exited and slipped on the gloves. Heading towards the sound of the waves, he pulled his sweatshirt hood up over his head. His eyes scanned in both directions. He could see a lone jogger far in the distance heading toward him. He slowed his pace and looked all around. There was no one else in sight.

The jogger was getting closer. Jack waited until the man passed, then he turned and quickly approached the runner from behind. He depressed the syringe into the rag, and just as the jogger realized that he was being followed, Jack swung his arm around the man's neck and slammed the rag over his nose and mouth.

Arms rose to fight, clinging at Jack's gloved hands, but the drug won and the arms lost the battle. Jack pulled the man up to a sandbar close to the parking lot then jogged over to his vehicle and backed as close as he could.

Hurrying, he returned to the man and lifted him, pulling him on his feet to the SUV. Opening the hatch, he pushed him inside. Jack folded down the back cubby and pulled out a large tarp that he kept stored in the van. Covering his victim, he closed the door, looked around confirming no one was around, slid into the driver's seat, and drove out of the park.

As he was leaving, he saw a BMW coming toward him. His timing was perfect. If he'd taken a few minutes longer the BMW would have been a problem. He knew he shouldn't take risks like this, but tonight the tingling in his skin was just too much. His loss today required action, and he was going to attend to it.

He removed the gloves as he drove, careful to obey all traffic signs. Jack followed the winding road back up the mountain and returned to his childhood home. He'd always dreamed of taking a person here, but he never had. Of course it was really his mother he had wanted to kill. All he had ever had the pleasure of experiencing here were a few small animals. Of course, that was all before Hope had caught him and made a pact with him. He shook his head, forcing the thoughts from his mind since they only deepened his anger as rage grew again inside.

Killing the engine, he got out of the vehicle after retrieving his medical bag. He went inside. He needed to assess a couple of things before bringing his visitor inside. Because of earthquakes it was uncommon for homes in California to have basements, but his home did. Built into the mountain, half of the home sat on a foundation, and the other nestled on top of a basement.

He went around to the entrance that opened from a mud room just near the back door on the main floor. Reaching inside the door for the light switch, he flipped it to the on position, flooding the entrance with yellow fluorescence. Descending the stairs he was pleased to see the area was free of clutter.

In the main room all that was there was an old workbench, that at one time had served as a laundry table. Next to it was a shelving unit that was now empty. Off to the left was a smaller room with a door. He remembered there was a shower in that room. His father used it after working in the garden. Another small room to the right contained a toilet and sink. He opened the door and turned on the sink then flushed the toilet. Everything seemed to still work.

Satisfied, he climbed the stairs two at a time and stepped out into the night.

Grateful for the solitude of his childhood home, Jack easily got the man into the house undetected. He found some duct tape in the garage and stripped the man of his clothing, then successfully secured him to the workbench. He stood and waited, watching closely, eager and with anticipation of what would come next. A half an hour later, the jogger was beginning to wake up.

Jack watched as his captive began to wake. He could tell the jogger was confused. He watched as the man shook his head, trying to remove the fog. The jogger attempted to raise his hand but struggled, not coherent enough yet to comprehend that he was taped down. Jack didn't like the fact that the workbench was made of wood. The porous surface certainly was not ideal. He also didn't like the old oil and grease stains that covered the surface and legs. It was not the usual sanitary condition that he was used to, but it was going to have to do, for now.

He gently slapped his visitor's face in an effort to help him wake up. "Wake up, my friend."

The jogger's eyes opened wide, and Jack could see the instant fear in his eyes. "Help me," the man pleaded.

"Not likely. In fact, you're going to help me." Jack watched the man's face change from hope to desperation and then fear. "Today has been an especially bad day for me. But you're going to make it better. Oh, yes, I have a need that you will fill very nicely."

For a moment Jack was reminded of Benz, the car salesman from Oklahoma. He had spent days with Benz. That had been one of the most successful times in warding off the darkness. Oh, Benz had been nice enough, but he could have told people about Jack and that just couldn't happen. So Jack followed the man then brought him back to his house and kept him for several days. Jack smiled as he recalled his time with the car salesman. That was before he had Hope back with him. He knew all he needed was his family, and then everything would be okay. He would figure it out, but for now he had something to keep him calm, and this jogger was just the right thing.

The man stared up at him and began to thrash against his bindings. "You can't get away, so you might as well calm down." Jack picked up the medical bag that he brought in from the car, unlocked the hasp, and reached inside for gloves. He pulled out a small leather roll and unsnapped it.

Retrieving a leather case from his medical bag, he rolled it open across the jogger's chest. Four different surgical knives of varying sizes were exposed. After slipping on the gloves, Jack ran his fingers across the shiny instruments. "Eeny, meeny, miny, moe," he said as he carefully made his selection while watching the jogger's expression.

The man really began to struggle now, his eyes bulging from the sockets. "I can see you're scared. Well, I should warn you that this is going to hurt. As a matter of fact, it's going to hurt a lot," Jack said as he took the number five scalpel and made an incision all the way down the man's torso from between the two clavicle bones to the pelvic bone. As Jack made the incision, the jogger writhed against the bindings, arching his back and curling his fingers into fists.

He cut into the jogger's body, and blood began to pool onto the workbench. But Jack didn't notice. He was far too interested in his pleasure.

With the incision complete, Jack began to talk, "Today my wife and child died for the second time. Do you know how that made me feel?" He paused and leaned over close to the man's face.

The jogger, in an obvious effort to somehow get out of the predicament he was in, finally able to find his voice gasped out, "I didn't," then grunts and groans followed.

"No, it's true you didn't, but you'll help me get over my pain. I lost my precious wife, Hope, and our beautiful daughter, Faith." As he talked about his wife and child the anger began to build. His frustration took over, and before he could stop himself, Jack pulled the man apart and forced his hands deep into the cavity of the jogger's chest. He intentionally squeezed the organs inside, angrily twisting and pinching.

At first the jogger's heart rate increased. His body squirmed against the bindings, and he screamed out in pain, fruitless efforts. For a moment Jack wondered if Vivian could hear the cries but gave little more thought to it knowing even if she could hear there was nothing she could do about it.

The man's heart began to slow, and as it did Jack squeezed the organ almost gently as if giving it stability again before he pinched it hard one last time, forcing it into a spasm before it slowed and finally stopped.

Jack screamed in release of his anger as the man died on the table in front of him. He screamed at his inability to savor the moment and at the anguish and loss he'd suffered.

Minutes passed. He wasn't really sure how long, but finally he pulled away. The man was now dead in front of him with his spilled blood pooling on the concrete floor. Jack sobbed as he removed his hands from inside the pale body. There was so much frustration inside him right now that he could barely control himself, but then he realized that he needed to get himself together if he was ever going to be able to be with his family again.

Jack began to busy himself with the cleanup. This part of the process had become as much a part of the ritual as the act itself. His surgical training and perfectionist demeanor would allow nothing less than precision.

An hour later he had the man and his clothing bundled in a sheet that he got from the hall closet. He needed better supplies, but this would have to do for now. Tomorrow he'd get to unpacking. He hadn't moved much, but his medical supplies were necessary. Looking around he acknowledged that he needed to get this room set up much more thoroughly.

After securing the bundle with duct tape, he lifted the jogger over his shoulder and prepared to head off into the woods again one last time for the day.

Chapter Nine

Max was waiting for Mark to come by and pick her up for an appointment with the social worker assigned to Heath's case. They'd already met with an attorney regarding emergency guardianship. There were some challenges, for sure. The first being that they were not yet married, and the second was their unexpected schedules and the nature of their jobs. The meeting with the social worker was to see what Mark needed to do to get qualified as either Heath's guardian or as his foster parent.

Over the past few days Max had given considerable thought about the proposal and the possibility of Heath becoming a very important part of the life she would lead with Mark. It both thrilled and terrified her. Marriage and a child were crazy, she knew, but she also knew Heath had really not been given a fair shake. Mark adored him, maybe even felt responsible for him somehow.

A few minutes later, Mark knocked on the door and pulled Max into his arms the minute the door opened. "Ready to do this?"

"I sure am," Max replied, applying a kiss on his neck.

"No reservations? No concerns?"

"Of course, I have both, but that's normal. I don't have reservations to the extent that I think we shouldn't go to this appointment. I'm counting on the social worker helping us better understand what we might be getting into."

"You're so logical about this."

"We have to be, Mark. I also want to be cautious. I'm trying to not get my hopes up until I understand more, and you need to be cautious too."

"I know. I'm trying to be realistic too."

"Well, let's go do this and see what she has to say. What's her name again?"

"Dana. Dana Thompson. Heath really likes her. She's one of the good guys. I actually think she really cares about the kids she's assigned to."

"Sad that you even have to say that or that any social worker wouldn't have the kids' best interest at heart, but I know there are so many that face their cases as the numbers on the file."

Mark looked at her for a moment then nodded. "We should probably get going. Our appointment's in forty-five minutes. Traffic may be heavy."

Max nodded and grabbed her keys from the small table that sat next to the door. "Let's do this."

The ride across town was slow going, but they arrived on time for their appointment. They sat for a moment in the car holding hands, their fingers interlocked in a silent embrace, before getting out and heading up the walkway. They smiled at each other before Mark swung open the door.

Inside, Mark stepped up to the counter and checked in with the plump, strawberry blonde woman that sat behind the window. She asked him to have a seat and explained that they would be called back in just a few moments.

They took chairs facing the door that people use when coming from the back office. That also gave them the view of the exit. This was a typical trait of almost anyone in law enforcement. Having a view on the door and any potential threat became second nature, more habit than conscious thought.

After about ten minutes, the door opened and a short, thin African-American woman opened the door. "Mark Wells," the woman called out, looking down at a clip board.

Both Mark and Max stood and greeted the woman who led them down a corridor, making a left and finally to a door on the right side. "Ms. Thompson will be right with you. Please have a seat."

They entered the room. It was quaintly decorated with soft colors and modest furnishings. Max found herself thinking that at least it isn't the institutional setting often associated with social and government facilities. She remembered Mark saying the woman was one who really cared, and this seemed to show in the décor. There were a few hand drawn pictures on the shelf behind the oak desk that seemed to be from former clients, based on the scrawled thank you messages in crayon.

Almost as quickly as they could be seated, the door opened again and in bustled a woman who appeared to be in her late fifties or early sixties. It was immediately apparent that despite her age she was a ball of energy. She approached them quickly, taking Mark's big hand into her much smaller one. "Special Agent Wells, it's good to see you again." Turning her attention and her smile to Max she continued, "And you must be the lovely fiancé I've heard about. Dana Thompson, it's a pleasure to meet you," the woman offered in introduction.

Max returned her smile and extended her arm, taking the woman's hand in her own. "I guess that would be me." Max hadn't heard anyone refer to her as a fiancé yet and suddenly felt shy and yet warm all over inside at the title.

"Please, get comfortable. We have a lot to talk about, and I want to make sure I answer all of your questions today."

The next hour was spent with Dana explaining to the couple how the social service system worked in the state of Virginia, which had jurisdiction over Heath. They were pleased to learn that an emergency placement could be made in the circumstance of abandonment or neglect.

In this case, both applied. Heath had been both neglected and abandoned by his mother. The father had been killed shortly after the boy was born, and there were no other living relatives. Heath would either have to be adopted by someone, or he would remain in the foster system until he aged out at eighteen.

Dana also explained the pros and cons of attempting to take on a child that had gone through the types of trauma that Heath had experienced. There was likely a need for long-term therapy, and there would probably be battles down the road as the yet unknown emotional traumas played out.

She explained the likelihood of a judge placing the child permanently with Mark. A single male was not good, but should the couple marry, she felt fairly certain they could apply for emergency placement, followed by temporary foster, and then ultimately adoption if that was the path they chose. In the meantime, she could allow visitation with Heath to ensure the connection was continuing to build with all three.

"You two need to really decide if you want to start your marriage off immediately with a child. I can almost guarantee you, Heath will no doubt present some challenges along the way. It won't be easy. These kids unfortunately just aren't easy."

Max jumped in, "We understand, and yes, we've been talking. That's all we've been talking about."

Mark added, "I think we have to decide if we're ready to be married right now so we can get the process going. Do you think our jobs will pose any problems?"

"As long as you can show proof that you can financially provide care for the child, I don't see that as an issue with placement. You might need a nanny or a relative that can provide care should both of you need to be out of state at the same time. Other people do it."

"How do we get started?" Mark asked looking over at Max for reassurance and getting the nod he was hoping for.

"You can take the paperwork with you now. That gets you started on the process of fostering. Either I or another social worker will come out and do home inspections. For emergency placement we come out first then make periodic stops in the first sixty days. Processing you should be pretty easy, actually, because all of the background checks and registration with CODIS are already complete through your jobs with the FBI. Sometimes that takes a while." Dana reached into the desk drawer to the right of her and began pulling out forms and putting them into a folder. Before she was done there was about a quarter inch stack of papers accumulated.

Pushing back from the desk, the energetic woman stood and handed the folder to Mark as he and Max rose from their chairs. "You can't take them back, you know. They're not puppies."

"We understand," Max replied.

"I just like my families to know what they're getting into. It seems all very romantic, but we're talking about a boy who has witnessed and experienced things no child should ever see."

"Honestly, we have no romantic notions. In fact, I think we expect this to be difficult," Mark offered.

"Well then, you have a lot of forms to fill out." Dana smiled at the couple. "I think you'd make great parents for Heath."

With that, she walked the couple back down the corridor and to the lobby. She handed Mark a business card and shook their hands, telling them to call any time if they had questions that needed answers.

Once back out in the car, they looked at each other. At first their gaze was just serious, and then smiles broke across both of their faces.

"So we have the day off. Let's do it," Max said.

"Do what?"

"Well, we're already downtown. City Hall has to be around here somewhere."

"Maxine Nichols, are you saying what I think you're saying?"

She smiled, displaying a mischievous lopsided grin and raised one eyebrow. Her head tilted slightly, and her green eyes twinkled in the spring sunlight in an obvious challenge. "I've never pictured myself having the whole princess wedding. Waaaayyyy too much attention for me," she said dragging out the sentence.

"You're totally serious?" Mark was stunned at her certainty.

"What about your family? My family?"

"My family will be pissed, and then they'll get over it," she shrugged and giggled. "I don't know your family well enough to know if they'll be pissed. That, my dear, will have to be your call."

Mark sat staring at her beautiful eyes and silly grin. Her confidence was unwavering in the moment, a trait that had drawn him to her from the moment they'd met.

He leaned in and kissed her tenderly, then started the engine and threw the car into gear.

Chapter Ten

Jack woke early. He felt better yet somehow disappointed in himself for not taking more time with the jogger. He allowed his emotions to get the best of him. He spent a few moments reflecting on the weeks after the…accident and how he had spiraled out of control. He had gotten drunk and lost. He couldn't let that happen again, or he would never be able to have Hope and his daughter back with him.

Last night after taking the jogger deep into the woods where he dug a deep hole, depositing the body and covering it with the soil, he returned to the house and carefully showered, making sure to remove any blood or dirt. Afterwards he made sure Vivian was set for the night and provided plenty of fluids and medication to get her through until morning. He spent about an hour reading to her until the medication took hold, and she fell into a deep sleep.

He threw his legs over the edge of the bed and forced himself to stand up. He needed to check on Vivian. Pulling on pants and a t-shirt, he went into the bathroom to freshen up before going upstairs to tend to her. He first went to the kitchen and prepared a cup of tea and an Ensure milkshake. He really needed to get something more than just ice and tea into her system. It was important to him to keep her strength up.

With the tea and shake on a small tray he found in the pantry next to the refrigerator, he took the stairs slowly, making sure not to spill anything. Outside of Vivian's door, he tapped lightly to announce his entrance before balancing the tray on one hand and swinging the door inward.

Vivian's small, frail body lay resting nestled into the pillows, but the sound of the door woke her. Her eyes fluttered open, and a slight smile curled at the corners of her mouth. "What time is it?"

"Oh, it's early, only a little after seven. I brought you some tea and a shake."

"Tea sounds nice."

"I really need you to try the shake too. I know it's hard, but you must keep your strength up."

"Why?" The woman's eyes seemed to plead with him.

"Because life is precious. You need to savor it."

"There is no value in it anymore."

"You are providing value for me."

The woman stared at him as if trying to assess whether he was telling the truth. Her eyes softened. "Tell me about you. Where were you before coming here?"

"Well, I've lived lots of places. Most recently, I was living in Scottsdale, Arizona."

"Tell me about it?"

Jack looked at her, studying the wrinkles around her eyes. Her blue eyes seemed to twinkle just a little. They were eyes that were filled with sadness. He assumed the sadness was a result of the loved ones she had loss. And there was pain in those eyes, both physical and mental pain.

There was a hint of something else in those eyes too, but he couldn't quite place what it was. Jack began to talk as he went about emptying the catheter and administering her medications. "It's very hot in Arizona. Air conditioning is a must. It's beautiful too though, or at least parts of it are. A lot of the buildings are the same color as the sand, so at times it can be very bland. But the rock canyons are lovely."

Vivian sucked on the straw Jack had placed in the shake, the effort nearly more than she could muster. With a ragged breath she prodded for more information. "Family?"

Jack realized she was seeking information about his past, and his mind raced on what, if anything, he could share with her. "I have some distant relatives that live in Arizona. I haven't seen much of them lately though. We weren't very close."

"You must fix that."

"Fix it? I'm not sure that's possible."

62

"You need to try."

Jack looked at Vivian. She forced him to accept her gaze and she nodded at him. "Okay, I'll keep that in mind. For now though I need to give you a bath, and we need to turn you again."

Jack began the process of gathering towels and a warm bowl of water. Then he gently sponged the woman, careful not to tear her tender skin. "I could go and get you some movies today. I have to run a couple of errands anyway. Do you have any favorite oldies but goodies that you might like me to pick up?"

"Gone with the Wind, my favorite," she rasped through her discomfort as he rolled her to one side.

"I'll get it for you. We can pop it in tonight." With a fresh gown on, Jack settled the small body back into the pillows.

"You're gentle."

"Well, I'm supposed to be gentle. My job is to provide you the best of care. Was my predecessor not gentle?"

"Not always."

Jack envisioned someone manhandling Vivian and instantly felt rage. The feeling unsettled him. It had been a long time since he'd felt any emotions about anyone other than Hope and Faith. Confused by the feelings, he suddenly excused himself and turned to leave the room.

"Movie tonight?" she asked sounding hopeful.

Jack turned back to face her. "Yes, Vivian, I promise," he said without facing her.

Leaving the room, Jack began to assess what he needed to accomplish today. He had to take the U-Haul back to the dealer. It was now after eight o'clock, and they should be open. He needed some coffee and hadn't found any in the kitchen. He saw a coffee pot, so he'd just need to stop by a grocery. He went to the bedroom to put on some shoes, grabbed his keys, and went out to the garage.

Looking around everything seemed to be in order. The hum of the freezer immediately caught his attention. He forced his eyes away from the reminder that his wife and daughter were gone, stolen from him again. He had to get them back. He wasn't sure how just yet, but he knew it was the only way he could survive.

63

Hitting the button to the garage door opener, he waited as the door slowly rose, letting the morning sunlight pour in. He walked outside, grateful for the beautiful day, and climbed in and slid behind the wheel of the U-Haul truck.

Pulling out of the driveway, he navigated the truck and trailer down onto Main Street. He went just a few blocks before pulling over next to a wide open space of curb. Climbing out of the cab, he locked the doors and walked across the street to the small bookstore that housed a quaint little café. As he opened the door he was greeted by the aromas of rich coffee and pastries. The barista welcomed him, and after a few minutes delivered him a steaming hot cup of coffee and a warm bagel.

He selected a table next to the window and enjoyed watching a pair of birds playing outside while he savored the coffee. He took a bite from the bagel, and his mind replayed the morning with Vivian. Suddenly, he knew what he needed to do. It was so obvious, but somehow she'd made it clear. He smiled as he finished off his breakfast and began mentally preparing how best to execute the plan to be reunited with his family.

Chapter Eleven

Mark and Max stood in the middle of the City Hall building. They obtained a marriage license and now were waiting for one of the authorized clerks to perform the simple ceremony. They were fortunate that in the state of Virginia a blood test was not required which could have delayed their sudden decision to marry today. The whole process was as simple as paying fifty dollars for a marriage license and filling out some paperwork.

Mark looked down into Max's emerald eyes. "You're completely sure about all of this?"

Max waved the marriage license at him and teased, "I wouldn't have this now if I wasn't sure, now would I?"

"That was only part of what I was referring to." Mark studied her face closely.

"I know," she replied, then leaned into him and raised up onto her toes to kiss him on the lips. Before she could say anything more, the door swung open, and they were joined in the foyer area by a plump man. The area was merely a large opening that was lavishly appointed with solid marble slabs.

The man that entered the room called out, "Wells and Nichols?"

The couple exchanged a glance and a smile, finding the formality of it amusing given the fact that there were no other people waiting in the area. Others had come and gone, but had walked on past to enter other rooms throughout the large City Hall building. There were people bustling about on their way to pay tickets, file land rights, or some other business.

Today they were the only couple waiting to be married. Max was relieved by this fact as it made it more intimate. On the way over in the car, she and Mark agreed that they would inform their respective families and have an official ceremony in a couple of months when things with Heath settled down.

Max hadn't ever really spent time fantasizing about her marriage like so many other girls. She'd spent her life imagining her life as a police officer solving crimes. She'd accomplished her dreams, and while she'd never dreamed of a fancy wedding with a flowing gown, she also hadn't imagined marriage in a court house either. The only thought she'd really ever given to her wedding day was that she wouldn't stand there and say "I do" unless she truly loved the person she was standing beside. Today she knew the only requirement in her marriage dream was being fulfilled. She did, in fact, love the man she would be standing beside.

Mark answered the man's question, drawing Max out of the flurry of thoughts that flew through her mind. "Yes, I'm Mark Wells, and this is my fiancée, Maxine Nichols."

Max barely had time to get used to the title of fiancée, and in just a few moments it would change to wife. Letting out a small sigh, she stepped forward with Mark as she took hold of his hand.

They followed the man through the door into a small room with four straight back chairs, presumably for witnesses, a non-requirement in the state of Virginia. They'd decided not to have anyone meet them here, allowing themselves a little more time to decide how and when to communicate with their families and their colleagues. The door containing a small four by four inch window closed behind them, clicking shut and leaving the room nearly silent. There wasn't much else to the room. It wasn't more than fifteen feet long with a small podium standing at the other end.

"My name is Dennis Chamberlain. I'll officiate your marriage today. In my role I will sign the marriage register, and I will submit the necessary documents to the Clerk of the Court. Those will then be sent to Vital Records. Once Vital Records completes the processing, you will be able to obtain certified copies at any time. Do either of you have any questions?"

Mark looked over at Max and smiled. "I don't believe we do." Max merely shook her head.

"Do you have any special vows that you would like to say or read to each other?"

Neither Mark nor Max had even considered this. Max could feel her cheeks flushing a bit. "No."

"We have a few traditional vows that you can choose from." Dennis reached to the podium and lifted a book that looked as though it had been thumbed through a least a thousand times. He handed the book to Mark. "Take a moment to select those vows that best suit you or your respective religious affiliation."

Taking the book, Mark started flipping through the pages as Max looked on. After a few minutes they agreed on a set of fairly traditional vows. Max pointed to the page that said "Husband and Wife" as opposed to "Man and Wife." Mark nodded to her in immediate understanding. Max was definitely not a subservient woman, and those words suggested that the marriage was not a union of equal partnership, but rather one where the man was revered as superior to the woman. Max couldn't picture herself saying those words and meaning them.

Turning back to Dennis, Mark returned the book, pointing to the page they selected. Dennis looked over the page briefly and nodded. "Do you have a ring?"

Max removed the engagement ring and handed it to Dennis. Mark looked a bit hurt for a moment until he saw the huge grin on her face. She was amused by the lack of preparation. They both giggled and instantly joined hands, fingers interlocking once again as they turned to face Dennis.

"Do either of you have any last questions or comments?"

In unison they replied, "No."

"Okay, well, then let's begin."

"…I now pronounce you husband and wife. You may now kiss the bride."

Their eyes had been locked the entire time. As unplanned as this was, it couldn't have been more perfect. They were the only two people in the world during those few minutes. Mark had been holding Max's hands the entire time, and now he pulled her to him, sweeping his hand into the small of her back while his other hand reached up into her long auburn hair and cupped the back of her head to raise her head. He gently bent to her and delivered an intimate kiss. Still lost in the moment, they only pulled away when there was a sudden sense of discomfort emanating from their officiator.

"I love you, Maxine Wells."

"I love you too, husband." Max grinned at the sound of the words coming from her mouth. "Now, let's go figure out how we petition for emergency custody of that little boy we've been talking about."

Mark shook his head. A smile spread across his face, and his blue eyes sparkled. "Okay, but we have to have a honeymoon night before we can have children."

Turning back to Dennis, he nodded and immediately began to busy himself with the paperwork. After a few minutes he presented them with a certificate of marriage, a few other documents, and a receipt for his services which contained the record number. When it was all complete, he turned and smiled for the first time since he'd introduced himself. "Congratulations, Mr. and Mrs. Mark Wells."

"Thank you," Mark responded then turned to face Max. "Shall we, Mrs. Wells?"

"Yes, let's do this." Max couldn't believe it. She felt great. Life was good. Her career was going well. Mark was more than the perfect man she'd always hoped to find, and soon they would have a young boy sharing their lives.

They left the room and proceeded back out to the parking lot to the car. Once inside they kissed for several minutes before agreeing that they better get going if they hoped to catch the social worker and get the emergency custody paperwork started. They both hoped within a couple of days they could take temporary guardianship of Heath. More formal paperwork would follow, but once he was with them they'd know he was safe.

Chapter Twelve

Jack returned to the house after delivering the U-Haul, picking up *Gone with the Wind* for Vivian, and grabbing a few other items including coffee for the next morning. He walked the few blocks from the U-Haul dealership after turning in the truck and trailer.

It felt surprisingly good to be back in Ojai. He relished the opportunity to reinsert himself into the familiar town. The old haunts felt right somehow. The morning alone gave him clarity, and he figured out exactly what he would need to do to make things right here.

In the last couple of hours a plan had come to life on how he could get his wife and daughter back home. There was only one problem; he was going to need to leave for a few days. Reaching for his cell phone, he placed a call to the hospice agency that had been caring for Vivian prior to him coming into town and taking over.

After explaining who he was he said, "I was hoping you could provide care for Vivian for two or three days. I have a family emergency and need to go out of town suddenly."

"We could have her prior caregiver out there tomorrow morning. Is that soon enough?"

"Yes, that would be fabulous. What time should I expect him?"

After waiting for the time and agreeing on the final arrangements, Jack hung up the phone. With lots to prepare now, he needed to check in on Vivian and get busy.

Jack spent the next few hours getting everything ready for Vivian's care while he was gone. The frail woman slept, so he turned on soap operas which seemed to help keep her awake and alert. She needed to stay alert at times, or she would surely give up. He wasn't ready for her to give up.

Tonight he was going to make sure she got another Ensure shake down when they watched their movie. While he sat and talked with her he realized the excitement of his plan was making the darkness creep in. Unfortunately, in his sadness and anger the jogger had gone too quickly, and he knew his desires wouldn't be abated for long. Only with Hope in his life and when he was working was he ever able to control the darkness. Without either, there was no way he was going to be able to keep things in check.

He needed a table; that wooden workbench would never do. He could set the basement up the way he liked things—clean and sterile. If he was going to live here for very long, he'd need certain things. He went to retrieve his laptop, and while Vivian watched her shows he sat nearby ordering supplies online.

With the table, small refrigerator, and a variety of pharmaceuticals ordered he was confident he could entertain guests for quite a while.

When a commercial came on he broke the news, "Vivian, I need to leave for a couple of days."

She turned to him, her eyes searching his face. "Where are you off too?"

"I decided to take your advice and try to reconnect with my family."

"Oh? Good for you."

Jack looked back to the T.V. as the show resumed. He stood and checked her IV's, and after checking his watch realized it was time to administer her medication. He was trying to time the drugs to allow her to enjoy the movie later. At this point it was important to keep her medicated heavily enough to keep the pain away. Unfortunately, that meant she slept a lot. Within a few minutes she had dozed back off into a deep sleep. Jack collected the dishes and quietly left the room without turning off the T.V. in case she woke again soon.

When evening came Jack returned to Vivian's room with a shake for her and popcorn and a beer for him. He settled in next to her bed for the long movie. She tried a couple bites of popcorn, letting the buttery puff balls melt in her mouth. Surprisingly, Vivian remained alert through the entire movie and seemed thrilled with the experience. It was the most animated she had been since he had returned to the home.

When the movie ended, he tended to her medical needs and promised to see her in the morning before leaving town.

"Thank you."

"For what, Vivian?"

"For the movie and the time."

"It was my pleasure." Jack brushed a stray lock of grey hair away from her brow and pulled the covers up around her. "Good night, Vivian."

Morning came with early signs of the sun peeking through the windows. Jack rose and went to the kitchen to make some coffee. A few minutes before seven o'clock there was a knock on the door. Jack was in the middle of packing an overnight bag and stopped to go let his relief caretaker in.

Standing back from the door, Jack assessed the younger man as he entered carrying an overnight bag and medical backpack. Reaching his hand out to assist, Jack introduced himself. "Tyler Thomas. Thanks for coming back for a few days."

"Jimmy," he replied. "Not a problem. I'm still waiting on another full-time assignment, so this is good. This lets me make a few extra bucks until that comes through. Besides, the ole' lady is nice and easy to care for."

"I'll only be gone a couple of days." Jack turned to the man, placing emphasis on his words as he spoke, "Let me be very clear with you, that *ole'* lady is to be given the best of care. Are we clear?"

The thick neck of the caregiver, who looked like he'd rather be surfing than caring for an elderly woman, showed signs of stress as the artery in his neck popped out. "Yeah, man, I only meant…"

Before he could finish his comment, Jack interrupted him, "I think I know what you meant. She told me you can be rough with her. I don't expect to hear that when I return. I expect you to spend time with her, stay exactly on schedule with her medication, and be gentle. Are we clear?"

"Yeah, man, relax. I'll be good to her. I promise."

"Good." Jack smiled. The charismatic smile that had aided him throughout his whole life though now altered, still held its charm. Immediately the surfer was put at ease. Jack knew he'd already made his point.

The next hour was spent finishing his packing and making sure Vivian was all set. Leaning over Vivian's bed, he handed her a small cell phone. "This is programmed for you to call me by dialing 1 and the pound sign if Jimmy here is not being nice," he nodded at the surfer. "You call me, and I'll take care of everything. I'll only be gone a couple of days. You be strong while I'm gone, okay?"

"Go find your family. Don't worry about me. I'll be here when you return."

Jack nodded before giving Jimmy a final look and turning to leave.

***

Jack arrived in town just before sundown. The drive had been fairly easy. It was Wednesday, and aside from the lunch hour, he hadn't hit much traffic the whole drive. He decided he needed to get something to eat, and besides, that would allow time for the sun to fully set. To work well, he'd need darkness for the plan that he was envisioning. He tapped on the GPS system in the center of the dash and selected the restaurant icon, then scrolled down until he found something that looked appetizing.

For some reason, The Arrogant Butcher seemed interesting to him. He smiled and made the selection to start the directional mapping that would lead him there. It was only a few miles away in the downtown area. He took his time winding through the city streets. He rolled the window down after exiting the freeway and was enjoying the freshness of the warm spring air and the beauty of the sunset over the desert sky.

Once in the parking lot he navigated the vehicle into the first available parking space. He exited his vehicle, clicked the remote on the key chain to lock the doors, and weaved in between cars across the parking lot. Inside the building, Jack indicated a table for one and accepted the opportunity to sit outside on the climate controlled patio.

The menu had some really appetizing and unusual choices. He knew from the name that it was a good choice. He wanted a cocktail but decided against it, knowing he needed to have his total wits about him. Now was not the time to compromise and risk being anything less than alert. After all, the future of his family depended on tonight.

A short while later the server brought him the appetizer of black mussels, which smelled amazing. He tore into the bread that accompanied the savory dish. Then suddenly he became aware that he was being watched.

At first he began to get nervous, and then he realized it was merely a woman trying to capture his eye with innocent flirtation. He noticed she was a very attractive brunette. Her long legs folded perfectly and stretched out just right under the table to give him a preview of what the rest of her body would likely look like.

Oh, he'd love to spend some time with her. In fact, the darkness would love to take her before the meal even came, but no, he would not be distracted now. Hope and Faith were waiting on him. He turned his head away and stared out the window, hoping she would take the subtle hint that he was not interested in her that way.

Plates were cleared then more came, and Jack enjoyed his time at The Arrogant Butcher, all while not allowing the woman to overpower the irony of the evening. The scallops that he ordered were succulent, and he devoured everything on his plate. Then the dessert menu came, and he forced himself to ignore the sound of the options, as he wanted to be satisfied but not sleepy. He still had a long night ahead of him.

He was also taking a lot of pleasure sitting out in public without concern. By now most certainly Jack, the man he used to be, would have been noticed. Cops would have come plowing into the restaurant with anxious rookies wanting to make their claim to fame and seasoned detectives or FBI agents fighting over the notoriety of the collar. This new look had given him the cover he desired, and it was working quite nicely.

Jack paid the bill, scribbling his latest name on the receipt. He smiled as he saw it in print. Tucking the credit card back into his wallet, he stood and began the walk back through the dining area. He nodded to the brunette as he left. She was truly lovely, and he knew she was just as lovely on the inside too. But that was not meant to be. It was dark outside now, and the moon had taken on a nice glow. It was just after eight thirty now. He needed to wait a while longer. It was too early and definitely not safe to proceed right now.

Deciding how to spend some time, he climbed in the vehicle and backed out, immediately heading to the top of the edge of town. He had always enjoyed the night sky and total darkness sprinkled with brilliant stars that twinkled like diamonds floating in the air. It would only take about thirty minutes to get to the top, and then he could look down on the city and enjoy the evening until it was time.

Two hours had passed since Jack had left the restaurant, and now he felt certain it was safe to begin the descent back into the city. He wound his way back down the hill and then followed the familiar path to the modest residential area.

The homes on the block were mostly dark inside. One had a light on in what appeared to be the back bedroom. He slowed down as he approached and noticed the homes on either side were buttoned up for the night. The home he sought was as snug as a bug too. Jack pulled along the curb as he killed his headlights and studied the area.

Chapter Thirteen

One week after Mark and Max had tied the knot, Max laid in bed relaxing. Mark was in the shower, and she realized she'd been so consumed by the marriage and the efforts to try to gain guardianship over Heath that she hadn't had much time to think about Dr. Jack Tyler. It surprised her somewhat, and she had to admit it pleased her too. Not having Jack consume her every waking moment was almost a relief.

Mark had asked for a few days of vacation to work with the social worker, and it was beginning to look like they would be granted guardianship within a week. They both would need to appear in court, but the social worker and their attorney felt their petition would be granted.

Max always struggled with anything that she couldn't control, and the waiting seemed ridiculously long, even though it really had only been a few days. She also struggled with knowing Heath was in a foster home with a lot of other kids and not likely getting the support he needed right now. All she could think of was that he was such a little guy to have been through so much, including the sudden death of his mother. She wondered about his long term mental health and hoped that together with Mark they could offer him enough stability and love to get him past the scars that, no doubt, existed.

Max had an assignment later today that was related to her case, but this morning they were heading over to Mark's parents' house. They'd not yet told them of their sudden marriage and plans regarding Heath. It wasn't that they had delayed the conversation. It was simply that time had gotten away from them. They definitely needed to have the conversation soon, or risk causing a rift in the relationship Mark had with his family.

Hearing the shower turn off, Max stretched and forced her body out of bed to take her turn in the shower. Since the day at City Hall, she was staying at Mark's full time. She couldn't believe they were married. They would definitely have some work to do on the living arrangements soon.

Fresh out of the shower, dressed, and ready for the day, Max could hear noises in the kitchen and followed the sound that seemed to merge into fantastic smells. Mark was making a valiant effort to cook omelets. She smiled knowing he was trying to domesticate himself, when in reality chasing bad guys was way more his thing. Stepping in, she took the spatula and directed him to the coffee pot. A short while later they were enjoying omelets, coffee, and toast.

"Have you thought about Jack lately?" Max suddenly asked, as if it was the first time she'd mentioned the killer in a few months.

"I think about him some, yes. We both want him. Bad, but Heath has just seemed to consume me. I've really tried to think about my motives to ensure we have been smart. There's no turning back once we bring him into our lives full-time." He studied her for a moment. "Have you thought about him?"

"Sometimes, but I've been focused on you, the marriage, and Heath too. You know, when you were on Heath's case I was starting to get very worried about you. You seemed so lost. I understand why now, but at the time, I wasn't sure what was wrong and didn't know how to help."

"Have you called Cortez yet?" Mark asked, changing the course of the conversation.

"No, I need to. I'll call her in the car on the way to your parents' house. I need to see if Bobby has come up with anything for me."

Mark nodded as he popped the last bite of omelet into his mouth. "You think we're making the right decisions with Heath, right?"

Max looked up surprised by the question. "Mark, yes, we're making the right decision. I've been thinking. I'm going to have to change my ways a little. I can't have a murder wall in my living room."

"I know that's how you work best. We'll figure something out. Maybe we can setup your own room in the garage. That way we can keep it locked to ensure Heath stays out. If having a murder board is how we'll catch Jack, then we need one."

Max smiled and stood to collect the plates off the table. "We need to get going soon."

Mark glanced at his watch and grabbed the cups and loaded them in the dishwasher. Max turned to head out of the kitchen, and before she could get past the counter Mark grabbed her hand. "Ready to do this with my parents?"

"I think so. Will they be angry with us?"

"Angry, probably is too strong, but they may not be happy about it. I don't want you to worry though. I can handle them, and they really do just want me to be happy."

Max shrugged. "I'll follow your lead, but you owe me a trip to see my sister. In the meantime, you drive. I'm going to call Cortez while we drive."

✳✳✳

A few hours later they were on the way back from Mark's parents' house. After the initial shock of the marriage had worn off, the visit had gone okay. Mark's father started to get upset, but Mark stood up for their decision and relationship. Mark's mother had wanted to see her son get married and was happy to hear there would be a ceremony with friends and family later.

Max had assumed they'd be more confused or concerned about Heath, but they seemed to have an instant understanding of Mark's draw to the young boy. Max watched the exchange as Mark explained the case, and how Heath had been recovered unharmed. She was surprised by their support of the unusual speed to a sudden marriage and family.

When they left the house, Mark's mother hugged Max tightly. Max returned the hug and promised to come back soon. They'd committed to keeping the parents posted on Heath's placement and agreed to bring him over to meet them as soon as they could.

On the way home Max took Mark's hand and began to fill him in on the conversation with Cortez. He'd heard one side of the conversation, but lacked some of the details, and she'd ended the call as they had pulled up to his parents' house, leaving no time to give him the update.

"Bobby has some names that are probable combinations that Jack might be using now. Cortez said he was not totally convinced it was viable data, but she was going to run with some of it and will send it over to me too."

"We could trace all those names. If someone is using the name and has recently relocated to a new area that would be a great first place to start." Max could tell Mark's mind was swirling on how they could use the data to find Jack.

"Oh, and she teased me relentlessly about getting married like we did."

Mark laughed out loud. "I'm sure she did."

"All she kept saying was, 'If you'd just listened to me.'"

"Well, we would have had more sex if you'd listened to her."

"What!"

"You barely even looked at me almost the entire time we were in Oklahoma. You were so angry with me."

"I wasn't angry with you. I was afraid to get close to you. I didn't want to get hurt. In my mind you were too serious and too handsome to not hurt me, and after our one encounter in California, I just didn't want to do that again."

Mark was grinning.

"Okay, I *did* want to do that again, but not just once."

"Well, I'm certainly glad you finally let down your guard."

"Me too, husband," Max teased.

"Did Cortez or Bobby have anything else?" Mark asked, directing the conversation back to finding Jack Tyler.

"No, that was it for now."

Mark's phone rang, interrupting their conversation. He answered the call and allowed it to pipe through the Bluetooth on the car speakers. "Agent Wells," he answered, assuming it was FBI related.

"Mark, it's Dana. Dana Thompson. I have some good news. I was able to get a meeting in family court tomorrow at one o'clock. Can you be there then? It'll need to be both you and Maxine."

Mark glanced over at Max and nodded. She nodded back at him, giving confirmation that she could arrange her schedule to accommodate the meeting. "Yes, of course we can both be there. What will happen at this meeting?"

"It should be pretty straightforward. The judge will review the petition. He'll ask you a few questions, and he'll talk to Heath. I'm going to meet with him to let him know what will be happening so he's not scared."

"Will he make a ruling on the spot?"

"Yes, he will. You should be able to take Heath home with you tomorrow."

"Can we see him today?"

"You could meet me over there. I'm heading there now."

"Okay, we'll see you there."

When Mark hung up Max said, "This is great news, Mark. Let's get my car. That way we aren't rushed. I have to report in at two o'clock, but I'd like to see Heath for a little while too. You'll be able to spend more time with him, if it's allowed, without having to rush to get me back."

Mark sped up the car a little to get to the house quickly. He pulled into the driveway and then leaned over, kissed Max on the lips, and watched as she swung open the door and got out. He waited until she started her own car before backing the car out of the driveway and heading towards Heath's foster home.

Chapter Fourteen

Jack waited longer, all the while considering his options. Finally making a decision, he rolled down the window before pulling the car away from the curb. He circled the block and parked half way down the street. While he was driving he listened carefully to the neighborhood sounds. He was specifically listening for any sign of neighbors being awake or dogs barking. Hearing nothing more than the normal comforting sounds of darkness he pulled over and listened again.

Reaching behind his seat, he pulled out a pair of gloves, three syringes of chloroform, and stuffed a roll of duct tape into his pocket. Sliding out of the van, he closed the door quietly, taking care not to make any noise. He silently glided up the sidewalk that lined the homes while he put on the pair of gloves. The street was silent and, short of the fluorescent lamps that lit the sidewalk every two hundred feet or so, the desert air was cool with stars dotting the clear black sky. A cool breeze came out of the west, highlighting the buzz he already felt on his skin.

His senses were on high alert. He felt totally alive, and he wondered why it had taken him so long to realize this was the only way he would ever really have his family back. He'd have to remember to thank Vivian for giving him the idea.

He approached the house and noticed the motion sensor on the porch light, so he slid to the right to avoid its detection. Outside the front door cloaked in the darkness, he rang the doorbell. His heart rate increased as anticipation embraced him. It was well after eleven o'clock now, and the residents would surely be sleeping or at least tucked in their beds.

Moments passed and then he heard footsteps. The door knob turned, and the door cracked open slightly. Jack could see his brother-in-law, Paul, in the light of the living room. However, Paul was struggling to see him on the darkened step. "Paul, good to see you. Sorry to stop by so late," he said pushing his way into the house and kicking the door closed.

Before Paul could respond or even fully comprehend what was happening, Jack pulled one of the syringes containing a fast acting sedative called methohexital from his pocket and plunged it into Paul's neck. His brother-in-law slumped at Jack's feet onto the floor.

A few moments later Jack heard a female voice call out from the back of the modest home. He immediately headed in that direction. He walked past two doors on the right side of the hallway, each adorned with letters spelling out girls' names, and another room on the left. The door was standing open, and as he passed he recognized it as the guest bathroom. From memory he continued down the hallway, knowing the room he was looking for was at the end on the left–the master bedroom.

He paused momentarily before entering. Pushing the door inward, he moved forward towards the bed. The room was dark enough that he could easily be mistaken for Paul long enough to do what he came for.

As he got closer the figure in the bed sat up slightly. "Paul, who was it?"

"It's Jack."

"Jack?" Delayed surprise filled her voice.

"I've missed you, Hope."

"Hope? Jack, how did you get in here?"

"We need to go right away."

"Go where? Jack, where's Paul?"

"He's sleeping. It's time for us to go home. Please hurry."

"Jack, what are you talking about? I am home."

"Paul let me in. I don't know why I didn't realize you've been here all along. I'm sorry it's taken me so long to come get you and Faith. Now, it really is important that we hurry. Please, get dressed so we can go."

"Jack, I'm not going anywhere with you." Mindy, Jack's sister-in-law and nearly an identical picture of Hope, reached and turned on the lamp on the night stand next to the bed.

"Hope, we must get Faith and go. We have a long drive ahead of us."

"Jack, I'm not Hope. It's me, Mindy, Hope's sister."

"I understand that you might be confused right now. That's okay. We have plenty of time to straighten this all out. But for now we need to go."

"Jack, you look different. The police have been looking for you. It's time to turn yourself in. Too many people have been hurt."

Realizing it would take her some time to adjust; Jack removed the second syringe from his pocket and approached Mindy. She was shaking her head and holding up her hands as he gently plunged the needle into her neck. "I'm sorry, darling. We can talk through all of this soon, but for now we have to get Faith out of here and go."

Mindy slumped over, her blonde hair spilling across the pillows. Jack brushed her locks away from her face and stared down at her. His heart raced as he realized how much he had missed his wife. He leaned down and kissed her. The warmth of her lips burned deeply, and he suddenly knew this was right. He would never need to store her away in the cold. They would be able to be together forever.

A smile crept over his face. "I'll be back in just a minute, sweetheart. I need to go get our daughter." Jack turned away from Mindy and returned to the first door in the hallway. Ignoring the letters that spelled out "Madison" on the door, he turned the knob and pushed in, immediately seeing a small bundle wrapped in the twin bed. He approached the bed and looked down at the child. Dark hair covered the pillow, and he recoiled and backed out of the room.

Continuing to the next door he repeated the process, again ignoring the letters that this time spelled out the name Allie. Inside the room he found the small treasure he was expecting. Blonde locks splayed out across the pillow, and light cream-colored skin shone like a beacon in the small amount of light that peaked in from the living room. Jack stared down at the angel. He wiped at the tears that flowed from his eyes.

Looking around the room, he saw a doll and a teddy bear. He lifted the child and each of the items and carried them out to the living room. Paul was still slumped on the floor. He'd have to deal with him in a few minutes. He searched the room and the kitchen until he found the car keys. He scooped them up and went out the door off the kitchen, which he knew opened into the garage. Pressing the button on the wall just inside, he activated the garage door opener. Sliding in the seat of the car, he turned over the engine and backed the car out. Depressing the button on the visor, he closed the overhead door and turned the vehicle down the street, leaving the lights off until he was around the corner.

Two blocks away, he parked the car, removed the garage door opener from the visor, and left the keys in the ignition. He could hope someone would steal it and take it all the way to Mexico, but it really didn't matter as long as he had time to get away.

Stepping out of the car he checked all around. He was still wearing the gloves, and felt certain there would be nothing connecting him to the vehicle. He walked along the streets until he was back at his own vehicle. Opening the door, he climbed behind the wheel, started the engine, and returned to the house, pulling into the garage using the remote. Once inside with the security of the overhead door closed behind him, he breathed a deep sigh. Now he could really start with his plan.

In Scottsdale he had traded the truck he used to escape Illinois and purchased a mini-van. He wanted to buy a SUV in the same model that he'd had in the past, but worried that it would somehow make it easier to track him, so he chose a mini-van. The seats folded flat into the floor which afforded him a lot of space. He had needed that before, and it would certainly come in handy tonight.

Opening the back hatch, Jack pulled the tarp out and laid it out in the back of the van, then went back inside the house through the same door he had exited earlier. Paul was still in the same position on the floor. It would be a while before the drug wore off.

He went to the master bedroom and lifted Mindy's petite body from the bed. He carried her down the hallway and out to the garage, gingerly laying her out on the floor of the van. She was wearing only a nightgown, and it slid up as he laid her down. He carefully pulled it down to cover her thighs. His eyes scanned her thin yet muscular legs. Hope always did have the loveliest legs. He forced his mind to focus on the plan. There would be plenty of time to enjoy each other later.

He turned and returned inside the house. This time he went to Paul. He stared down at the muscular man. He would love to spend some real quality time with Paul, but in order for his plan to work he needed to control his dark desires. Shrugging, he bent down and pulled the man up by his arms, slid his own arms around Paul's chest, and tugged him backwards, heels dragging on the carpet down the hall. Inside the master bedroom, he hoisted the man into the bed. He made sure he had a pillow under his head and covered him with the blankets.

Walking around to the side of the bed where Mindy had laid just moments earlier, he folded the blankets back as if someone had tossed them over as they exited that side. Looking around, he grabbed the purse that sat on the dresser and removed a pair of jeans and a blouse from the drawers along with the women's tennis shoes that sat next to the closet. He looked around and smiled. *Perfect.*

With Paul dealt with, he returned to the living room. The child was sound asleep. Unfortunately, he needed to be sure she remained that way, and though he regretted needing to do so, he knew he must make her sleep. Removing the last syringe from his pocket, he rolled the sleeping beauty to one side and stuck the needle into her neck. She moaned but responded with nothing more than that before she was locked into a full slumber that would last for a while.

Lifting the child, he carried her out to the garage and placed her next to her mother on the van floor. Oh, they were so beautiful he could hardly believe his eyes. His Hope and Faith were truly right there in front of him. They were even more perfect than he'd remembered. Not wanting to do so, but knowing there was simply no other choice; he covered the two sleeping beauties with the edges of the tarp.

After closing the door to the van he went back inside. He walked through the house and made sure nothing was disturbed. He returned to the child's bedroom and gathered clothes and shoes before returning to the living room. He retrieved the toys he'd set down earlier, and then before leaving he made sure the front door was locked and all the lights were off. He carefully returned to the garage, allowing the lights on the stove to illuminate the path, and slid back into the van. Pressing the remote control one more time allowing him access to the street, he backed out of the garage and onto the street and closed the garage door as he pulled away.

He retraced the route back to the car he'd left earlier two blocks away. With his headlights off he pulled next to the car and quickly got out and placed the remote back on the visor before driving away into the dark of night with the sleeping woman and child tucked under the tarp behind his seat.

***

Jack immediately left town, travelling for two hours before he pulled off the highway again. He chose an exit that was in a remote area to reduce the possibility of anyone seeing him. He found a lone gas station that was open and pulled off to the side, making sure that he parked far from any lights. Getting out of the van, he checked his surroundings. The station was in ill repair and wouldn't likely have too many vehicles pulling in. There was only one other vehicle in sight. The driver was pumping gas into the tank and should be on his way soon.

Keeping an eye on the other driver, Jack went to the rear of his van and opened the back about half way then leaned inside. He laid his hand on Mindy's leg to see if she responded to his touch, a sign that the drugs were starting to wear off. He needed to keep both sedated until he could get them back home.

Just as he thought he could travel for another couple of hours, Mindy groaned slightly. Convinced that he needed to give her more of the medication, he went to the side door and retrieved his medical bag. Inside he had four more syringes. Selecting one, he slid into the back seat and closed the door then pushed back the tarp to expose Mindy's head.

"Hope, you are so beautiful. I can't wait to get you home, our home where we can be a family again. It's going to be perfect."

Mindy moaned slightly again. "Honey, I know it's uncomfortable right now, but it will only be like this for a while. Then everything will be wonderful, just like it used to be." Jack

86

comforted her as best he could then slid the injection into her neck, putting her back into a deep sleep.

While he was there he took a quick peek at Faith under the tarp. She too seemed to be sleeping peacefully. She would likely sleep quite a bit longer given her size. Deciding things were under control for now, he carefully covered them up and exited the van.

The patron who had been getting gas was long gone, and now Jack had the station to himself. Pulling up to the pumps, he decided now was as good of time as any to fill up. The next stop would be several hours. Leaving the van parked at the pump while the gas was flowing, he locked the van, listening for the chirps to indicate that the vehicle was completely secured, and went inside the station. A large cup of coffee was certainly in order. Driving for a minimum of another five hours before he made it back home was going to be difficult. He needed to stay clear and had already been up for going on twenty hours now.

The man working behind the counter was in his mid-twenties and seemed bored out of his mind. Jack paid for his coffee with cash, thanked the man, and turned to return to the car. He was nearly certain the employee would never remember him because he barely looked up from his cell phone the entire time. There were security cameras, but Jack could tell they weren't functioning. There was no red light indicating recording, and no motion sensors. The whole setup was a cheap ruse to deter would-be robbers. Jack smiled as he left the store. He could be comfortable that anyone looking for Paul's family would never know he rolled through here.

Removing the pump from the tank, Jack felt pretty reassured that he could make it to Ojai with only one more stop. He would wait a couple of hours before calling Vivian's caretaker to tell him what time he'd be back so he could go on home. Jack certainly didn't need anyone at the house when they arrived. His life was finally going to be exactly the way it was supposed to be again and he certainly wasn't going to let the surfer dude get in the way.

Back in the van and on the highway, Jack realized he needed to be very careful. He couldn't allow his excitement about the future to cause him to speed. Forcing himself to remain focused, he set the cruise control at the speed limit and settled back into the seat, sipped on his coffee and dreamed of the life he was about to enjoy. *Oh, life was going to be good again.*

Chapter Fifteen

The court room was small compared to the impression one would have from watching courtroom action on television. The only people present were Mark, Max, Dana, the judge, and Heath's court appointed guardian ad litem. Heath was brought in briefly. After about forty-five minutes of reviewing documentation and asking questions, the judge ruled in favor of emergency placement into Mark and Max's custody.

When it was done Heath was brought back in and was told that he would be able to go home with the newly-wedded couple. A huge smile covered his small face. Max realized it was the first time the boy had smiled that big since she met him. She watched as Mark hugged Heath and could tell a weight seemed to be lifted off his shoulders. Being able to help Heath was allowing Mark to settle the past.

Dana explained that a social worker would come by their home soon and periodically check in with them over the coming weeks. Bursting with pride, Mark and Max left the courthouse, each holding one of Heath's little hands in theirs. Heath chattered all the way back to the house and asked if they could have pizza. His random and simple conversation made Max smile, and Mark promised him pizza for dinner.

When they arrived home, Heath roamed the halls and bounced on the bed in the room that would be his. They had some decorating to do to make the room suited to a child, but Mark and Heath could work on that over the next couple of days. Mark was still arranging the sitter service. They had a lead on a nanny that was the sister of a fellow agent. It felt good to have a referral rather than trying to rely on a total stranger to care for Heath.

Max was frustrated that she was not going to be able to help make those arrangements, but her case was starting to heat up and they were close to narrowing in on the drug trafficking operation. The plan was to raid a drop and bring in people that could lead them to the organization that was heading the entire operation.

In some ways she felt overly conflicted. There were so many things to do, and new priorities were driving her now. She had her main work responsibility, her husband, and a child, and she wanted to have some time to run down the names Bobby had provided as potential leads on Jack Tyler. She was being forced to prioritize her life now in ways that were never necessary when she was single and with her career as her sole focus.

She was also seeing a softer side of Mark that was pleasing. When they met he was this totally serious, tough guy. It was sexy and all masculine, and now what she was getting to know was the layers and depth of the man she had grown to love. Those layers were going to provide the substance in their relationship that would enable her to remain in love and desire to stay with him forever.

After spending a while just settling into the house, Mark ordered pizza, and Max went to the bedroom to get comfortable. As she came back into the living room after changing, she could hear giggling, and she peeked around the corner to catch a glimpse of Mark holding Heath up in the air. The muscles that popped under Mark's shirt challenged the seams, and she realized that watching the way he interacted with Heath was the most attractive she'd ever seen him.

The days following Heath's court appointed custody were filled with new beginnings and learning how to care for a child and settling into a life of balance between family and work. Family had all been very supportive, and friends brought toys and clothes over. Soon Heath's room began to look like a child's kingdom.

On the surface everything looked perfect, but Heath often had nightmares. Max took turns with Mark going to him when he needed support. He would settle back down after a few minutes of comfort. He wet his bed at times, so they purchased plastic sheets to protect the mattress. Finally, after getting Heath added to the health insurance they began therapy sessions and were hoping to see some progress soon.

Max's case had turned up millions of dollars in the recovery of pharmaceutical drugs, and after an aggressive gun fight at a truck stop just off of Interstate I-40 they'd made a number of arrests and were now tracking the owner of a large pharmaceutical company located in California. She'd been lucky. So far there was only one overnight trip required, and the nanny recommended by their co-worker was working out very well.

Mark went back to full duty, and Heath started school. He was making friends and would come home filled with stories of other boys and playground antics. Things were settling nicely. Max notified her landlord that she was giving up her lease and, as time permitted, was slowly moving her things over to Mark's house.

Once Heath was tucked into bed, the passion that had first pulled Mark and Max together was stronger than ever. There was a familiar excitement that seemed to constantly sizzle between them. Life was good. They were happy, and things were going pretty well with the ready-made family.

Max took down the murder board in her living room at the apartment and began setting up a similar area in the garage at the house. They spent a day adding in a wall and door. The room was still crude, but it allowed Max to have the space to focus in the way that seemed to work for her. Heath wouldn't be allowed in that room. They agreed to keep it locked at all times.

Now that her family was stable and a routine was established, Max set up a desk and a computer in the room. She got home early and now had an hour before Heath would be home from school. She sat staring at the murder board stapled to the studs in the wall. She was considering the names Bobby had provided to Cortez. *Time for me to re-focus. Jack, where are you?*

Chapter Sixteen

Jack returned to California after giving Jimmy instructions to go home. He spent the next few days getting the basement established, fully furnishing the main room with a bed, TV, small kitchen table, and couch. He added a stainless steel table in the side room, setting up everything exactly the way he needed it to be able to take care of Hope and Faith while ensuring no one interfered with their safety.

He left Arizona with Mindy and her child and returned to California with Hope and Faith—his cherished family back together again. So far keeping them comfortable had been his only real concern. He knew it would take a little time before they settled in, and he really just wanted everything perfect for them. He was certain that he finally figured out the ideal way to have his life back.

Vivian continued to hang on, and it seemed Jimmy had taken good enough care of her that she hadn't felt the need to dial the phone number he'd given her. And now that he had his family back with him, there would be no reason for Jimmy's services again.

Early in the day he drove across town and followed Jimmy from the agency to his house. The fact was that Jimmy hadn't taken all that good of care of Vivian the first time around, and Jack knew he would not be able to allow that to pass. He was biding his time between feeding Vivian and caring for Hope and Faith. Waiting patiently until after midnight, it was time to pay Jimmy a visit.

"Hope," he said to Mindy. "I know we've always agreed to not hurt innocent people and that I'd use my skills for good versus simply feeding my dark impulses. But Jimmy is not innocent. He hurt Vivian when he cared for her, often not staying with her like he was supposed to, or leaving her far past the point of discomfort and in pain."

Mindy sat on the couch where he'd placed her, staring back at him. She could hear him perfectly but was not able to express her thoughts or feelings. No matter how hard she fought, the drugs won out, keeping her in an alert yet paralyzed state.

"You do understand, Hope darling, don't you?" Jack asked, his eyes pleading with her and waiting for a sign that she understood and supported his choice. "I followed him today. I know where he lives, and I believe he needs to pay for his transgressions."

Mindy couldn't respond, but Jack saw something in her eyes. A flicker, maybe even a sparkle and he knew. "Oh, thank you, darling. I knew you'd agree with me. Hope, I never want to disappoint you or defy the agreement we made when we were kids. I love you so much, and I only want what's best for you and our beautiful daughter."

He glanced over at the chair and smiled at the little girl he saw staring back at him. Her right arm dangled off to one side, and her blonde curls trailed over her shoulders. "She is so beautiful. Isn't she, Hope? Our adorable little Faith. Maybe one day we'll have that son we dreamed of. Do you remember talking about that?"

Not waiting for an answer that couldn't come, Jack leaned in and kissed Mindy, offering a deeply passionate kiss. Excitement filled him as he realized the enjoyment he felt in the warmth of the kiss. His Hope was truly alive, perfect in every way. He had finally done it, and he couldn't be more pleased.

Leaning back, he pushed a lock of hair out of Mindy's face and gave her another quick peck on the lips, then checked his watch and clicked his tongue inside his cheek. "I've got a couple of hours before I can leave. Do you think it's time I checked up on Agent Maxine Nichols? We certainly don't want her to ruin our plans. I'll be right back. Don't go anywhere." He chuckled and then turned and left the room.

A few minutes later he returned to the basement with his laptop. He plopped down on the couch next to Mindy. "It's so fun that you can do these things with me now. Agent Maxine Nichols has tried to keep us away from each other, Hope. We just can't let that happen."

Jack opened the lid to the computer and tapped away on the keys. With his wireless connected and Google open, he typed the agent's name into the search field. His first few attempts yielded nothing new, her graduation from the FBI academy being the most recent result. He tried a few different approaches and suddenly leaned forward as his eyes scanned the result on the screen.

"Why would a woman like Maxine Nichols suddenly get married?" His mind raced. "Do you think she's pregnant? Do you think while she was in Illinois trying to find me she laid down with Agent Wells? She married him at a court house, no ceremony, and no family present. Odd, don't you think?"

***

Mindy looked on, a steady blank stare cast over the screen. While she couldn't move, her eyes attempted to scan the page, searching for anything that might indicate someone was looking for her.

She saw nothing other than the small legal announcement of the union between Mark Wells and Maxine Nichols in the state of Virginia. She remembered the agent coming to her home in Arizona asking questions about her brother-in-law Jack Tyler. Mindy had been unable to provide details of his whereabouts. At that time she hadn't had contact with Jack for almost a year. She was stunned to hear they thought he might have been involved with the murders of six people that had been discovered in a grisly burial site in the Malibu canyon.

Despite her concerns about Jack's odd behavior as a boy, Mindy never thought him capable of murder. Now though, she knew full well of his capabilities. She had followed the news stories and knew he was connected to murders in three states. He killed children and was believed to have used the body parts of his victims to create replications of his dead wife and daughter—her sister and niece. The horror of that knowledge terrified her for the fate of herself and her child. Her eyes shifted to the little girl sitting across from her. Their eyes met momentarily, and she tried to comfort her in that moment.

95

She was terrified and could only imagine how scared her young daughter was.

She shuddered internally at the thought of how Jack considered her to be Hope. It was true, the sisters had been often asked if they were twins, but the fact that he had gone so crazy that he believed she was Hope scared her. He had already shown signs of wanting intimacy with her, and she knew it was only a matter of time before he wanted more. And she would be unable to do anything about it.

She wondered what he had done to Paul and their other child. She prayed they were okay, but she feared Jack had killed them both. A lone tear escaped the corner of her eye and rolled down her face. She could feel it but was unable to wipe it away. Fear filled her, worrying that Jack would see it and become angry with her. She mustn't show weakness around him if she hoped to survive this.

She hoped that in time he would not sedate her. If she got the opportunity, she would work to earn his trust. She just needed the opportunity. For her daughter's safety, she would do whatever Jack wanted from her.

***

Jack continued to surf the Internet trying to glean any more information he could about why a sudden, private wedding ceremony for Agent Maxine Nichols had taken place. Several attempts at searching had given him no results so he decided to change the criteria and searched on Mark Wells instead. He was astonished by what he found.

In the legal notices there was a single line indicating a court appointed guardianship of a five year old male child to Mark Wells.

"Hope, she's not pregnant. They got married so they could take custody of a young boy. Very interesting, don't you think? I assume they couldn't do it while single and living together," he said as Mindy continued to watch the computer screen.

He searched in vain to find a picture of the boy. Deciding there weren't any images for him to find, he finally gave up, satisfied for the moment. *So, you got married and have an instant family,*

Maxine. With these recent events, have you forgotten about me? That would be too good to be true.

Turning to face Mindy he asked, "Remember we were talking about having another child? We hoped that we would have a little boy, a playmate for Faith. We never got the chance. But now we're being given a second chance. It's funny how life creates chances. Don't you think, Hope? We're so lucky."

Jack stared into Mindy's eyes and mistook the fear that was clearly evident as approval of his comments. He smiled back at her, still ignoring the signs of terror that only her eyes could convey as she remained in a paralyzed state.

✱✱✱

A few days passed, and all the while Jack could barely remove his focus from that boy. He had become so focused on the idea of having a son, which thrilled him, that he had not yet handled the situation with Jimmy. He was so envious of Agent Maxine Nichols. He imagined how rewarding it would be to have a five year old that looked exactly like Hope. A boy he could teach and play with in the woods. A boy who could enjoy the playhouse the way he had enjoyed it as a child.

In between fantasizing of having a son he began to slowly wean Mindy and Allie off of the drugs, allowing them to move around on their own, like the ability to take food and water. This prevented him from having to feed and water them intravenously as he had been doing up until now. He wanted to get to a point where they could care for themselves.

He spent hours building security features into the basement that would ensure they would not be able to escape as they became more mobile. Confident that over time he would be able to allow them to have full range of not only the basement but also the home, he patiently waited for signs of compliance to their new life as his wife and child. On a sub-conscience level he knew they were resistant, but consciously he convinced himself that they were his loving family and everything was perfect now. There was just one thing missing.

As Mindy became more capable of participating in daily life his attraction and sexual desire grew. He was missing the intimacy he always shared with Hope and even considered conceiving a child now. There was just one problem…He remembered that Mindy had some issues following the birth of her children and knew that she was not capable of carrying a child. Oh well, there were other ways. Soon a plan began to form. There were a few things he would need first so that he could proceed. Excitement grew.

"Hope, Faith, my lovely family, I have an errand to run. I'll be back soon. Maybe I'll pick up some food from Boccalli's. Hope, I remember how much you loved the lasagna. We won't be able to sit out under the trees and enjoy the stars like we used to, but we can enjoy the savory food. Faith has never had the pleasure of trying it, so that will be a special treat. Don't miss me too much. I'll be back soon." He nearly skipped out of the room after planting a kiss on the top of Faith's head and Hope's pursed lips.

At the top of the stairs he applied the deadbolt and the strong arm across the steel door he'd recently installed. The strong arm was essentially a steel bar that locked across the door, affixed deeply into the concrete wall making it impossible to push the door open from inside. The entire basement was assembled from concrete block set deeply in the ground. The door was the only exit point. With the deadbolt and strong arm in place, Jack was quite confident there was no way out.

After checking in on Vivian and finding her alert and watching *Judge Judy*, he left the house and locked up behind him. Winding his way through town, he decided it was a good opportunity to check in on Jimmy. Swinging the vehicle out onto Main Street, from memory he returned to Jimmy's house. Making the final turn, he slowed as he passed by the small single-story corner home, taking notice that Jimmy's car was sitting in the driveway. Jack smiled, a familiar feeling rippled through his body, the darkness wrapping in on him like a thick cloak.

Continuing down the road, he retraced the route back to Main Street, through town to Matilija Street, and pulled into the Radio Shack parking lot. He assessed his surroundings and felt good that there were only a couple of other cars in the lot. He hoped those were employees' cars. He exited his vehicle, closed the door, and approached the store. Entering caused a chime to announce his presence.

Jack was greeted almost immediately by a young, geeky looking man who appeared to be barely in his twenties. His large, thick framed glasses seemed to be a shield for the heavy acne that covered his entire face.

"Good afternoon, sir. What may I help you with today?"

Jack smiled. His allure and natural charm immediately engaged the young lad and put him at ease.

"I am looking for some security cameras, basically a monitoring system. Do you have anything like that?"

"We sure do. Do you want something that is just internal to your home or business, or a system that can be monitored by the local police and fire, as well?"

"I think just internal to my home. I want to be able to ensure my kids are safe." Jack smiled again. "Getting to those teenage years and having friends over more, you know how it is?"

The pimply faced man laughed and nodded. Jack assumed he didn't really know what it was like. He likely wasn't invited to participate in many of those events.

"We have a unit over here that provides monitoring for four rooms, and it can be viewed on your cell phone," the young man replied, leading Jack to the other side of the room and picking up a large box from the bottom shelf.

Jack listened as the pimply faced man awkwardly explained how the device worked. His interest was in the monitoring ability and the feed he would get to his laptop and cell phone. He needed the ability to see what was happening in the basement from anywhere.

"Is there any audio capability that comes with this or as an add-on?"

"You mean you would want to be able to speak through an intercom of something like that?"

"Correct." Jack felt compelled to continue with an example based on the blank stare he received through the thick glasses. "Imagine if my teenage son has a girl come over and things get a little too hot. I want to be able to tell him to settle down and send her home." Jack had to refrain from laughing knowing the picture was making the guy horny at the very thought of it.

99

A bit flustered, the sales clerk pushed his black framed glasses up on his nose and then quickly moved to another shelf, turning his back to Jack seemingly in an effort to regain his composure. "We do have this. It's not part of the video unit, but it can work in conjunction with it." He carried the box over to the glass checkout counter and set it down then flipped open the box to display the contents. He spent the next few minutes describing the contents and how they would work.

Jack learned that basically, speakers could be mounted to the wall and an app could be downloaded for iPhone or Windows compatible devices, allowing the user to talk through a speaker and into the room where the speaker is mounted. It could also be used as a room to room intercom.

"Can the person inside the home turn off the device? I definitely wouldn't want my son turning it off, basically overriding the point of it in the first place."

"No, sir, that's the beauty of it. You can set it up to be controlled from a certain device. So for example your laptop would be the administration device, and the setup changes require a password to override the configuration. It gives you complete control of what and how you want to monitor or interact with the intercom. The video system works the same way." Pushing his glasses up over his pimply nose again, the sales clerk seemed pleased with himself.

"Great, I think this will work perfectly for controlling my kids. I'd also like to install a front door intercom with a monitor. You know where you can see who is outside the home?" Jack said, pulling his wallet out of his back pocket prepared to make a purchase.

After a few more minutes of the clerk showing him a few choices, Jack selected the intercom system too. It was a last minute thought, but after the way things went down with Dale in Illinois he didn't want any surprises like that again. He needed to protect his family in every possible way.

The sales clerk seemed ecstatic with the purchase as he bagged the boxes. Just as they were finishing the transaction and Jack was signing his alias onto the credit card slip, the door chime rang announcing the arrival of another customer.

A tall blonde woman entered the store. Jack grabbed his packages by the handles on the bags and turned to exit. As he passed, the woman stopped him. "Hello. Do I know you?"

Jack stopped, startled by the exchange. "Excuse me?"

"I'm sorry, you just seem so familiar. I thought I might know you from somewhere."

"I don't believe so," Jack replied rushing to the exit.

Getting to his vehicle as quickly as possible, he placed the packages on the back seat and climbed into the driver's seat as fast as he could. Backing out, he headed down the street and slammed the steering wheel with his hand, shouting, "Damn it, damn it, damn it!!!"

Anger rose in him. That woman recognized him. He knew who she was. Her name was Rebecca Tillman, or Reb as she liked to be called. She and Hope had remained friends until their sophomore year when Reb had expressed her concerns to Hope about him. Oh, she'd gone on and on about him being odd, strange, or creepy even. Hope hadn't listened, of course, and had severed the friendship just before they had gone off to college together.

As he drove he wondered what would happen if she remembered where it was she knew him from. He could not allow that to happen. He would have to take care of it. Oh, he would have fun with that, for sure. Deciding she was more of a risk than Jimmy, he looped back towards the Radio Shack, and rather than pulling into the parking lot he stopped about half way down the street and pulled in behind a Mercedes Benz that was parked along the curb.

For a moment his mind flitted back in the past to Benz—the used car salesman he spent quite a bit of time with in Oklahoma. Benz had been the perfect house guest. Jack had certainly enjoyed his time with that man. Maybe Reb could offer the same type of pleasure. The corners of his mouth curled slightly at the thought of it.

A few minutes passed, and then he saw her. She exited the store carrying a small bag. He watched as she climbed into a Lexus SUV and backed out. As she started down the street, he waited until a car merged in behind her and then he pulled out.

Keeping her car in his sights, he stayed back far enough to not be detected. He watched as she turned down a side street, and he slowed before identifying the street was not a cul-de-sac. He followed her, watching the SUV closely as it weaved through the trees that created shadows on the street from the late afternoon sun.

He continued to hold back far enough that he almost lost sight of her, and then watched as she pulled into the driveway of a ranch style home that sat at a great distance off of the street. The home was surrounded by trees and an ample yard. *Little Ms. Reb, you've done okay for yourself. What'd you do? Sleep with the rich quarterback?*

As he passed he saw the mailbox at the front of the driveway. He noticed the numbers and the name Tillman in block letters across the side. *Interesting, you're not married. Still have your maiden name. Or, have it again. What happened? Did someone hurt you real bad?*

He continued down the street and followed the winding path until it met with another and then hooked his way back out of the neighborhood. Once he was a good distance away, he stopped on the side of the street and pulled out his cell phone. He Googled "Rebecca Tillman, Ojai, CA" and waited for his 4G network to deliver the results. A few moments later he had a few options to choose from. He quickly selected the option to run a background check and logged into his previously established account to keep track of Agent Maxine Nichols. When he set it up he had no idea how handy it would be.

Within a few minutes he had the details about Rebecca Tillman. The records indicated that she was divorced and the mother of a child that had died at birth. Maybe that was the reason for the divorce. She changed her name back to Tillman a year after the divorce. Jack clicked "yes" on an advanced search and learned that she was the only name on the title of the house she led him to. Her mother died three years ago, and her father resided in Iowa. All indications were she lived alone in that home. *Oh, it is going to be a good night.*

Jack drove out to Boccali's and picked up the promised food before returning back home. He spent some time with Vivian before going downstairs to enjoy dinner with his family. He prepared the table and then assisted Mindy and the young girl to sit down for the meal. Although each day Jack was backing off on the medication, neither was able to completely walk on her own. Within a couple of days they would be able to move more freely. He assisted them with the food, which surprisingly they each readily accepted. Hunger must have finally overcome their resistance to him.

"Hope, it really is good to see you with an appetite back. I've terribly missed our dinners together." Turning his attention to Faith, he smiled and brushed his knuckles gently against her face. She flinched slightly, but he didn't notice. "What do you think of the lasagna? It's almost like your favorite, macaroni and cheese. Don't you think?"

The scared child looked at her mother. Mindy grunted out, "Good," before the girl could answer. The child gave a quick nod, following her mother's lead. Mindy watched in terror then relaxed slightly as her daughter answered the question correctly.

Jack chattered away throughout the dinner to the two half-immobile people sitting at the table. When the food was nearly gone and the two slowed down their acceptance of the food that he spooned their way, he began to clear the dishes.

"Well, I need to begin the installation of the equipment I purchased. I selected several items that will absolutely ensure you are both kept safe. You won't ever need to worry about your safety again. I bought equipment that will allow me to see where you are and what you're doing at any time of the day or night, even if I'm not home." He looked back and forth between the woman and child. "Isn't it great, Hope? I never have to worry about you leaving me ever again. Never can someone take you from me. We'll be together forever."

Leaving Mindy to contemplate the finality of his last statement, Jack left the room. He spent the next few hours working diligently to setup the video monitors and intercom systems. When he finally had everything installed, he downloaded the recommended apps to his cell phone and laptop. With everything in place he began monitoring his captive wife and daughter in the basement. Since they were both still sedated, he lost interest quickly but was pleased with the manner in which he could check their status on his cell phone. Now he had a visit to pay to Reb, but before leaving he needed to ensure his family knew they were safe.

He unbolted the door and descended the stairs. He didn't notice the subtle shudder that ran through Mindy as she saw him enter the room. "Hope, I just wanted you to know I got everything set up. Look how cool this is," he said showing her the view on the cell phone, which now displayed him standing in the room next to her showing her his phone. "I'll truly be able to be with you no matter where I am. You'll always be safe now, Hope. Nothing can

103

ever happen to you again. I just wanted you to know I'm watching before I go up to check on Vivian."

Mindy's head gave a slight snap at the name. "Oh, you didn't know she was here with us, did you? Yes, she's not all that well, but I'm caring for her. She's bedridden, pretty frail, actually. I'm doing the best I can with her. She resists eating some days, and so I'm focused on keeping her comfortable."

He smiled down at Mindy and saw a frown on her face. "Oh, don't worry, darling. I'm fine caring for all of you. I'm just sorry I have to divide my time. And I forgot to tell you, I saw your old friend Reb today. Remember her, that dreadful bitchy girl that tried to separate us? Anyway, she may come to visit soon. I think I'll invite her over." Jack laughed at the irony of his comment. "Okay, sweetheart, it's getting late. You need your rest, as does our little girl." With that he lifted her onto his feet by pulling her up by her arms and forcing them to drape around his neck. With her body pressed against his, he gazed down at her and passionately kissed her. Leaning back, he smiled and whispered in her ear, "Not now, darling, Faith is watching. Maybe once she falls asleep. I love you, Hope." He assisted her in walking across the room to the bed, laid her down, and kissed her again.

"Okay, Faith, time for bed," he said, turning to the child, lifting Allie up and carrying her to the couch to lay her down. After carefully covering her up, he kissed her small cheek and said his good-nights to each before leaving the basement.

He didn't really have plans with Vivian. She'd fallen asleep for the night long ago, but he didn't want his wife to worry about him being out in the middle of the night. She needed to feel safe in knowing that he was in the house with her at all times. He double checked the door to the basement, looked at the monitors, and checked the app on his cell phone before turning to leave.

Outside in the night his body tingled. He felt alive. Things were going so well. He just had a few loose ends to clear up before he could proceed with the rest of his plans.

Chapter Seventeen

Max got home before Heath returned from his afternoon Kindergarten class and before Mark returned from the office. She went in during the wee hours of the morning to meet with the task force as they monitored the drug company CEO. He had unusual comings and goings during the middle of the night, and they were trying to get a fix on what he was up to. There was some concern that he was rebuilding his trafficking network faster than they could gather enough evidence to prove he was the mind behind the entire operation.

Lately though, Max was spending a lot of time in the private room in the garage. She went in and locked the door behind her, making sure Heath wouldn't enter on accident. She was trying to make some sense of the names that Cortez had sent over. So far she came up empty. She worked through the list one by one looking for anything unusual, but given the fact that the names were somewhat common and that she had no idea where to look for Jack, it was a slow process.

The first thing she did was cross-reference the names against the locations that she had previously identified as the most likely cities that he would live in. This was still based off of the list she had put together when she first started tracking Jack after he killed six people in California.

The discovery of his magazines under his playhouse from when he was a boy in Ojai had been instrumental in creating the list. Later, he had in fact turned up in Tulsa, Oklahoma, the number three city on her list, and then again outside Bloomington, Illinois. She knew those cities held special meaning to him, and she hoped that she would be able to tie him to one of them again. If one of the names matched one of those towns and anything out of the ordinary jumped out, she just might have a lead.

She tried to narrow down the searches by sorting the names associated to the list in fewest to highest order, hoping she would get lucky and not have to work through the high numbers at the bottom. It was a long shot, but she had to try. Letting Jack Tyler remain at large just simply was not an option. Not realizing it, she said out loud, "I'm coming for you, Jack, and I will find you."

After going through the data, Max heard the door open to the garage. Glancing at her watch, she realized the nanny must have just brought Heath home. She decided it was time to wrap up for the day and saved all her files then turned off her computer.

When she opened the door she was startled to see Heath standing there. "Hi, Max. Whatcha doin'?" the boy innocently asked her, curiously trying to peer inside the room.

"Oh, hey there, big guy. I was just workin'. Whatcha' doin'?"

"Lookin' for you. Wanna play with me?"

Max chuckled, putting her arm around the small boy's shoulders and leading him away from the room, locking the door behind her. "Sure. How about we get a snack first?"

Heath smiled up at her, his crooked little grin glowing at her. He slipped his little hand into hers as they entered the house.

Once inside Max got them each a banana, Heath's favorite snack, and cut it up in little pieces. They sat face to face at the dining room table as they popped the mushy, white bits into their mouths while Heath chattered about his day. Max smiled at his resilience. Life had dealt him a very bad hand, and yet anyone looking at him right now would have thought he never suffered a sad moment. As she sat watching him lick his sticky little fingers, she felt grateful for having the ability to be there for him now when he needed someone the most.

A few minutes later the front door swung open and Mark came in carrying Chinese food. Heath jumped down from the chair and ran to him, nearly barreling him over. "Yea, chicken sticks," he yelled as he clung to Mark's waist.

Mark laughed at the greeting as he held the bags of food over the boy's head and out of the way of a possible spill. Once Heath settled down Mark leaned over to kiss Max, who had joined Heath at his side, then continued on to the kitchen counter to set down the bags.

"You don't like chicken sticks, do you, Heath?" Mark teased the little boy.

"Yes, I do," Heath answered with emphasis on his words in a sing-song way.

Max chimed in with, "I bet you don't want any since you just had that banana."

Heath gave her a look then said, "I could eat a whole chicken."

Max laughed at the assuredness the little guy presented. "I bet you could!"

A few minutes later the group offered the nanny the evening off and settled down to eat an early dinner. Heath practiced with his children's version of chopsticks with the shape of elephants at the end, and instead of being two separate sticks they were connected at one end, making it much easier for small hands to hang on to. Even still, as he tried to navigate noodles into his mouth, a good portion fell back onto his Sponge Bob plate and down the front of his shirt. Mark and Max exchanged a glance and each smiled at the certain mess that would be the result of the dinner selection. The small family continued to eat, chatter, and share stories throughout the dinner until the food was nearly depleted and Heath was sufficiently covered in gooey sauces.

Finishing off with the fortune cookies, Mark let Heath pick his own before handing one to Max and taking his. Heath attempted to read the words by calling out a few letters that he knew. For all of his struggles he was doing pretty well. He was able to recognize most of the alphabet and was progressing well ahead of where he needed to be to enter first grade.

Finally, after letting Heath attempt to read his own cookie Mark read it to him. "A new perspective will come soon."

"What does it mean?" Heath asked with obvious curiosity and excitement as if the fortune could truly predict the future.

"Well, it means that soon you will think about things differently," Mark replied.

"Oh." The boy was clearly thinking hard about the message. His young mind obviously churning. "Like being a big boy in first grade?"

Both Mark and Max laughed out loud. Mark replied, "Exactly like that."

Heath seemed satisfied and listened anxiously as Max read hers, followed by Mark reading his. They each explained what theirs meant, and once he was satisfied with the responses, they began to clear the containers and plates away from the table. Max started to do the dishes when Mark stepped in and offered to assist while she helped Heath with his bath. They often took turns with the household chores and Heath's care. Tonight it was Max's turn to handle bath duty.

With a sufficient bubble bath drawn at the perfect temperature, Heath settled deeply into the foamy water and played with a variety of toys that lined the tub wall. As he played Max sponged him clean, washing his hair with no tears shampoo. A half an hour later Heath was dried and dressed for bed, complete with a nighttime pull-up required for his bed wetting problems. They'd discovered early on that Heath wet the bed nearly every night. She'd be lying to herself if she said the bed wetting wasn't concerning. She could only hope that as the emotional scars healed this would improve.

Her mind drifted to Jack Tyler. He had been a bed wetter, she was certain. She thought about his abusive mother and his troubled life, how Hope at such a young age had reached into the dark torment and had given him a life preserver to cling to, and how that life preserver was snatched away so quickly. She smiled as she thought of Mark being the life preserver for Heath. Together they would give this boy something to cling to and keep the evil from coming after him again.

"Max, are you going to tuck me in and read me a story?"

She smiled at his innocent request that snapped her out of her thoughts of Jack and the horrible childhood he had endured. "You bet I am. Why don't you go pick out a story? I'll be there in just a minute."

Heath ran off down the hall to his room, and Max hurried to clean up the towel and clump of clothes that lay on the floor. When everything was back in place she followed the path the child had taken and found him kneeling in front of his small bookcase. He was holding the story of *Little Red Riding Hood,* and though she didn't really know why, the book sent chills up her spine.

Shaking it off, she chastised herself for having such strange thoughts over a children's story that she herself had adored when she was a child. Heath crawled under the covers and pulled the blankets up to his chin and listened, only occasionally interrupting her as she read the story.

When the wolf had been successfully conquered Max kissed Heath on the head. He wrapped his arms around her neck and whispered in his sleepy state, "I love you, Mommy."

Max's heart raced. This was a first, and she almost didn't know how to feel. They'd only had the boy a few weeks, but clearly he was settling in.

"I love you too, Heath," she replied hugging him tightly.

"Will Daddy come in too?"

"Yes, I'll send him to tuck you in too."

"I know what the tortune cookie means," he said, pronouncing fortune cookie wrong as he had always done. "It means I feel different for you. Good different." His eyes were starting to close and Max patted the covers around his sides before standing up to go and get Mark.

In the living room she found Mark tapping madly at his laptop. "Problem?" she asked.

"No, just finishing up something."

"Heath wants you to tuck him in, though I think he's already in dreamland."

"Right. On my way," Mark said, standing up and turning to the hallway.

"And, he called me mommy and you daddy."

Mark stopped dead in his tracks. "He did?"

Max nodded in confirmation. "He did."

A huge smile crossed over Mark's strong and almost always serious face as he turned back to the hall and towards the boy's room to say his good night.

Chapter Eighteen

Jack stood under Reb's bedroom window. He peered in long enough to determine that she had a small dog. There didn't appear to be any other movement in the home. Reb lived alone. Well, other than the dog.

He felt his pocket, confirming he had what he needed, and then slipped around the end of the house, his gloved hands checking windows. So far he hadn't found any open, but he wasn't discouraged and wouldn't let a few locks stop him.

By the time he decided it was safe to move forward it was well past midnight. He checked the monitors back at the house on his cell phone. Hope and Faith were sound asleep. He smiled at the peaceful scene.

Satisfied his family was fine, he continued along the side of the house, making his way back to the bedroom. He peered into the window and waited for his eyes to adjust from the cell phone glow to the darkness. After a few moments the pupils in his eyes adjusted, and he could see Reb snuggled into her bed. He watched carefully. The little dog was tucked in the fold of her knees.

Deciding it was time, he moved around the house to the furthest window from the master bedroom. He looked around on the ground and found a rock, then reached in his pocket and pulled out the rag he had shoved in there before leaving his vehicle. He wrapped the rag around the rock, and with one more look around, he tapped the rag-covered rock against the corner of the window. The glass gave way with a quiet shatter.

Jack stood there frozen as he listened for any movement inside. He heard a few small barks that seemed to start towards him then turned and went towards the back yard instead. Jack sighed then began removing the remaining glass fragments. Shoving the rag back in his pocket, he dropped the rock on the ground. After making sure there was nothing to get cut on, he pulled surgical booties and a hair cover from his pocket and put them on before hoisting his muscular body up through the window and dropping in on the carpeted floor. Glass crunched under his feet. He hovered and listened before moving. His eyes quickly adjusted to the light inside the home. It was dark, but a light shone in the hallway and a clock cast an eerie blue haze on the floor from the stove.

Jack could hear the dog barking outside and saw that there was a doggie door next to the back patio door. The flap was still swinging slightly. He treaded softly over to it and quickly slid the panel closed to keep the pet outside. He felt relieved that he wouldn't need to deal with the woman's pet. He wasn't interested in animals anymore. No, he had moved far beyond that dark pleasure years ago.

Reaching into his pocket, he pulled out a syringe he'd tucked away before getting out of the van and began slowly creeping down the hallway. Just outside the door he stood still with his back up against the wall and waited.

The dog continued to bark occasionally, probably wanting back inside now that the noise it had gone in search of had not been discovered. The woman remained still in the bed. Jack leaned in far enough to see which direction she was facing and found her back to him. He contemplated his approach briefly and then silently pushed off of the wall and entered the room.

Next to the bed he stood staring down at the woman—Reb. He hated her then, and he hated her now. *This is going to be fun*, he thought. He pulled the rag from his pocket, along with the syringe, and depressed the plunger into the rag.

"Hey, Reb," Jack said just loud enough to wake the sleeping woman. He watched as in her confused state she shook her head trying to make sense of what she was seeing. The surgical hair cover likely added further confusion. He could only imagine that her initial thought was that she was in the hospital. That was if she could make him out at all.

Well, plenty of time for her to catch up later. Right now, it was time to get Reb home where he could fully teach her all the lessons she deserved all along. He leaned forward to press the rag against her face and was startled when she shot out of the bed and lunged at him. Before he knew what happened, his vision was blurred from an intense pressure against his eyes.

Reb dug her thumbs deep into his eyes sockets, forcing him to drop the empty syringe as he grabbed at her wrists and slammed her back down onto the bed. Clinging to the rag in his hand, he slid his knee up under himself and used it to push hard down on her chest while wrestling her wrists into the hand that was free of the rag. She arched her back and tried to push against his muscular frame.

Finally, he was able to lock her arms under his while working her thin wrists tightly together. He could feel her pulse pounding against his thumb as he wadded the rag into a ball and pressed it against her mouth as he leaned even deeper into her abdomen, forcing the air from her lungs. The lack of oxygen caused her to gasp for a breath, taking in a deep dose of Chloroform. A few moments later her legs and arms went slack, and the wrestling match ended. She'd fought hard, but she was no match for his strength.

Being sure that she was completely unconscious, Jack slid off of her and stood staring down at her body, his face red from the struggle; his hand shook with anger. "That wasn't very smart, Reb my dear. You just sealed your fate. I might have been nice or at least gentle with you, but now you'll pay. We're about to have a whole lot of fun together."

Jack rolled her out of the bed, and with his adrenaline still pumping, he slung her over his shoulder. Her arms and hair dangled behind his back as he walked through the dark hallway to carry the woman to the garage. He lowered her to the floor by dropping the bundle with a thump. "Oh, that probably hurt. I'd say I'm sorry, but I'm not."

Jack left Reb laying there and went back into the house. Using the door to the garage, he entered through a small room connected to the kitchen. He cautiously slid through each room while searching for her purse. He found his bounty sitting in an office next to the master bedroom. Digging through the bag, his fingers curled around a set of car keys. Snatching them out, he turned and went back out to the garage.

Sliding in behind the wheel of the Lexus, he turned the key in the ignition and flipped the visor down to look for a garage door opener. Finding a programmable feature in the ceiling panel next to the rearview mirror, he pushed the button and smiled as the door began to open. Backing out, he pulled the car on the opposite side of the driveway, then exited and walked quickly to his own vehicle just at the edge of the property.

Jack looked around. The neighborhood was still quiet with the exception of Reb's small dog. He needed to let that dog back in the house so he would quiet down. Deciding he'd deal with that once he had Reb secure, he pulled forward and turned into the driveway, pulling his vehicle into the garage. The lights were on inside, so he quickly hopped out and walked around the front grill of the vehicle, and hit the remote mounted on the wall next to the garage door.

Protected by the privacy of the garage, Jack went back inside and opened the doggie door. He was faced by a small mixed breed dog. The animal immediately approached him, quickly demonstrating his lack of watch dog skills. Jack patted the small, wiry haired dog on the head then went back to the garage with the dog's nails clicking on the floor behind him.

Back in the garage Jack opened the back hatch of his vehicle and then walked back to the front of the garage and pulled Reb's body over to the back of the vehicle. He slid the end up into the back and then pulled the tarp out to carefully cover his new cargo.

The small dog was still hovering around. It sniffed at the blanket on the floor and whimpered slightly. "It's okay, little guy. She's just sleeping for now. Don't worry. Nothing bad is going to happen to you." Jack watched as he spoke to the little dog. His tail wagged and tongue draped to one side.

Jack went back inside the house for one more look around. Then suddenly he remembered something. He walked quickly back to the master bedroom, and once near the bed he knelt down, feeling around under it until he felt the syringe. Careful to not stick himself, he scooped it up then stood looking around in the dim light. Feeling confident that he didn't leave anything in the bedroom, he turned to leave. As he passed the office next to the master bedroom, he grabbed Reb's purse, then remembered the broken glass.

He carried the purse to the kitchen counter and set it down, then took a few minutes to look through various closets until he found the vacuum. He lifted the device labeled Eureka, which instantly triggered a flash of memories of the small town he'd found in Illinois.

Focusing, he turned and went back to the area where the glass fell in and was crushed into the carpet. He unwrapped the cord from the vacuum's handle and squinted through the dim light until he found a plug in the wall behind him. He plugged in the machine and carefully sucked up the debris, listening as the chards made pinging noises as they whirled up inside the canister. Once the noise subsided he looked at the locking hasp on the front of the vacuum and removed the canister. Carrying it into the kitchen, he looked through drawers until he found a grocery sack. He dumped the debris into the small plastic bag, being careful to not allow anything to fall onto the floor. Then he walked the canister back over to the vacuum to reinstall it.

Unplugging the item from the wall, he wrapped the cord back around the handle and carried the vacuum back to the closet where he originally found it. He walked back to the kitchen and lifted the purse from the counter, pausing briefly as his mind worked through each room. With the bag containing the glass still in his hand and satisfied that he left nothing else, he returned to the garage and closed the door behind him.

Hitting the remote on the wall, he lifted the little dog and carried him to the driver's side of the vehicle. He opened the door and set the small animal on the seat next to him. Starting the engine, he backed the car out far enough that he could pull Reb's car back in.

Jack quickly made the swap of the cars inside the garage, and then backed his vehicle out of the driveway and wound his way out of the neighborhood. When he was a few blocks away he sighed. "We're safe now, little guy," he spoke to the dog as he drove.

Within a few minutes Jack arrived back at his home and quickly tucked the vehicle away inside the garage. He went to the back of the vehicle and immediately pulled the woman out of the van, hoisting her onto his shoulder so he could carry her down to the basement.

The little dog followed at his heels as they entered the house through the garage. With the keys in his hand, he removed the bar from the basement door and unlocked the deadbolt. A step at a time he carefully descended the stairs, glancing into the room where Hope and Faith were sound asleep. The medication made them rest a lot.

Neither one stirred at the sound of his footsteps. He continued to the room that he had prepared for his special surgical needs.

After depositing Reb onto the stainless steel table, her body making a thumping noise as he dropped her, he returned upstairs to secure the door just in case one of his family woke up. The little dog stood at the top of the steps waiting for him.

"Come on, you can do it. These steps aren't that big," he encouraged the pup as it danced back and forth working up the courage to take the first step.

Jack watched as the dog finally pushed against his fear and began easing his way down the steps.

At the bottom Jack patted the little dog on the head and praised him, "Good job. I told you it wasn't too hard."

Returning to the surgical room, Jack closed the door behind him, and he could feel the adrenaline begin to pump again. It had been a while since he'd been able to allow the darkness to rip through his veins, and he was very much looking forward to the euphoric release that came with his exploration. Reb was going to be especially satisfying. That little bitch had tried to ruin his life, and back then he'd ignored it. Now his patience was paying off.

Jack spent the next few minutes removing his clothes and pulling on scrubs. Properly dressed for the occasion, he worked Reb's clothes off of her, and once fully nude, he retrieved zip ties from the shelf on the wall and tightly secured her hands and feet to the table legs. With her fully fastened in place all he had to do now was wait.

As expected, a few minutes later Reb began to stir. Jack smiled as he watched her eyes flutter and try to open. He didn't apply a gag to her mouth, not yet. He wanted some time to talk with her first.

Reb rolled her head to the side as she tried to shake off the effects of the Chloroform. Finally, her eyes opened and scanned the room, stopping on his face. They grew wide.

"Well, hello, Reb. Remember me?" he asked.

Reb tried to talk, but nothing came out at first. Her tongue flicked across her lips. "Store," she managed to get out, her voice raspy and dry.

Jack laughed out loud as he realized she was talking about the Radio Shack. "Well yes, I guess you did see me there, but no,

Reb, that is not exactly what I was talking about. We go way back, but you don't recognize me, do you?" He was nearly gloating in the success of the surgical modifications that had been made to his facial features.

Reb's eyes scanned his face. She was clearly confused by his comments. Jack leaned in closer. "Familiar," she choked out, fighting her hands and feet against the pressure of the zip ties which held her tightly to the table. Within moments she'd worked herself into frenzy and began to scream.

The little dog stood at Jack's feet and whimpered. Jack bent down and lifted up the little dog. Reb immediately stopped struggling when she saw her beloved pet. Her head began shaking furiously, and tears poured down her cheeks.

"Oh," Jack said, "I'm not going to hurt him. I like him. I think he likes me too." Jack looked at the little dog, and the dog took a quick lap with his tongue, landing a puppy kiss on Jack's nose. "See, he does like me."

Reb continued to fight against the restraints. "What do you want from me?" she forced out while continuing to study Jack. Her eyes scanned down and landed on his hands, and a hint of recognition sparked. He could tell she had seen something familiar about his hands. He had meticulously manicured nails with perfect half-moon crescents.

"I really don't want anything. It's just payback time," Jack said as he watched her eyes looking for anything to help figure out who he was.

"Payback?" Reb asked clearly puzzled.

"Think about it. I'll give you a hint. You tried to destroy my relationship."

He watched as Reb stopped fighting, and the wheels began to turn in her brain. Slowly a mild yet confused recognition came over her face as she seemed to remember. Her eyes dropped to his hands again. "Starting to figure it out?"

"Hope?"

"That's right. You tried to ruin the beautiful thing Hope and I had. But it didn't work, now did it? Today when I saw you, I knew you would try to ruin us again. I can't let that happen."

Reb stared at him, tears rolled from the corners of her eyes. Her eyes searched his face. "Hope... dead."

117

"Oh, she was, but I took care of that. She and our daughter Faith are asleep in the other room, sorry, but there won't be any reunion for the two of you."

Reb began fighting again as the realization set in that the man hovering over her was Jack Tyler, nationally known as a wildly insane killer. A shudder coursed over her. Jack could only imagine that she had read stories in the paper about him. He'd been pursued by the authorities in several states and had made national news.

"Well, about that reunion. I'm glad you know who I am. This is going to be so much fun for us." Setting the little dog back down, Jack pulled on a pair of surgical gloves, and then picked up a scalpel from the tray that hung suspended on an arm over the surgical table. Light glinted against the polished tool. Reb began to scream again, but Jack was too busy making his signature incision to notice.

Blood flowed out of Reb's body and puddled on the table at her sides. Jack throttled his desires. He desperately wanted to dive his hands deep into her body, but he knew if he did then the fun he planned on having with Reb would end abruptly. He couldn't have that since he planned on having a long relationship with her.

He looked down at the woman's nude body, and without allowing his eyes to explore the private areas, he assessed her condition and realized he needed to stabilize her. He went to work quickly suturing up the incision he made down the center of her abdomen.

A few moments later, he had stopped the bleeding. Although she had lost a fair amount of blood, and there was no doubt organ damage from his invasive probing, she would not die. He wouldn't allow her to die. Though she'd gone slack at some point and had fallen unconscious he wasn't aware of when that took place. He'd been too focused on his own enjoyment that he'd missed that moment.

Jack began cleaning up. He looked down and watched as the little dog lapped at a small pool of blood on the floor. His paws were now a bright crimson. Jack smiled. "Hey little guy, what are you doing?"

He lifted the small dog, rinsed him, and then toweled him off. Afterwards he rinsed the blood off the floor and down the drain in the center of the room. "Now stay out of stuff, okay?" Jack said setting the little dog back down.

118

Moving over to the other end of the room, he opened a small refrigerator that sat in the corner and pulled out an IV bag. He returned to the table and carefully inserted the IV into Reb's right arm, then hung the bag on a portable stand. He would hydrate her enough to keep her alive. After all, he wasn't finished with her yet. He double checked her breathing and was satisfied that even though her breathing was labored, she was stable. With that he pulled off his scrubs and deposited them in a laundry basket next to the door, then hosed himself down, scrubbing at his skin and washing himself thoroughly with bleach.

Finally, satisfied that everything was perfectly cleaned, he picked up the little dog and exited the room. A quick peek in on Hope and Faith showed they were still sound asleep. He wasn't sure what time it was, but he was tired and hungry. Ascending the steps, he unlocked the door and stepped onto the landing. Setting down the little dog, he closed the door and applied the bar across it, sealing in his family and guest.

After going to the kitchen, he immediately cracked several eggs into a skillet. The clock on the wall indicated it was three o'clock in the morning. He usually ate much healthier than this, never eating at this time, but his late night adventure left him famished. He scooped a couple of spoons of the fluffy yellow scramble into a small bowl and set it down for the little dog then quickly devoured the rest himself. The dog licked his chops and stared up at his new master, wagging his tail in approval of the snack.

Jack rinsed the dish he used for the eggs and filled it with some water, setting it on the floor again, allowing the small dog to lap up the liquid until he was satisfied. Placing the dish in the sink, he led the little dog over to the back door and let him outside. The dog watched Jack warily at first, then stepped out into the night. A few moments later he returned inside.

Jack patted him on the head. "Good boy. I guess I need to give you a name. I don't even know what kind of dog you are, but you sure are a scruffy little guy. Scruffy, that's it. Come on, Scruffy. Let's go check on Vivian and then it's off to bed for us."

Chapter Nineteen

Jack woke with a start. He looked over at the alarm clock on the bedside table. It was nearly ten o'clock. He started to sit up but felt a weight at the back of his legs. Looking down, he saw the small dog curled next to him. The dog's brown eyes looked into his, appearing eager to see what would be next.

"Well, good morning, Scruffy. We have to get moving. Vivian, Hope, and Faith need us." Jack lifted the little dog off of the bed and quickly went about getting breakfast ready for Vivian while the dog explored the house. He went up the stairs with the dog following right at his heels.

After tapping lightly on Vivian's door, Jack entered. She lay propped up on the pillows with her eyes closed. Each time he entered the room his heart jumped as he thought she'd passed, but then she'd stir slightly and he would smile as relief washed over him.

"Good morning," he said softly.

Vivian opened her eyes and smiled slightly. She looked around the room, her eyes settling on the small dog. "You have a friend?"

"This is Scruffy. He lost his owner recently and needed a new home."

Jack checked Vivian's catheter and vitals while asking, "How are you feeling?"

"Like a teenage girl," Vivian teased.

Jack gave her a disapproving look. "Seriously, how are you feeling? What's your pain level?"

"The same, I guess."

Jack administered meds to her and offered the tea he'd brought up. He spent the next thirty minutes trying to get a protein shake down her before she dozed off again. He tucked the blankets around her before quietly leaving her to rest.

The next stop of the morning was to check on his wife and daughter and Reb. Once in the basement, he was pleased to see both Hope and Faith were awake. For the first time he allowed the medication to wear off completely, so they were sitting cuddled together on the couch. When he entered the room they shrunk deeper into the cushions.

"Good morning. Sorry, I didn't mean to frighten you. No need to be afraid, but we do need to talk. It's time we started acting like a family again. I want to allow you freedom here." He swept his arm across the room.

The woman and child sat staring at him, their eyes wide with fear. It tore at his heart that they would be frightened of him, but he knew it was time for them to settle in. He knew how to make them more cooperative. Holding up his finger, he said, "Stay here."

Jack went to the surgical room and swung open the door. Reb lay still tied to the table. Her nude body was pale and her breathing labored. The incision down her torso looked raw and angry. Jack's breath caught as he saw her. His adrenaline immediately ramped up. Reminding himself he needed to focus on his family, he continued to the refrigerator in the corner. Swinging open the door, he looked at the vials in the cool interior.

Jack selected the bottle labeled Phenobarbital. He stared at the bottle for a moment and then closed the door, trapping the cool air inside. This would keep everyone in the right frame of mind so they could reconnect as a family. He certainly understood why this was so hard. They had been ripped apart. His wife and child had suffered severe trauma, and now they were healing. It would take time.

Returning to the room, he was pleased to see that neither the child nor mother had moved. Scruffy was on his heels as he went back and forth between the rooms and now stood at his side facing the couch. Jack approached, and while they had the energy to get to the couch, neither was willing to put up a fight as he injected them each with a mild dosage of the drug from the vial. They would be able to function but would remain passive and relaxed. This was the way he needed things to be until they got used to this arrangement.

"Hope, I love you so much," he said after removing the needle from Mindy's arm. She just watched as he brushed her hair from her face. "I bet you're getting hungry." Jack knew what he needed to do and went upstairs for his next task.

Within a few minutes he made breakfast and delivered it down the stairs. He helped them move over to the table, and they sat as a family to eat the food he had prepared. The woman and child ate slowly. Their navigation of the fork to their mouths was somewhat impaired by the drugs in their system.

Jack rose and left the table, quickly climbing the stairs. He returned a few moments later with his laptop. He opened up the computer and logged on. After a few minutes he successfully ordered a small refrigerator, electric stove, and a microwave to be delivered the following day. Tomorrow he would set the rest of the basement up to accommodate food and cooking. He needed Hope to begin resuming some of her duties of feeding and caring for Faith. The sooner she started acting like a mother again the sooner she would begin to realize this is where she belonged.

With the items ordered he decided that while he was logged on he would check on his favorite person–Special Agent Maxine Nichols. After a few minutes he was unable to find anything new on the beautiful agent. Next he logged onto a home page for the Phoenix news to see if there was any report on Mindy. He hated it, but he knew he needed to make sure his new identity was still protecting him. He could never let anyone get close enough to hurt his family again.

His eyes scanned the screen as he sat across from Hope and next to Faith. They continued to eat slowly as they watched him click away on the computer. Finally, his search found what he was looking for. In a headline that read "Husband/Father Suspect in Wife and Daughter's Disappearance," Jack skimmed through the article carefully and nearly laughed out loud when he realized the police believed that Paul had caused his own injuries to cover up a crime committed against his wife and daughter.

"Hope, this is perfect. Honey, we're safe. No one is even looking for us. We can relax and truly be a family."

Mindy's eyes met his. A mild tremor rushed through her, but Jack barely noticed. He was too focused on the story and elated by the report.

Hitting the back button on his search page, the screen returned to his lookup on Maxine Nichols. His eyes again scanned the page, and then he typed in Mark Wells and re-read the stories he read before about the little boy. Maxine Nichols and Mark Wells were the proud guardians to a little boy. Jealousy filled him.

He looked across the table at his wife and daughter, and a smile formed on his face. Life was going to be so good. He had a few things he needed to do, but suddenly he felt so happy about what the future would hold.

Later that evening after dinner, Jack sat for a while watching TV with his family. Scruffy took turns sitting on his lap and Faith's. It was cute to see her cuddled up to the little dog. It seemed to make her happy, and he wondered why he'd never gotten her a dog before. The day quickly got away from him, between taking Scruffy out, checking in on and caring for Vivian, and being with his family. It was evening, and the darkness was calling for him. It was time for his family to sleep and time for him to make another visit to Reb.

Hope and Faith were carefully tucked into bed for the night. Jack tucked Scruffy in with Faith, and then left them to rest and entered the surgical room. Reb lay on the stainless steel table. Her eyes popped open at the sound of him entering the room. "Well, it's good to see you're feeling better. You were a little under the weather earlier," he said referring to her unconscious state earlier.

Reb's eyes grew wide, and her feet started to twitch as fear pulsed through her nervous system. "You better keep yourself calm. You could cause yourself to have a stroke. You know, getting it all worked up."

Unable to calm herself, Reb's feet continued to twitch. "Well, I do understand your concern because you're right after all. What I'm about to do is in fact going to hurt like hell."

Jack snapped on gloves and slipped out of his clothes and into a fresh set of scrubs. Within moments and despite Reb's screams and pleas, he snipped and pulled away each of the sutures, depositing them onto the surgical tray. Reb arched her back against the pain as Jack slid the scalpel into the opening that just barely began to heal. Blood oozed out of the new opening. Jack slid his gloved fingers into the cavity and touched organs. Still he resisted the urge to push his hands fully into the woman's battered body, as he wanted to enjoy more time with her. Killing her now would be a disappointment.

With his immediate needs met, Jack once again stitched the woman's body closed and secured a new IV bag. Like before, Reb passed out from the pain at some point during the violation of her internal organs. Her breathing was labored, but once again she would survive. Jack knew the pain must be excruciating, but he didn't really care. Only once had he ever really cared about the pain he inflicted on his victim. He smiled as he remembered little Jessie. He had stolen her mouth, but let her live.

For a moment the memory made him feel sad as he realized the procedure had ended up being unnecessary a complete failure. Things hadn't gone as he had planned, but for a while Jessie had brought Faith back to him, long enough for him to realize he had been going about it all wrong. And now he'd found his real family.

Reb was once again stitched and resting. Exhausted from the adrenaline, he washed everything down the drain. His body washed and clean he went upstairs to pull on some boxers before returning down stairs.

He moved Faith and Scruffy to the couch then slid in between the covers of the bed and pulled Hope to him. She was sound asleep and didn't respond, but it felt good to hold his wife again. Her skin was so soft, and her hair smelled of honeysuckle. He felt himself becoming aroused and forced himself to push those feelings back. He would wait for her to feel more comfortable. Relaxing, he let out a sigh and spooned against her. Soon he was fast asleep.

***

Mindy woke to the warmth of a body snuggled tightly against her. She felt lips kiss the back of her neck and for a moment she leaned into the feeling. Her mind clearing from sleep and drugs she suddenly realized where the warmth came from and rolled over to pull away. Her body went rigid.

"Good morning, darling. I hope you slept well. How does a good breakfast sound? I'll make Faith her favorite pancakes. Then later we're going to get some appliances delivered here so you can prepare meals yourself. I'll have to go out to get some groceries. I'll stock up everything. I want you to have everything you want."

Mindy stared at him. She wanted to gash his eyes out, but she couldn't seem to bring herself to have the strength to do anything but lay there paralyzed by her fear. Her mind felt like quicksand. She knew she needed to pull herself together for her daughter Allie, *Oh God, where is she?* Her eyes searched the room, finally finding Allie still asleep on the couch. There was a small dog wrapped in her daughter's arms.

Mindy's heart pounded deep inside her chest, and her head hurt. Jack lay close to her talking, but she really had no idea what he was talking about. *I have to get out of here,* she thought, but she had no idea how to make that happen when lifting her head off the pillow seemed insurmountable.

"Today, I'm going to start slowing down the meds so we can begin to act more like a family. I think you're sleeping too much. I want you to be able to care properly for Faith. She needs you. I know you experienced a lot of pain from the accident, but you should be healed now. After all it has been well over a year since that horrible day. You both have been through so much, but I promise you nothing but the best now."

He was still talking. *Did he say he was going to let up on the drugs?* If he did that, maybe she could find a way out of here. Where is *here*? She tried to find something in the room to help her understand where she was, but nothing looked familiar. She started to wonder about Paul, but she made her mind come back and focus as best she could on Jack.

Suddenly, Jack was moving. He slid out of the bed and leaned in, and he was so close she could smell him. He kissed her mouth and pushed his tongue between her lips. She wanted to wipe her mouth but struggled to raise her hand to her lips. Her mind recognized it would not be a good move. She would have to play along.

She watched as Jack left the room, and then returned a few moments later and forced a pill in her mouth. She swallowed reflexively, and the pill nearly lodged in her throat. He handed her a glass of water, and she sipped it slowly as the pill slid further down her throat. *What did you give me, Jack?*

Jack walked over to where Allie slept and patted the dog on the head. Then he leaned in and kissed her daughter on the head. She sighed when she realized that her daughter didn't stir and that he hadn't touched her. Thank God she was sleeping.

"I'll be back in a little while with some breakfast. I'm sure you're hungry."

She watched as he left the room. She could hear footsteps that sounded like they were going up stairs then a clicking and scraping sound. When she couldn't hear anything else, she forced her head up and worked her body up on the pillows. She needed to get up and get to Allie.

✳✳✳

When Jack returned to the basement he found Hope holding Faith in her arms. Scruffy was sitting next to them wagging his tail. Jack smiled. He couldn't believe his eyes. He truly had his family again.

Jack set the table and then invited his wife and daughter to join him. He was glad to see they were able to walk to the table on their own. Neither spoke, but they did slowly eat the breakfast he had made them. He looked down and saw Scruffy looking up at him with wanting eyes, so he took a pancake and tore it into small pieces, feeding the small dog who took the food eagerly. Jack made a mental note to get dog food.

Clearing the table, he called the dog which followed him without question up the stairs. Locking the basement door behind him, he entered the kitchen and set the tray with the breakfast plates on the counter, then opened the back door to let Scruffy out. He watched for a moment as the dog scampered out into the trees.

Jack washed the dishes before checking on Scruffy and finding the dog patiently waiting at the door. As he was letting the dog back in, he heard a knock at the front door. With Scruffy following right behind him, he went to the door and found a delivery truck outside. He invited the driver to the garage where he had the appliances unloaded. He could handle taking the items down into the basement himself.

With the items unloaded and the driver gone, he made a trip up to check on Vivian and got her setup with the required meds and her daily soap operas. He hoped that soon he could share his family with her. It would be nice if they all could spend some time together.

With Vivian taken care of, Jack let Scruffy out once again before putting him back in the basement with Faith. He noted that his family was asleep again. The drugs were obviously still thick in their systems. Good, this was a perfect time to take the appliances downstairs. Retrieving an appliance dolly from the far corner of the garage, he strapped the refrigerator in place and muscled it through the doorway and slowly down the stairs one at a time.

An hour later Jack had the refrigerator, stove, and microwave set up in a mock kitchen at one end of the basement's main room. Things were really starting to look homey now. Satisfied that he had everything working properly, he secured the basement and made a run to the grocery store.

It felt good to be out of the house. The sun was shining, and the air was brisk. Occasionally he caught a hint of the ocean air that had managed to make its way up the mountain and into the Ojai valley. At the store he packed a cart full of items he knew his wife loved to use in cooking. He bought spices and milk and juices for Faith, a big bag of dog food for Scruffy, and a few dog treats and toys.

In the aisle that had automotive and other hardware accessories he searched for a padlock he needed for the surgical room. As Hope and Faith got stronger, he wouldn't want them entering that room. That was his special place. Even though Hope fully knew about his needs, Faith wouldn't understand, and it would most certainly frighten her. He needed to protect her. Her innocence was very important.

He bought special items for Hope, fragrances she liked for her hair and lotions for her body, and then picked up a couple of toys for Faith, including some crayons and coloring books. There were a few more things he needed, but he would have to get them at the hardware store.

Making another stop, he got PVC pipe, a utility sink, a shower head, and the appropriate hose connections. He could route water lines from the surgical room at the end of the basement into the smaller room and improvise a shower and kitchen sink for the girls. It wouldn't take too much to set it up. He considered a shower curtain rod, but thought about it again. He wouldn't buy anything that could be used as a weapon or tool.

Looking around the store quickly once more before deciding he had everything he needed, he paid and took everything outside and loaded it into the back of the van around the groceries. It felt good to get out, but he wanted to get back home to his family. Vivian was due for her medication, and it would soon be time for lunch. It seemed time flew by these days. Being back with his family, he was alive again. He drove through the familiar streets, and happiness filled him.

Unloading the groceries, he took them down into the basement and filled the refrigerator and the shelves that had in years past held his father's paint cans or tools. For now the shelves were a mock pantry.

Quickly connecting the electric stove in the corner of the soon to be makeshift kitchen, Jack popped a pizza in the oven while Hope, Faith, and Scruffy watched from the couch. The TV droned on in the background as he began fabricating the wall adjacent to the surgical room into a shower for the bathroom. He added a sink next to the stove and mounted the microwave onto one of the shelves.

The timer on the new oven dinged, and he was pleased when he saw Hope get up and take the pizza out of the oven. She worked slowly and with intense focus, as if it took all of her energy to do the menial task.

She got the pizza out of the oven and worked to slice it with the plastic utensils Jack had provided. Then she set the pizza and plates on the table and assisted Faith to her chair at the table. Jack continued to watch from where he worked.

With the items installed and plumbed, he tested the water flow, drainage, and pressure. They had both hot and cold water and would be able to comfortably shower now. The drainage wasn't perfect, but with concrete floors and block walls, it was good enough. The dishes could now be washed here too. No more carrying them up and down the stairs.

After placing two dog dishes on the floor near the stove, he filled one with water and one with dog food. Scruffy immediately ran over to investigate, smelling the food and gobbling away at the small kibbles. His tail wagged the whole time.

Jack washed his hands and joined his family at the table. Hope seemed to be settling in nicely. He smiled. It was good to see her doing some normal tasks of a wife and mother.

Finishing his slice of pizza, Jack pushed back from the table and thanked Hope for the delicious meal. He leaned back in his chair and studied the scene. Faith sat next to him and Hope was across the table. Scruffy was curled up next to Faith's chair. Across from Faith sat an empty seat. It was a table for four. Knowing Hope could care for Faith—at least her basic needs now—and with the surveillance in place, he knew what he needed to do. Jack went upstairs, secured the basement, and made a phone call.

Several hours passed before Jack's phone call was returned, and his head was buzzing with excitement. He could barely contain himself as he sat with Vivian watching some movie from the *Leave It to Beaver* era. She was thrilled that he stayed and watched the movie.

He'd already given her a bath and had made sure she was comfortable. He fed her crushed ice and held her hand as the pain medication took hold. Some days the pain was worse, and this was one of those days. For now she was at ease, and the movie was a great distraction.

Checking his phone to monitor the basement, he saw Hope and Faith watching TV together. Scruffy was sitting between them. Each had a hand on the little dog, gently patting his soft, wiry fur. His family was doing well.

The medication was coming out of Hope's body, and she was beginning to be capable of caring for Faith. For something to do after lunch he had encouraged them to take showers, so he checked in on their progress while he waited for his call. Hope had helped Faith wash her hair, so right now they sat there looking shiny. They each had a freshness that he could almost smell from two floors away.

He continued to sit with Vivian, but the noise from the movie was simply a buzz in the background of his mind. He was planning. He really couldn't believe his luck. The blood was pulsing through him at a nearly deafening rate. His ears throbbed, and the more he tried to calm down, the more excitement he felt at the possibilities.

"Are you okay?" Vivian squeezed his hand.

"Oh, I'm sorry. I guess I let my mind wander," Jack answered a bit startled.

"Thank you for sitting with me."

"My pleasure," Jack answered smiling at the frail woman.

"Is it time yet?"

Jack felt a tug inside his chest. Moments ago he was nearly exhilarated. That feeling was crushed under her simple question. It was a question with so many implications.

"Not yet, Vivian. I want you to meet my family first."

"Your family? I thought…"

"I know, but remember you told me to reconnect? I did that, and it's wonderful. You'll love them. There's only one problem. I'll need to move you. I'm going to have to make a little trip soon. Just a day, maybe overnight, but I won't be gone long. You can stay with my family while I'm away."

Vivian smiled. "I'm glad you worked things out. Family is important."

"Yes, it is," Jack said. He watched as Vivian's eyes drifted closed. Moments later her mouth opened slightly, and she took deep yet short breaths as she fell into sleep influenced by the illness and medications.

Jack stood and tucked her hand gently under the covers before he slipped his away. He watched for a few more moments then silently turned and exited. Once outside the room, Jack was again able to allow his thoughts to run wild in his head. The information his contact had given him was simply too good to be true. Opportunity was knocking, and he damn sure was going to answer.

Chapter Twenty

Mark surprised Max with tickets to go see her sister in California, eager to introduce Heath to his new family. That day had quickly arrived. The trip would be short, just a long weekend, but Max was thrilled to be heading to see her sister Shauna.

Max held Heath's hand while Mark presented their boarding passes and special firearms permits and guns to the airline agent. The agent highlighted each with a pen and scanned their identification with a strange purple light. He peered over his glasses, looking them over with obvious scrutiny, and then handed back the items before telling them to have a safe trip.

Putting the identifications away, Max dropped Heath's hand for a minute before continuing to the security checkpoint behind Mark. Heath asked a million questions about everything from why the man had the purple light to why they had to take their shoes off, and if the machine could see all of his insides. The last question made both Mark and Max laugh out loud—would he look naked when he went through the scanning machine? It took a brief moment to convince him that no one could see him naked.

They spent the next few minutes riding the tram and making their way to their boarding gate. Confident they had plenty of time, they agreed to get something to eat before the long flight to Los Angeles.

Heath shoved a chicken nugget in his mouth, chewed happily, swallowed, and then asked, "Will your sister like me? Can we go to the beach when we get there?" Shoving another nugget in his mouth, he bobbed in his seat anxiously awaiting an answer.

"Slow down, tiger," Mark said. "Max's sister will like you just fine. And, yes, we can go to the beach. It may not be right when we get there, but for sure it will be soon. Deal?"

"Okay, deal." Heath continued to pop nuggets and fries into his mouth and gobbled away at the food.

"Are you getting as excited as he is?" Mark asked Max.

"I am. It's pretty exciting to see my sister and for her to meet Heath."

"A lot has happened since you last saw her. You've moved, sold your house, graduated from the FBI, got married, and took in a foster son. You sure do know how to live."

Max laughed. "Yeah, well I think a couple of people helped me on this wild ride." She looked between Mark and Heath. They laughed with her.

After finishing their meal, the trio stood and followed the signs towards the gate. They arrived to find they were just ten minutes from boarding. Max encouraged Heath to walk with her to the restroom while they waited, and Mark took a seat near the gate.

Returning from their walk, Heath bounced on his feet as he anxiously anticipated getting onto the plane as the gate attendant started calling the boarding sections. The plane filled quickly, and they settled into their seats as Heath checked out the sliding window panel, the folding food tray, everything in the seat back, and finally settled down a little to study the airplane exit plan.

Unfortunately, they would have to do it all again before making it to their final destination because the only reasonable rates included a connection in Minneapolis. Fortunately for them, the layover was pretty quick, and her sister would be there to pick them up upon arrival in Los Angeles.

Max was really starting to get excited now about seeing her sister and her family, as well as meeting up with Cortez. The trip was entirely pleasure, but she intended on getting some time with Cortez and Bobby to go over some of the files they had been sharing back and forth on Jack Tyler.

There's no way she could be in L.A. and not see Cortez, much less avoid spending some time focused on Tyler. After all, L.A. was where it had all started, and while she had a lot of fond memories of L.A. for so many other reasons, the one that stood out the most, and because it was unresolved, was Jack Tyler's six buried bodies in the Malibu hills. She had to admit to herself that she would never fully rest until Tyler was either dead or behind bars.

She also wondered if he was still living with the decomposing bodies of what he obviously believed were recreations of his wife and daughter. The thought made a shudder roll through her body.

"Are you cold?" Wells asked noticing the tremor.

"No, just a chill I guess," she replied not wanting to tell him that she was thinking about Tyler in front of Heath.

Several hours later and after changing planes, they finally landed in California. The passengers wrestled luggage out of the overhead compartments and from under seats, and one by one each exited the plane. Heath continued to ask question after question, typical of a child's quizzical mind. Finally off of the plane, they worked their way through the throngs of people that bustled in every direction through one of the busiest airports in America.

Max texted her sister that they were on the ground and on their way out, and Heath's excitement seemed to grow with every step. "She's waiting just under the United Airlines sign at the curb," Max explained to Mark after receiving a returned text.

Mark nodded and pointed to the exit sign. "What will she be driving?"

"A white Lexus SUV," Max replied.

"What's a trexis UUV?" Heath asked, scrambling up what he had heard.

"It's a kind of car."

"Oh." He seemed satisfied for now and less excited when he realized it wasn't necessarily something really cool.

The doors slid open, and they were greeted with a whoosh of warm air as they stepped outside. Max searched the parking strip and then pointed at a few cars to the right where a woman stood waving from the rear of the vehicle. "There she is," Max said.

Within a few moments Max and her sister, Shauna, were locked in an embrace. As Max pulled away, she immediately turned to Heath and introduced the boy. "Heath, this is my sister, Shauna. Can you say hello to her?"

Heath shyly kicked at the ground before softly saying hello. Shauna kneeled down to eye level. "I bet you're hungry after your long trip. Would you like to go get something to eat?"

"Okay, I guess so, but can we go to the beach too?"

Shauna laughed. "I figured that was the first thing you would want to do. We just need to drop your things off at my house and pick up my son so you have someone to play with. How does that sound?"

Heath was smiling from ear to ear now and obviously very excited about the idea of having a playmate to share in the beach experience. He nodded his head up and down.

"Okay, well let's get going then."

They piled into the car, and Shauna wiggled through the heavy traffic and out of the airport. Heath talked the whole time until they arrived at Shauna's house, located just off of Santa Monica Boulevard. Max smiled at the sun and the ocean. It truly felt good to be back here. She watched as businesses flew by and thought of the first time she and Mark had lunch together.

Less than an hour later, the two young boys suited up for the beach with sand pails and shovels, they were on their way to Zuma Beach. Heath could hardly contain himself and was becoming fast friends with Max's nephew as they ate fruit snacks in the matching car seats Shauna had installed in the back.

Max and Shauna chattered almost as much as the boys while Mark sat and listened to the noise around him, enjoying the warm breeze that flowed through the window. It felt nice to be on vacation and not have a case hanging over his head. Heath's case had taken a toll on him, and this week here in California was certainly going to help wash out some of the pain that had come in the wake of working that case.

Shauna navigated the SUV into a parking space at the far end of the lot, allowing them some open beach space away from others. They piled out of the vehicle and unloaded a picnic basket and blanket from the back. The boys were already kicking their way through the sand with Max and Shauna calling out after them to slow down and to not go in the water until they all get there. Knowing Heath had never been to the beach before and wouldn't have any concept of the power of the waves, Mark chased after them to ensure they didn't go in.

Mark led Heath by the hand as he put his toes in the water for the first time. He squealed as the cold water splashed up his legs and pulled his feet deeper into the sand. The next hour was spent digging for sand crabs and playing with the strange, wiggly crustaceans, followed by building sand castles. They only stopped playing to eat.

***

Jack watched from his vehicle. His heart rate raced as he saw the beautiful, light haired boy playing in the sand with his dark haired friend. His eyes bounced between the child and Agent Maxine Nichols. *Oh, wait. Her name is Wells now, isn't it?* He couldn't believe the agent was back in California, but was relieved to see that it appeared to have nothing to do with him. He relaxed as the realization settled in.

When his contact had told him that the agent had flight plans to California, he was afraid she was onto him and was planning to sneak in on him when he least expected it. With the flight schedule in his hands, he had been at the airport and watched them arrive. He'd followed them to the house and assumed it was Maxine's sister but couldn't be sure. He watched as they had put the picnic basket in the back of the vehicle.

His eyes returned to watching the boy—a son. A son, just like he and Hope had talked about. They'd been planning to have another child, and he just knew it would be a boy—a little brother for Faith to play with. Jealousy of Max and her new family filled him.

Focus! He told himself, realizing emotions like jealousy were useless and even reckless. He continued to watch the family play until they started to wrap up the blankets and collect their items. Max toweled off the little boy, tousling his blonde curls. The boy laughed and danced about in the sand.

Jack's eyes scanned Maxine's muscular body. He'd almost forgotten how attractive she was. His eyes shifted to Mark Wells. He was the epitome of tall, dark, and handsome. Jack sized him up in comparison. Not that he wanted Maxine, no; he had Hope. And he would never be unfaithful. His devotion and commitment to his wife was for life. He wondered if Mark Wells would be dedicated to Maxine for life. *What would you do to keep her with you, Agent Wells?*

The family loaded everything into the SUV and backed out of the parking lot. Jack waited then pulled out behind them. He knew where they were staying and didn't dare risk being noticed. With two FBI agents riding in the car, he wondered if they would instinctively realize they were being followed and then notice that it was the same model of vehicle that had followed them earlier. He wasn't willing to risk this, so he dropped from behind and went a different route. It was time for him to get something to eat. Maxine and her family would likely go back to the house and spend the evening together. They were all covered in sand and salt and would need showers.

Feeling confident that he had some time, he drove down Santa Monica Boulevard and found a restaurant that looked appealing. It was time to check on his family back at the house. He was sure they would be fine or he wouldn't have left them, but he still wanted to check in with the video system.

While inside the restaurant and after placing his order, Jack logged onto the surveillance system through his phone and watched Hope, Faith, and Vivian through the various camera selections. He could see the main room where he had placed Vivian's medical bed.

Knowing that he had to leave, and not trusting anyone in his home, he had made the decision to move Vivian down into the basement where she could be with Hope and Faith. He had temporarily placed her on the couch while he relocated the bed. Once he had everything in place for her, he gingerly carried Vivian down stairs and introduced her to his family.

He watched the security feed as Hope checked on her and suppressed a smile, not wanting anyone to notice him. His family was doing just fine, and he would be home soon. His plan was to be home before Vivian needed any more medication. Just before leaving, he had given Vivian a pretty heavy dose of morphine and had added a morphine push to her IV where she could push the button herself when she needed to, without any risk of allowing her to over medicate.

Hope was doing exactly what he had expected. She was still moving slowly, but her motherly instincts drove her to care for Faith and Vivian. They needed her, and he knew she needed them too. It was those traits that he had always admired about her the most.

He flipped the camera to the surgical room and watched for a moment, being careful that no one could see over his shoulder. He saw Reb lying there attached to the table. He leaned in and saw shallow breaths and knew she was still alive. *Good.*

Confident that things were fine back at the house, he closed the app right as his food was delivered to the table. He thanked the plump server and turned his attention to his meal, suddenly realizing how hungry he actually was. He watched the sun setting outside through the windows while enjoying the food. His mind swirled about his family and the wonderful future ahead.

After a rich cup of coffee, Jack paid the bill and went back out into the night air. It was cooler, and the darkness smelled of fresh, salty ocean air. He felt as if he could hear the waves slapping happily against the sand, but he was actually too far to really hear it. The image made him feel alive, happy, and good. His senses were on full alert, and he was ready to execute his plan.

Once back inside the vehicle he relaxed back into the seat and waited. A while later he looked at his watch and saw that he still had time since it was only nine o'clock. To kill time, he logged back on to the surveillance app on his phone and observed his family. They were watching TV curled together on the couch.

After a few minutes Hope got up and checked on Vivian. Using his fingers to spread the screen, he zoomed in. He watched closely as Hope gently tended to the old woman. He waited and realized that she must have been satisfied because she returned to the couch.

Reaching behind the seat, he retrieved the ear buds that were carefully stored in the side pocket of his laptop bag. Plugging them in and applying the buds to his ears, he listened. They were watching a movie. He waited a moment then recognized some of the lines of *To Kill a Mockingbird*. Great choice for Faith.

Jack could remember watching that movie himself when he was about her age. He listened more closely and wished he'd installed some more robust speakers to support the video. He could hear Faith's sweet little voice slowly asking questions.

Closing the app again, he decided there was plenty of time to take a drive. He pushed the gear shift into reverse and backed out of the space, then propelled the vehicle forward out of the drive and headed towards the Malibu Canyon.

Thirty minutes later he was on his way up a familiar winding road. When he passed the entrance gate for Shalom Camp, his pulse raced as he neared the familiar spot. He recognized the spot as a large oak tree loomed over the road out of the darkness. He pulled the vehicle over onto the shoulder.

Reaching across the vehicle, he retrieved a small flashlight out of the glove box and clicked it on. Within moments he exited the vehicle, crossed the asphalt, and dropped off the opposite side of the road into the thick brush. It was obvious no one had been here in a while. He counted his paces instinctively until he was deep into the thicket. He stopped, knowing he was standing in the exact spot where he had buried six bodies over the period of a few months. He wished those bodies were still there, but knew... yes, he knew Agent Maxine Nichols – no – Agent Maxine Wells had stolen them.

It was cathartic being here right now, as he was beginning a new chapter in his life. Filled with emotions, he forced himself to move from the spot and return to his vehicle. Before getting in he reached under the driver's seat and pulled out a small tool box. Removing the screw driver, he went to the back of the vehicle and removed his license plate, then did the same for the front.

Getting back in the van he returned the flashlight to the glove box, the screwdriver into the tool box, and then fired up the engine to make his way back down the mountain.

He looked at the clock on the dash and noted the time now was after eleven. Perfect. By the time he got back down the mountain and to the house, it would be nearly midnight. He assumed the agents would tuck in early tonight given the long travel and day at the beach.

Forty minutes passed before he turned onto the street and pulled over at the end of the block. He watched the neighborhood for a few minutes. It was quiet. He assessed the house. There were no lights on inside. The street lamps illuminated the sidewalk by casting long, blue shadows. His eyes scanned each house along the path that led up to the two story brick-faced home where he watched the family enter earlier.

Every home had a perfectly manicured yard. The homes were better than middle class, and Jack suspected most of these people lived close to bursting at their financial means. Everyone in L.A. was always trying to compete with each other—nicest cars, most beautiful home, best schools or bodies. It was a bit ridiculous, really, and nearly always led to over spending and high debt.

He was grateful that his success had afforded him luxury and lack of need to worry about those silly competitions. No, his needs were fulfilled through caring for his family and the feelings he achieved when surgically invading another person's being. It was the fact that he both took and saved lives that drove him. Nothing material could even remotely compare to what he had accomplished.

Deciding the silence in the neighborhood was the perfect cloak of safety, he slid his car up the street, just in front of the house neighboring the one that was the point of his focus. He needed to be cautious since there were, after all, two FBI agents inside. He had to assume they were good with details like the make and model of a vehicle. He had intentionally removed the plates in case they woke. His vehicle was common enough that they would never find him without the actual plate. He made a mental note to put the plates back on before his return to Ojai later. He certainly didn't want to make any long trips without plates on. *No room for error.*

He reached behind his seat and pulled his medical bag forward, retrieving a syringe and rag. Before sliding out of the vehicle, he slipped on latex gloves and checked his pocket for his Swiss Army knife then quietly exited, softly clicking the door shut. Slipping up the sidewalk, he took a sharp turn up the driveway to the side door leading to the garage. It was a long shot, but he was hoping that it would be unlocked and make his job easier. Past experience told him that the side door was the most commonly forgotten exterior door.

His hand grabbed the knob, and he took a deep breath as he turned the knob. Giving the door a slight nudge, he stopped, shocked when it in fact pushed open. He slipped inside. The garage smelled of engine oil and soil.

Standing just inside the door with his back against the wall he listened. Every sense was tingling with excitement and anticipation. Other than the normal sounds that any home would emit, it was silent. He needed to be most careful now. Taking a moment to let his eyes focus on the items in the garage he made a mental picture of everything in his path, on the floor and walls. If he tripped or bumped anything on his way in or out, it would cause a great deal of noise, and he couldn't afford any mistakes.

Slowly starting across the floor, he passed in front of the SUV that occupied one side of the garage. Then he passed a smaller vehicle shrouded in a car cover and based on its shape it appeared to be a sports car. He approached an interior door on the opposite side from where he just entered. He reached for the door knob and turned it, but unfortunately, it was locked.

He quickly overcame his disappointment and went to work on the lock with the smallest blade of his pocket knife. He had learned after a few times of not being really successful that he needed to bring small tools with him, which was why he always carried a Swiss Army knife in his pocket. It only took a couple of minutes before he had successfully turned the tumbler and was standing inside a laundry room.

Sucking in a deep breath he waited, listening again—still nothing. The house remained silent. Moving forward and paying close attention to every detail, he remained acutely aware of everything. Nothing had excited him in this way. Every minor noise resonated through the pounding of his heart in his ears—the sound of the refrigerator, a clock ticking, the house settling. He made his way through the kitchen guided only by his instincts and the glow of the moon shining through the light-weight curtains.

Finding a set of stairs that he could tell led to the second floor, he turned and climbed slowly, deliberately paying special attention to the possibility of any creaking steps. He paused for a moment when a fan kicked on somewhere in the attic. Recognizing it as the air-conditioning system, he continued on.

Arriving on the landing at the top, he followed the hallway until he found the first bedroom. The door stood slightly ajar. Waiting briefly once more, he allowed time to listen again. His ears tuned for every noise. *Can't be too careful.*

He knew he shouldn't but unable to resist the temptation, he slid through the small opening. Out of fear that it might squeak on the hinges, he turned his body sideways making sure not to touch the door. Inside the room he moved with slow, purposeful, light steps across the carpeted floor.

The curtains on the far side of the room were opened maybe an inch, offering enough moonlight that he could see the bed in front of him. He focused on his breathing, controlling it with small draws through his mouth. He'd learned through exercise routines how to not allow adrenaline to cause hyperventilation—a technique that had aided him in moments like these.

Slipping closer to the edge of the bed, he peered down at the two figures curled into each other. His heart raced as he stared down, his attention focused on the female. Her long, auburn hair cascaded out over the pillow. He knew all along that she was a stunning beauty, and seeing her in person confirmed it even in the dim lighting. This was a moment he had pictured time and again, but never thought would actually come to fruition. He had to quell the visions of his hands deep inside her body, touching and exploring. Oh, how good that would be.

Not able to resist the urges coursing through him, he reached out and almost tenderly touched the locks of hair that seemed to be caressing the pillow. His eyes darted to the man next to her, and imagines of him split wide open on a shining stainless steel table immediately entered his head.

Sliding his hand in his pocket, he removed the Swiss Army knife he always carried and gingerly folded open the scissor part of the tool. He leaned forward then very carefully lifted a few strands of the hair that splayed out on the pillow and made a small cut. The knife made a quiet snipping sound as the locks fell free and into his fingers.

The sleeping man stirred, pulling the woman closer to him, causing Jack to pull his hand back. *So protective, Agent Wells.*

Realizing he'd spent as much time as he could allow, he took one more gaze down at the lovely Maxine Nichols—or Wells, and slowly backed away from the bed, retracing his steps to the door and slipping out without making a single noise.

Once out of the bedroom, he re-oriented himself and noticed another door a little farther down the hall. This one stood all the way open. He paused briefly again to listen for any motion from the room he just left.

Satisfied that the house was still in rest, he entered the second room. He saw an airplane hanging from the ceiling and toys on the desk under the window on the far wall. Approaching the bed, he saw two small figures under the bundle of blankets. Scanning the first pillow, he saw a dark ball of hair and moved his eyes to the other pillow where his gaze landed on the lighter hair.

His heart was racing again. He wanted to reach down and push the hair back so he could see the child's beautiful face, but he knew better. Removing the rag and syringe from his pocket, he injected the liquid into the rag and then quickly and deliberately placed the rag over the boy's face while pressing his body down on top of him. In doing so, he managed to restrict the amount of movement to no more than if the boy had turned in his sleep. The other child stirred slightly, but did not awaken.

After being certain the boy was properly sedated, Jack lifted the boy from the bed and retraced his steps back down the hall, down the stairs, and out the garage door, intentionally leaving the doors wide open. He slipped back out into the darkness and to the van where he laid the sleeping child down in the back and shut the hatch. He got behind the wheel and drove off into the night without looking back.

Jack made sure to put good distance between himself and the house before pulling over in a parking lot to reinstall the license plates on his vehicle. It was late, and he certainly couldn't risk getting pulled over with the boy in the back of his van.

Looking around to make sure he was alone and seeing no one around, he secured the plates. But before getting back inside he took another syringe from his medical satchel and gave the child an injection of Rohypnol, commonly known as a Ruffie. The drug would help ensure the boy had no memory of what had taken place this evening, protecting both the boy and himself.

Knowing the child would sleep easily until he made it back to Ojai, he slipped the tarp that he carried in the cargo net over the small body, then got back in the van and traveled through the palm tree- lined residential streets to the freeway where he entered the ramp heading north. Within two hours he would be safely home. He smiled. Tonight had truly been one of the most important moments of his life.

Chapter Twenty-One

Max woke with a start as her cell phone rattled on the nightstand. For a moment she was confused, her surroundings not immediately familiar. She shook off sleep and reached for the phone that buzzed again, insisting on being answered.

"Nichols," she answered still using her maiden name.

"Hey, it's Cortez. Sorry to call so early, but we have an issue."

Max glanced at the alarm clock next to the lamp on the nightstand where her cell phone had moments ago rested and read five thirty-two. "Jesus, Cortez," she muttered just as her mind realized Cortez would not be calling this early unless there was a valid reason. She sat up, propping the phone under her chin as she pulled on pants, then slid off the bed and slipped into the adjoining bathroom.

"I got a call this morning from a missing person's detective in Phoenix."

Max felt her blood start to pump. "Phoenix?"

"Right, listen up. Mindy and her youngest daughter are missing."

Max was still trying to shake off the sleep and wasn't quite following. "Mindy?"

"Yeah, Max, as in Jack Tyler's sister-in-law."

"Shit."

"Shit is right. She's been missing going on three weeks."

"What the hell. Why wasn't I notified sooner?"

"Slow down, girl. I just got the call. Apparently, the local police didn't make the connection to Tyler and have been totally

145

focused on the husband. He said he was attacked, and the other child was left sleeping in the home. He called the police and reported the wife and child missing. The police thought he staged the whole thing and have been trying to get him to confess. The scene was clean. It totally smells of Tyler."

Max was completely alert now. "Where and why would he take them? Mindy was never a big Jack fan. That could be really bad for her."

"I don't know why, and of course, we can't be sure. But I thought you'd definitely want to know. I was looking forward to spending time with you, just didn't think it'd be like this."

"Let me fill Mark in, and I'll call you back."

"Okay. The chief is not sure we have any jurisdiction in this case. There's no way or reason to know that Tyler is back in California. He could have taken them anywhere."

"I know. I'll call you back in a few."

Returning back to the bedroom, Max tapped Mark on the shoulder. "Mark, wake up."

"Max, what's up?" Mark sat up startled by the urgency in her voice.

"Jack Tyler's sister-in-law is missing. She and her daughter have been missing for nearly three weeks."

"What?" Mark asked, but was already slipping out of the bed.

"Cortez just called. She received a call from a missing person's detective in Phoenix. Apparently, they've been looking at the husband this whole time. And unfortunately, there's nothing connecting Jack to the case, but the detective thought it was too much of a coincidence and called me."

"Call Cortez back and ask if there's a place where we can meet and get the case details. Can your sister watch Heath for a while?"

"Sure. No need to wake the whole house. I'll leave her a note and have Cortez pick us up."

Mark pulled on clothes, while booting up his laptop and put on his shoes then pushed a stored number on his cell phone. "This is agent Mark Wells. We need everything we can get on the missing person's case for Mindy Prescott in the Phoenix area," he said referencing a file on his computer for the name. There's a child missing too. I want everything there is on the case faxed to Detective Lorraine Cortez at the LAPD."

While Mark was talking, Max was back on the phone with Cortez asking her to come pick them up. Cortez confirmed she'd be there in fifteen minutes.

Max went into the bathroom and ran a comb through her hair and brushed her teeth. Mark entered and stood beside her and took the other toothbrush from the travel kit. They spit into the sink in unison then shared a towel to wipe their mouths. Max grazed Mark's mouth with a gentle kiss then turned back out of the room and rifled through her luggage to retrieve her Glock 45. Even though they had come here on vacation, as an FBI agent neither of them traveled without their service weapons, even though it meant they had to gain special clearance for each flight.

Mark returned to the bedroom as well, and Max handed him his service weapon. Within five minutes the two were heading quietly down the stairs to go outside. Max turned toward the kitchen where she found a pen and paper and wrote out a short note to her sister to call her as soon as she was up. Just as she was about to join Mark outside, she turned to find her sister Shauna standing there with her hand on her hip.

"Sneaking out? Have you had too much of me already?"

"It's a case. I'm sorry. Will you keep Heath busy until we figure out whether there's anything to the information we got?"

"Of course, do you need a car?"

"No, Cortez is picking us up in a couple of minutes."

"Okay, don't worry about Heath. I'll keep the boys busy."

"You're the best."

"Max, does this have to do with Tyler?" Shauna asked, concern showing on her face.

"Yes." Their eyes met briefly before Shauna nodded in acceptance and understanding. Max acknowledged that Shauna knew her well enough to know she could never rest until Tyler was captured or dead. Max gave Shauna a quick hug. "I'll call in a couple of hours to give you an update when I know more."

With that she turned and was about to leave when Shauna asked, "Did you open this door?"

147

Turning back she noticed the door leading to the garage was standing open. "No, I didn't really notice it. Maybe we left it open last night when we came in."

Shauna looked at Max then shrugged before closing the door. "Call me when you can and be careful."

"I will, thanks, sis!" Max said before crossing the living room and exiting through the front door where she joined Mark outside. He was on the phone again asking questions when Cortez pulled up to the curb.

The two agents walked quickly to the curb and climbed into the police issued Crown Victoria. Cortez sped away as they exchanged greetings.

Chapter Twenty-Two

      Jack drove the van into the garage and closed the rollup door behind him. Within a few minutes he had removed the small, limp bundle from the vehicle and carried him inside, laying him down on the living room couch. Jack sat down next to the child, kicking off his own shoes. Exhausted and finally able to fully relax, he pulled a blanket Vivian had perfectly folded over the back of the couch and spread it out covering both Heath and himself then laid his head back. Sleep took him almost immediately.

      Light shone through the kitchen windows and the glow poured into the living room over Jack's face. He woke and shielded his eyes with his hand then worked at the stiffness in his neck. He looked down at the boy lying next to him. He'd taken a Chance and it had worked out perfectly. *Chance ... yes it was perfect...*

      Glancing at his watch, he was surprised to see it was almost noon. He'd slept longer than he'd wanted to, obviously needing the rest, but he needed to get up and get moving. Despite the discomfort of sleeping sitting up, he'd slept peacefully and knew it was because his family was now perfect. *Everything is going to be perfect from now on.*

      Slipping his shoes back on and after spending a few minutes combing Chance's hair down with his fingers and straightening his clothes, and despite the fact that the child was still quite sleepy, he decided it was time to introduce him to the rest of the family.

      Unlocking the door, he carried the boy's limp frame down the basement steps. At the bottom of the stairs, he approached the

149

couch and laid the boy down before returning up the steps two by two to lock the door once more. He descended the stairs again and was faced with Hope standing there looking between him and the blonde boy on the couch.

"Jack? Who is this boy? Whose child is he?"

"Hi, honey. You're looking so much better. I'm sorry I had to leave you for so long. But I'm back now, and finally we can have everything we ever wanted."

Mindy's eyes grew wide. "I don't know what you're talking about."

"Hope, darling, I've brought our son home. His name is Chance. He's perfect, don't you think? Just like we always talked about" Jack approached Mindy and pulled her into his chest. He looked down at her. "Your heart is racing. Are you feeling okay?"

Pushing her hair away from her face and keeping her eyes away from Jack's gaze, Mindy replied, "I'm fine. I'm just surprised, that's all."

"Of course, it's a lot to take in—a new child, a brother for our little Faith. But finally we're all together, you, our children, Vivian, Scruffy, and me. All together here in this home, where we belong, where it all began."

Mindy averted her eyes. Her lip trembled slightly, though Jack didn't notice. "Yes, the way it's supposed to be," she said forcing the expected response.

"Chance should wake up in a little while. He's been asleep for quite a while. When he does wake he may be a little confused about where he is. This will pass in a few days. Soon he'll understand that we are his true family and that he should have been with us all along."

Mindy nodded, and Jack smiled accepting her approval. "I'll bring him along slowly. Hope, I can see worry in your eyes. Please, don't worry. He'll be fine, and Faith will help him settle in." Jack turned to focus his attention in the opposite direction. "How is she doing?" he asked, nodding towards Vivian.

Mindy's voiced hitched slightly, but Jack didn't notice. "She sleeps a lot. She asked for you earlier. I told her you'd be back soon."

Jack walked across the room to the bed where Vivian lay. He felt her pulse and brushed her hair from her forehead. Her breathing

150

was a bit labored but steady. His heart tugged at him as he realized time with Vivian was limited. Forcing his mind back into the happy times, he looked towards the bedroom area. "Where's Faith?"

Mindy quickly walked over to him and stood between him and the bed. "She's sleeping. She'll probably wake up just in time to play with Chance." Mindy forced a smile and placed her hand on his arm, her fingers trembling slightly.

"Of course, well, no need to wake her, I guess."

Taking a chance Mindy continued, "You know, I'm worried about Vivian. We probably should have her in a facility where she can get full time care."

Jack's head snapped back in her direction. "Hope, do you think someone else can take better care of her than I can? She needs to be with people who care about her." Jack had never lost his temper with Hope, but he couldn't believe she would suggest such a thing. He felt his pulse pumping in his neck and had to concentrate to keep his temper under control.

Mindy recoiled slightly at his response. "Of course, you're right."

Jack reached out, not noticing how Mindy flinched at his touch. He lifted her chin until her eyes met his gaze. "Hope, I love you so much and now that we're all finally together, I just want to focus on our family. With Chance here we're finally complete. We have everything we dreamed of, and there's no reason Vivian can't share these moments. I know her time is short, and that's all the more reason for her to be with people who truly care for her. I know you have her best interests at heart, but I truly believe she is right where she needs to be."

Mindy blinked back tears and nodded. Jack leaned in and kissed her tenderly still holding her chin in his hand.

***

Mindy internally shuddered as Jack's lips closed in on hers. She closed her eyes and accepted his kiss. She'd tried to use the suggestion of moving Vivian as a possible means to escape. It hadn't worked. She'd taken a risk and failed.

151

While Jack was gone she had spent some time trying to find a way out, but with the cameras on her she'd been unsuccessful. She wasn't sure when Jack was watching and knew she had to be very careful. She'd been too afraid to take too many risks.

The cloud that had been in her head for…how long?…was finally clearing, though she knew the medications he continued to give her kept her from being totally clear. It was only while he was gone that the drugs really started to wear off. She glanced to where Allie slept and considered that a blessing. She could only hope they could get away before the fog cleared for her. She prayed her child would not remember any of this.

There was only one thing Mindy knew for certain; she would do anything she had to do to protect her daughter. Jack obviously believed she was her dead sister, Hope, and that her daughter, Allie, was her dead niece, Faith. Though she had always thought of Jack as odd, she knew Hope adored him, and she knew he had absolutely cherished her sister and their daughter. Knowing he would never hurt either of them gave her a bit of comfort. She had to play the role, whatever that took.

She had to ignore the images of bodies buried in the Malibu hills and in the country in Oklahoma; the horror of the children killed; and of the mouth removed from an innocent little girl in Illinois. She had to stay in the present. She most certainly knew what her brother-in-law was capable of, but she had to believe that as long as he thought she was his wife everything would be okay.

She stood frozen, facing the madman that had once been her sister's husband, and waited for his direction. She forced the trembling in her body to cease by focusing her mind on her daughter and making a mental promise in moments like these to think of Paul, she would escape. *Oh, Paul, I hope you and Madison are okay.* Choking back the images of her husband and oldest daughter, she couldn't help but wonder if Jack had killed them or if they were alive and trying to find her and Allie. Knowing she couldn't become distracted by despair, inside her mind she screamed out, "Stay focused on Allie!"

Suddenly, she realized Jack was talking to her and forced her attention back to him, willing herself to pretend to be Hope.

"Hope? Are you okay, dear?"

Mindy's eyes rose to meet Jack's. "Yes, I'm sorry. I guess I was just wondering how soon it would before Chance wakes up. I'm anxious to spend time with him," she lied.

Jack smiled and felt his body relax a little. "Well, we'll slowly encourage him. It may take just a little time."

"Well, for now I have a few things I need to do. Why don't you prepare us something to eat? I'll join you in a little while. Will an hour be enough time?"

Mindy briefly looked at him. "Sure." She started to turn away but was pulled back.

"I love you, Hope. I've always loved you," Jack said, his hands holding hers tightly and pulling her into him. He leaned in and kissed her passionately. Pulling away, Jack smiled then released her and turned to leave the room, heading towards the surgical room. "I'll be working, so please don't disturb me."

***

Jack unlocked and opened the door to the surgical room with the keys he kept in his pocket. He slipped into the room, closing and locking the door behind him. On the table Reb's pale body lay motionless. The jagged incision down the center of her torso seemed to glow in the sudden light.

Jack approached her and placed his index and middle finger on her throat. His heart rate increased slightly as he felt a weak pulse. He leaned in close to her ear. "I see you're still hanging on, Reb. For that, I thank you."

Reb blinked, obviously straining against the lights and struggling against the pain. "Good girl, wake up now. I'm sorry I wasn't here to spend time with you the past couple of days. I really would have liked more time with you, but I had something far more important than you to deal with."

Reb's head rolled from side to side. Her breathing labored. It was clear she was distressed. "I think it's time for us to rendezvous. Have I ever told you how much I always hated you? Well, never mind. That really doesn't matter much now."

Jack continued to riddle her with questions he knew would never really be answered. "Are you ready to have some more fun? Strange, isn't it? I hate you, and yet you have given me quite a bit of pleasure since you've been my guest."

Reb's eyes grew wide, and with the little bit of strength she had left in her body she struggled against the restraints that still held her arms and feet to the stainless steel table. Jack ignored her struggling efforts and prepared the room for surgery.

Realizing the lunch Hope was preparing should be nearly ready Jack looked around the room. Satisfied that he had everything prepped and despite the fact that his adrenaline was already pumping he didn't want to disappoint Hope. "Reb, I know you are likely anxious to get started and while I would love to oblige you, I can't let my lovely wife wait, but don't worry I won't make you wait long. I'll be back to see you later today."

Jack left the room locking the door, dropping the keys in his pants pocket, leaving Reb lying naked, cold, exhausted and filled with terror.

Mindy already had the table set and was just ready to dish food into bowls. She'd made a homemade soup and prepared a fresh salad, the room smelled amazing, of fresh herbs.

"Honey, you really do spoil us, this looks like a really great lunch." Jack said as he entered the room. Nodding to the couch he asked, "Has Chance started to wake?"

"No, Not yet," Mindy answered her eyes darting to the couch.

Chapter Twenty-Three

Mark and Max were greeted at the door by Chief of Police Harding who appeared to instantly stifle the pride he obviously felt in the accomplishments of his once young detective. "Well, look at you, Nichols. All grown up into a FEEB," teasing her with a nickname commonly used by local authorities for FBI agents. Everyone knew there was no love lost between the local and federal organizations, and though he would never tell her to her face, using his gruff exterior to hide his pride, Max could tell he was nearly bursting.

"Yeah, yeah, Chief. I see you're still a funny man," Max tossed back at him.

Immediately turning to business Harding asked, "Well, what do you think? Is your boy Tyler at it again?"

"Honestly, we haven't had much time to get caught up on the events around the Prescott abduction. I don't feel I can really answer that question yet." Max nodded towards her ex-partner. "Cortez filled us in a bit in the car on the way over." Just as Max was finishing her sentence, her cell phone started buzzing. "Excuse me," she said looking at the display. "It's my sister. It must be important."

Stepping away a few feet, Max answered her phone, "Shauna, is everything okay?"

"Max, I don't know. I can't find Heath anywhere. The garage door to the outside was open, and I've looked everywhere." Shauna was rattling as fast as she could and was obviously out of breath.

"Whoa, slow down. He's not in bed?" Max's mind reeled at what she was hearing.

"No, he's not. Max, he's not in the house or the yard. I've called for him outside. He's gone!"

"Okay, slow down. We're coming right back." Max hung up the phone and faced the group who had turned their attention to her as they clearly heard her side of the call. "Jesus, Mark. Heath's gone!"

"What do you mean gone?" Mark asked in his usual calm, but direct manner.

"Shauna went to check on him, and he's gone. The garage door is open, and he's nowhere." Max could feel tears starting to well in her eyes, and she forced herself to gain control. "We have to go back right now."

Cortez and the chief both were immediately in motion. "I'll get some squad cars over there to canvas the neighborhood," the chief offered.

"Max, it'll be okay. He probably just got curious and wandered off. Let's go!" Cortez encouraged.

Racing back out to the parking lot, they piled into the vehicle Cortez had used to bring them to the station. Before they could even get their doors closed, Cortez had slapped the temporary police lights on the top of the car and was pulling away with the siren blaring.

Cortez was an expert driver and navigated the city streets with ease, pushing people out of the way and respecting the urgency of the situation. The ride to the station had taken them nearly twenty minutes, but they returned to the house in just over seven.

As they were nearly to the house, a chilling memory hit Max. "Mark, the kitchen door to the garage was standing open before we left. Shauna asked if I'd opened it. We closed it without thinking too much about it. He may have already been gone when we left," Max said, her heart pounding in both her head and her chest.

Cortez screeched the car into the driveway at an odd angle, and they all poured out onto the lawn. Before they could even get to the door, a panicked looking Shauna raced towards them.

"Max, I don't know where he is. I'm so sorry!" The fear took over her and tears poured down her cheeks.

Max hugged her sister then pulled back. "Shauna, I need you to keep it together. You're going to have to tell us everything you can remember." Leading Shauna into the house, Max took her inside and lowered her onto one of the dining room chairs. Reaching for a note pad, she began to ask questions, repeating them over and over, attempting to stimulate any additional memories. Max knew sometimes it was just little details that helped.

Mark was in motion and began the process of having an Amber Alert released to the local radio, TV, and freeway notifications. Within the hour the neighborhood was crawling with police vehicles and officers who were going door to door searching yards and talking to neighbors.

When nothing turned up from the search, Max began to really panic. She couldn't imagine that Heath would wander off on his own. After all, they weren't in their home town, and where would he go? Terror filled her. Could someone have come into the home while they were all sleeping and have taken him? It seemed nearly impossible.

With no leads and nothing else to go on, Mark called for a crime scene analyst to come in and dust the doorframes and windows to see if there were any signs of forced entry.

Max had given Shauna a break, but now resumed her questions. She was trying to get Shauna to remember whether or not the garage exterior door had been closed and locked. They walked through the questions over and over again, but Shauna couldn't remember.

They talked through what she remembered. They had gone to the beach. She had been excited about the visit, and she couldn't remember the last time anyone had actually accessed that door. Nothing. They had a big, fat nothing!

Mark approached Max, and she could see the terror in his eyes. She knew he was thinking of Tommy and how this could not be happening all over again. He took her hand. "The Amber Alert is out. We'll find him," Mark said with a confidence she didn't personally possess. She nodded but wondered if he was saying that because he really believed it or because he needed to hear it for himself.

While they stood there together, the chief arrived on the scene. He could see the grave look on their faces as he approached. "What do we know?"

Mark responded, "Not much. Both the kitchen door and garage door were open. The kitchen door was open before we left to come to the station. If that's the exit point, it puts him out of the house prior to our departure. We didn't check on him because it was too early and didn't want to wake him. Shauna checked on the kids shortly after we left. She wondered if our leaving might have awakened them and was considering breakfast for them. When she entered the room, only her son was in the bed. Heath was gone. Assuming he'd wandered downstairs to play, she started looking for him. After searching the house she went outside, both the back and front yards, then into the garage. That's when she discovered the door standing open. She can't remember if it was locked or when the last time it was accessed. Her husband had left for work already, but he's on his way home. He may be able to help fill in the blanks on the door. In the meantime, the analyst you sent over is taking prints from doors and windows. We need to rule out whether an intruder forced his way in." The words hung in the air. Mark stood unmoving. His typically warm, blue eyes appeared frozen like ice on a pond, locked with the chief's.

"Okay, the Amber Alert is out and is running on every local station. It'll hit national news soon, and I think social media is already grabbing it." The chief paused for a moment. "Cortez," he barked, causing her to immediately appear from the next room. "What has the canvas gotten us? Do we have anything?"

"I'm sorry, sir. It was early. So far no one saw a little boy walking the neighborhood around dawn. School has started now, so it's getting harder as we're starting to get reports of sightings. We're working those leads, but so far they've proven to be other neighborhood kids."

"Max, where have you gone since you arrived in town? Is there anywhere the boy may have wanted to go back to?"

"The beach." Max turned to Mark, feeling hopeful for the first time. "Mark, do you think he would have tried to go to the beach on his own?"

Mark turned to the chief. "Can we get a canvas going on any route headed towards the water? He may remember what direction we came from."

"I'm on it, Chief," Cortez called out before he could even respond.

Harding nodded at Cortez then turned his attention to Max. "We'll find him, Nichols. Stay focused."

158

With that comment he was gone. Max knew him well enough to know he was on his way to apply pressure to the tip line and to the canvas. She tried to sigh, but her breath seemed to be stuck deep inside as if strangled by her rib cage. Her head began to throb, and then suddenly another terrifying thought began to edge its way into the outskirts of her mind. She refused to let it in, but it sat there as if taunting her.

***

The day had blown by and still there were no solid leads on how or where Heath had disappeared. Max felt as if her mind was crumbling around her, and she could see despair beginning to settle in on Mark. Shauna had all but turned into a ball on the couch, barely able to even care for her own child. Their beautiful world was crashing around them, and there was nothing Max could do.

It was beginning to get dark out, and everyone agreed to move to the station where they could start working the case in the manner they would if they didn't know the child that had gone missing. "You should stay here in case he comes back," Mark offered to Max even though he knew the likely answer he would get.

"Shauna is here. I need to keep working. We need to work the case, Mark. I feel paralyzed."

"They're going to isolate us. You know that. We're too close to be assigned to this case. They're going to continue to question us, and they should," Mark warned. "It's what I would do."

"I know. I'm okay with that too. It's part of it, and it helps keep them focused in the right places."

Mark stared into her eyes and resigned himself to their situation. "Let's go."

"Shauna, we need to go. We're going to the station. There's a lot we can be doing, and staying here is not going to help. Are you going to be okay?"

Shauna nodded as her husband brought her a glass of water. "I'll take care of her. We'll be fine," Shauna's husband reassured.

"They may want to ask more questions, but for now they feel confident either Heath left on his own or an intruder...," Max couldn't complete the sentence. She hugged her sister then turned to leave with Mark.

***

It was two o'clock in the morning before Max was able to be reunited with Mark. They were separated and questioned for hours. Finally, they had been cleared of any suspicion and were able to begin working with Cortez. They weren't allowed too much access, but the chief was allowing them to remain involved, keeping them well informed. The news was not good though. Two miles in each direction from the house to the shore had been under surveillance for hours. The Amber Alert tip line was lit up with callers, but nothing surfaced as a solid lead.

"They want you to do a press conference and speak out on the morning news. Top story. We need to make a plea. If Heath was abducted. His abductor may not see him as a boy, but rather an object. We need to change that. Both of you need to be there, but Max, you need to be the one that talks. Make it personal—he's a boy; he does boy things; he likes the beach; and cars—whatever applies."

Max nodded and turned to Mark.

The chief continued, "We've had a picture of Heath blown up and will have it beside you. Speak to that photo as much as you can and then directly into the camera. You know how to do this."

The next few hours seemed to crawl by. But when six A.M. rolled around, all the local news stations were gathered on the steps of the police headquarters. When signaled, Chief Harding led Max outside onto the steps with Mark behind. It was there that she delivered the speech of her life time.

"…If you have him, he's a little boy. He's been through a lot already, and we love him and miss him. You see, we took him into our lives because we need him as much as he needs us. He got to go to the beach for the first time just a day ago. He giggled at the sand crabs and the way the sand pulled away from him, squishing between his toes. Please, let him come home to us."

160

Throughout the conference Mark stood behind Max with his arm on her waist and offered a few final words for the camera. "He's our son. We adore him and want him home safe. I plan on teaching him how to ride a bike and to fish. Heath, if you see this you know we love you."

Chief Harding concluded, holding his hands up, "No questions," and guided Max and Mark back into the building.

Once inside Max broke down and cried for the first time. This was real. "Mark, what if...?" She stopped, unable to bring herself to finish her thought.

"What if what, Max?" he pressed her.

"What if Jack did this?"

Mark stared at her for a moment, a look of disbelief on his face. "How would he know we're here? How would he even know about Heath?"

"I don't know, Mark, but something is not right and my gut tells me he's involved somehow."

By now Mark had come to trust Max's instincts. So often when she had that feeling, she was dead on. He had not accepted her thoughts before and had later regretted it. With Heath's life in the balance, he could not afford to second guess her now.

"Chief Harding, Max has a theory. Tyler may be involved in this. We need a full team, and we need it now. I'm going to bring in some more agents from Quantico to assist. This is still your case, of course, but we have to align our teams. If she's right, we don't have a lot of time. Tyler has only left one survivor ever, and that victim is scarred for life."

Chief Harding stood facing Mark. Their eyes locked in a dead-on stare as the chief seemed to be thinking through everything Mark has just said. "Okay, Wells, you got whatever you need from my team. We'll find your son, and if that little bastard Tyler did this we'll take him down once and for all."

Chapter Twenty-Four

After lunch Jack had spent time with Hope helping cleaning up the kitchen and watching TV before returning to the surgical room. Inside the locked room with his scrubs on, he lifted the scalpel from the tray next to the table as Reb's eyes followed his hand. Her body gasped out a few ragged breaths as a single tear fell from her right eye and trailed down her shallow cheek. He ignored her and focused on the deep incision along the half-healed cut as he used the scalpel to tear through the flesh for a third time.

This time he merely sliced right through the sutures with little regard to the tiny wire-like strings. Reb was thrashing about now, but Jack didn't notice. He was far too focused on his process and what was to come. With the incision complete, he turned to the shelf behind him, lifted the surgical saw, and turned back. Using the tool, Jack sawed right through her sternum. He set the saw down and inserted a rib spreader into the opening and pushed apart her body, giving him access to a variety of prizes.

His heart thumped inside his chest, beating against his ribs like the flapping wings of a caged bird, as he slid his hands deeply into the cavity of her body and thoroughly explored her vital organs. His fingers sought out her heart and gingerly pressed around the beating organ. He reveled in the triumphant energy that flowed into him from within her body. He squeezed the slippery muscle, slightly driving an erratic reaction. The beating increased at first then slowed to a near stop. He squeezed again. This time the heart reacted wildly in his hands, and he rejoiced in the power and control he felt in the moment. His ecstasy came to an abrupt stop as the firm, yet soft treasure stopped reacting to his taunts.

163

Jack leaned back and looked down recognizing that Reb was now gone, and he felt both vindication and disappointment. She had betrayed him and deserved this. His disappointment came only from the realization that he would not be able to spend time with her again. He also knew the darkness would never let him be free.

Even though he had Hope back with him now, his family whole and very much alive, he still was missing his required use of skill that kept the darkness away. He couldn't ignore his impulses without having his surgical outlet. His mind wandered as he began to clean up. There was still Jimmy to deal with. After all, he hadn't treated Vivian right. With that thought he began to whistle softly.

The surgical room was restored to its normal sterile shine. Jack grabbed Reb's personal belongings and carried her ravaged body out of the basement, past Hope who watched with wide eyes. He didn't take time to acknowledge her gaze. Carefully locking the door behind him, he went through the kitchen and out the back door that gave access to the garage.

Jack grabbed the shovel from the corner of the garage while balancing the nude woman's body half-hoisted over his shoulder. He exited the back door of the garage and navigated his way through the underbrush and along the path to the play house. After a few moments, he decided the woman who years ago had nearly broken apart his relationship with Hope had no right to be buried near the bodies he'd once thought were those of his family, so he pushed past the playhouse he loved so dearly as a child and continued on deeper into the woods. When he arrived at the edge of the creek he stopped and looked around. Deciding this was as good as any place to bury the body; he dropped the frail corpse onto the ground and began to dig next to the narrow bank of the creek.

The soil was soft this close to the water, which made his job easier. It only took thirty minutes to have a hole dug deep enough to properly conceal the body. Using his forearm, he wiped the sweat from his brow, and after assessing the area, he lifted the body just enough that he could drop it into the dark space he had created. The body crumpled against the walls of dirt. He dropped in the bag containing her purse and clothes and began covering it with the soil he had just removed moments ago.

Ten minutes later he had the soil piled on top of the body. He took a few minutes to scatter leaves over the area to make it look more natural. Standing back and looking around, he noted that nothing looked as if it had been disturbed. With the task of burying Reb complete, he became relaxed enough to be aware of his surroundings. He could hear the creek trickling nearby and the birds chirping in the trees. Remaining perfectly still, he allowed himself time to enjoy the beauty of the area.

The sun was starting to set. Jack had spent more time with Reb than he'd realized and it was time to get back inside. Dinner would certainly be ready soon, and hopefully Chance was beginning to wake up. He'd slept a lot longer than Jack had expected and would, no doubt, have a lot of questions, and he certainly wanted to be there to welcome his son home. Turning away from the creek, he retraced his steps through the woods.

After entering the house, Jack went upstairs and took a shower and dressed in comfortable clothes since he wouldn't be leaving again tonight. The shower was refreshing, and exhaustion from the last twenty-four hours and sleeping on the couch settled into his body. Despite his tired state he felt peaceful. Reb had helped push away the darkness for now, and a complete calm seemed to be embracing him.

As he approached the basement stairs he was greeted by a wonderful aroma. He smiled, realizing Hope had prepared a family meal. It would be the first one with their son. Chance might not be feeling up to the task of eating right away, but even still it was the first one together as a whole family. His chest burst with pride and excitement.

He entered the basement and locked the door behind him, taking each step with purpose, and was met at the bottom by Hope. He was pleased to see she seemed alert and relaxed.

"I made a roast. I hope you like it."

"Thank you, darling." Jack leaned into her and swept her into his arms. He kissed her passionately. Her body felt warm as if teasing him. He suddenly was aware they were being watched and pulled back to find Faith looking at them.

"Mommy?" Faith looked at them and sounded confused.

"Faith. Honey, are you hungry? I know I sure am," Jack teased. He walked over to where she was standing and kneeled down to eye level. "Mommy made us a roast, and I bet it's the best we've ever had."

165

Faith just stared at him. He brushed a lock of hair away from her eyes and then turned to the couch where Chance still lay, though he seemed to be stirring.

"Has he been awake yet at all?" Jack asked Hope.

"Not yet. He's made a few noises, stirred a little, but has not yet awakened."

Jack turned his attention to Vivian and spent a few moments tucking the blankets in around her fragile body before saying, "Okay, well let's eat, and maybe Chance will wake up soon enough to join us." Taking Faith's hand, he led her over to the table. She went willingly.

Mindy watched as her daughter took Jack's hand, and she silently prayed that her small child would willingly accept the situation they were in. Allie was finally starting to be more alert, and Mindy knew soon she would have to try to explain to her young daughter how important it was for her to just act the part that has been given to her.

Jack had carried that woman's body out past her earlier, and it was in that very moment she understood what she needed to do. Everything from here on out would be exactly as if she really were Hope. She had to make Jack believe she was Hope and live the dream he'd created in his head. He was obviously delusional, and she was certain that as long as she and Allie played their roles in his crazy fantasy, they would be safe.

Her mind kept returning to that woman's face and how the head twisted in a way that it had been grossly staring at her as Jack carried her body out of the room. That face. It was familiar, and it took her half way through making the meal for her to make the connection. That woman had once been Hope's best friend. She could remember when Reb had warned Hope about Jack and how strange he was. Hope had become very angry and had stood up for Jack. Seeing him carry her out of the basement terrified her beyond anything she had ever experienced.

166

Mindy could remember many conversations with Hope about Jack when they were kids still living at home. As teenagers she had warned Hope a number of times that there might be something not quite right with him.

A tremor ran down her spine as she considered what would happen if he realized she was not really Hope. For now his desire to have Hope back with him was over powering reality. Clearly, he knew he came into her home and took her and had the presence of mind to do that, but now he seemed convinced that she was Hope and that Allie was Faith. She had to keep it that way. Her life and Allie's life depended on it.

Realizing she hadn't been paying attention, she returned her focus to dinner. Dishing the meal onto the plates, she served Jack a good helping of the savory roast and potatoes. On the side she had prepared a fresh salad and mixed vegetables. Setting the plate in front of him, she watched as he smiled up at her. It took everything in her to return a smile that she hoped felt genuine.

Once all the plates were filled, Mindy took her seat. It was difficult to eat even though the food smelled amazing. Realizing she needed to look every bit the happy wife, she forced bites of the succulent meat into her mouth. The food did taste good, and knowing it was important that she keep her strength up, she ate nearly everything on her plate. She certainly didn't want to have a chance to escape at some point and be too weak, causing her to fail to save her daughter because of it. She would never forgive herself. Those thoughts allowed her the focus she needed to continue to eat and nourish her body.

She watched as Jack scooped mouthfuls of the food, obviously really enjoying the meal.

"Faith, isn't this delicious?" Jack asked breaking the silence.

Allie looked confused, and Mindy nodded to her, hoping she would understand to just agree. She nearly sighed out loud when Allie spoke, "I like it."

***

Pushing back from the table, Jack rubbed his stomach with his left hand. "That was by far the best dinner I've had in months. Thank you, darling." He stood and picked up his plate, as well as Hope's and Faith's, and carried them over to the small kitchen. "I do believe it's my turn to clean up. You clearly have done plenty lately, what with caring for the kids and Vivian. Why don't you take a shower and freshen up?" A flirtatious smile covered his face as he winked.

Mindy looked back at Allie, who had moved from the table to the couch next to the boy and turned on the TV. Returning her gaze back to Jack, she nodded in agreement and headed to the small bathroom. As she passed, Jack curled his arm around her waist and nuzzled her neck. "You make me so happy, Hope. I love you so much." He released his grip and swatted at her butt as she pulled away and continued across the room.

Jack busied himself with the dishes, and once they were all clean, dried, and put away he went to the bed where Vivian lay. He gently took her pulse and observed her breathing. She was stable but obviously weak. The medication offered her what comfort she could gain. Unfortunately, that meant she slept a lot. Her eyes fluttered open at that moment, and he smiled down at her. "Well, hello, sleepy head."

"You're back from your trip," she said in a barely audible mumble.

"I am. I'm sorry I had to leave you, but I wasn't gone long, only a day. Hope took good care of you, I'm sure."

"Hope?" A confused look crossed the woman's face momentarily before her eyes closed again.

"Sleep well, dear," Jack offered, though the old woman clearly had dropped back off into a medicated rest.

Turning his attention across the room, he approached the couch where Heath and Allie sat. "How are my two favorite children?" he asked, gaining Allie's attention. "What are you watching, Faith?"

The girl gazed at him for a moment as if she didn't quite understand the question then replied, "TV."

"Well, I know that, silly, but what show are you watching?"

The child's eyes returned to the TV nearly in slow motion. "A cartoon."

"Fantastic. I love cartoons. Can I watch it with you?"

She raised her shoulders in a subtle shrug. "I guess so."

"Do you remember how we used to get up on Saturday mornings to watch cartoons together?"

The child looked up at him, her big blue eyes connecting with his for the first time since he'd brought her to the basement. She nodded then turned her attention back to the TV.

"That's my girl." Jack pulled her close to him, requiring her to rest against his chest.

Mindy returned from the shower to find them somewhat cuddled together on the couch.

"Hey, honey. We're watching some cartoons. Why don't you join us?"

Heath stirred a few times on the end of the couch, and Jack slid the boy's small body closer to him and rested the child's head in his lap. Mindy joined them on the couch next to Allie, and Jack stroked Heath's hair.

After one hour and two cartoons later, Heath opened his eyes and stared up at Jack. "Well, look who's waking up. Hello, son."

The boy blinked his eyes several times and appeared to be trying to cast off what might be the remnants of a dream. He tried to sit up but was not able to muster the energy to do so, so he rested back onto Jack's lap.

"Hey there, take it easy, big guy. It will take you a little bit to wake up. Take your time. We're watching some TV together. Do you want to watch some too?"

The boy's eyes moved around the room and stopped on the bed on the other side. He tried again to sit up but once again wasn't able to compel his body upright.

"Are you hungry? Mommy made some really great pot roast. We saved you some."

The boy's eyes darted around at the word mommy, and then stopped on the woman at the end of the couch.

Jack followed his gaze. "That's right, Chance. That's your real name, and she is your real mother. I know that probably seems a little confusing. You see, we had to keep some secrets from you to keep you safe. But finally you're home with your *real* family," Jack said applying emphasis on the word *real*.

Heath looked at the little girl next to the woman, and then his eyes moved once again to the bed across the room.

"That's Vivian. You can call her grandma. I'm sure she won't mind. She's been a little sick lately, but she loves little boys like you."

Mindy watched as Jack spoke to the child in a soothing and convincing manner. Her eyes dropped down to Allie who met her gaze. The girl's eyes were filled with questions. Mindy slowly shook her head at the young girl. Allie's eyes dropped to the floor as if she understood the subtle warning.

Heath's eyes returned to the little girl. His head nodded slightly towards her.

"And, that is your sister Faith. You two have been apart for a long while now, but you'll be fast friends. Your job will be to watch out for her. Even though she's a little older, you'll be stronger. Brothers need to take care of their sisters. Do you understand?"

A small nod came from the boy before he looked back up at Jack, their blue eyes connecting with each other. Jack did everything he could to express comfort and safety to the boy in that moment. He felt the child's body somewhat relax and watched as he drifted back to sleep.

"He's had a long day. For that matter, so have I. Why don't we all turn in? Tomorrow will be a really special day." Looking to Faith, he asked, "How would you like it if Daddy makes special pancakes tomorrow?"

Allie looked up and gently nodded before dropping her eyes to the floor again.

"Good deal. Then let's get your bed ready." Jack stood and turned to leave, taking the stairs two at a time. The basement door closed, and he returned a few minutes later with a set of sheets, a couple of blankets, and two pillows.

"I got the fold-out couch because I just knew we were going to need some more space. You two are young enough that you can sleep together for a little while. Of course later…well, we'll see how that goes. We have a whole house to grow into with time. You two want to give me a hand?" Jack set the bedding down on the floor.

Mindy and Allie stood, and Jack lifted Heath off the couch and then gave Mindy instructions on how to pull the couch out into a bed. A minute later the room was filled with a queen sized bed, aligned pretty closely to Vivian's bed.

"I know this is a little crowded, but it'll have to do for now," Jack said while looking to Mindy to put the sheets on the bed.

"Al… Faith, why don't you go get your jammies on," Mindy said nearly slipping up and calling her Allie.

Allie did as she was told, and as Mindy got the bed made, the little girl reappeared just as Jack was laying Heath down.

"Okay, honey, climb in," Jack said. He seemed to suddenly realize something and turned to quickly climb the basement stairs. When he returned he had a book in his hand. "We can't expect you to go to sleep without a bed time story, can we?" Jack lifted Allie into the bed and tucked the blankets up to her chin, then sat on the edge next to her, and opened the book filled with bedtime stories. He picked one and began to read. Within a few moments Allie dropped off to sleep. Jack turned to Mindy. "Look at our kids. Aren't they beautiful?"

Mindy nodded as she offered up a forced smile.

"Now, it's time for us to turn in." Jack reached out and took Mindy's hand in his as he led her to the room just off where the kids and Vivian were fast asleep.

***

Mindy's heart raced as she felt herself being led to the bed, which she had until now shared with her daughter in the dank basement. She was hopeful that Jack would be too tired for what she was certain he had on his mind. After all, he had been up all night and all day. Her mind reeled as she considered her options.

"Are you tired, darling?"

She jumped, his voice pulling her out of her thoughts. "Yes, it's been a busy couple of days," she replied hoping it sounded convincing enough.

"Me too," he answered.

Pulling back the sheets, Jack tugged at his shirt and pulled it over his head. Then he kicked off his shoes and socks and tossed his pants over the back of a chair, his keys fell out and landed on the floor next to his shoes. He stood before her in nothing but his briefs and Mindy's heart pounded even harder at the sight of his muscular body. Fear enveloped her, making her feel light-headed. Suddenly, she had an idea. "I'll be right there," she said as she went to the bathroom.

Inside the small room, she took a moment to regain control of her emotions, flushed the toilet, and then splashed cool water on her face. Feeling a bit more in command of her body, she slipped on the pajama he'd bought for her then opened the door and returned to the bedroom where her heart immediately took flight again, pounding wildly in her chest when she saw him in the bed propped up against the pillows.

She compelled her legs to move forward. Her mind focused on protecting Allie as she slid under the sheets next to the madman her sister had married.

Jack turned to her. "God, you're stunning."

She pulled the blankets up tightly around her neck and snapped off the table lamp beside the bed, knowing her eyes would give away her fear. Suddenly, a memory invaded her mind. She recalled how Hope would rub Jack's neck and back—something he seemed to really enjoy. She decided it might be the only way to protect herself, at least for tonight.

"You've had such a long day. Why don't you let me rub your back? You know how it always relaxes you." After making the offer she lay in the now dark room, unable to see his face and waiting with anxiety for his reply.

"Oh, that sounds really fantastic. I'm very tired."

Mindy felt his body rolling in the bed and knew he had turned on his stomach. Sucking in her breath, she turned to him, placed her small hands on his back, and began to pray that her touch would not deceive her. All she could think of as she began to move her hands over his broad, muscular back was getting her and the children out of here alive. Somehow she must find a way.

It wasn't long until soft snores filled the room, and Mindy began to relax. She continued to massage Jack's back for a few more minutes, wanting to ensure he was fully asleep. Finally, she moved as far away from him as she could, being careful to not stir too suddenly, and curled her body into a tight ball. She lay there wondering what she could use in the room to kill him. *Could she kill him?* She wasn't sure, but then thoughts of him hurting Paul entered her mind. She wept softly in the dark. Sleep eventually took her.

***

Jack stirred in the bed. His arm reached to the place where he knew Hope would be resting next to him. His fingers found a crumple of soft blankets and pillow. Opening his eyes, he scanned the room while blinking out the sleep and welcoming the morning light. His gaze rested on Hope in the small kitchen as his nostrils filled with the scent of bacon and coffee. A smile covered his lips, and his chest welled with love. Tears filled his eyes. Suddenly, he realized his dreams had become a reality. He truly did have his family back, and the proof of it was right before him.

Rolling over in the bed, he scanned the rest of the room and saw Faith already awake on the fold out sofa with her little head propped against the big pillows. Scruffy was wrapped around her and lifted his head when he saw his master moving around. His tail made several thumps against the sheets. Chance was still asleep next to the girl and the dog. Jack looked at the boy and thought that today he should become much more alert as the medication wore off from his system. That big breakfast Hope was making was certainly going to help with the absorption.

Sitting up, Jack swung his strong legs over the side of the bed then stood, rubbing his eyes and stretching his muscles out. Grabbing his shoes and keys he went straight up the stairs seeking clean clothes.

Returning to the basement he went to Vivian's bedside to check on her. She too was awake and seemed fairly alert this morning.

"Well, good morning, sunshine. You look pretty chipper today."

The old woman smiled up at him then struggled out a raspy, "Good morning."

At the sound of his voice, there was a loud clatter from the kitchen. Mindy dropped the spatula and turned to face him.

"I'm sorry, dear. Did I startle you?" He looked at her with obvious concern on his face.

"I guess I didn't hear you get up," she quickly responded while recovering the kitchen implement from the floor and quickly moving to the small sink to rinse it off.

Moving away from the old woman, he crossed to his wife and wrapped his big arms around her waist from behind. "You know I would never do anything to intentionally frighten you. I'm sorry. I'll be more careful."

Mindy stood in his embrace, frozen in place. "It's okay," she choked out.

"This breakfast smells amazing. You're really spoiling me."

"Would you like some coffee?" Mindy asked, pulling away to reach for a cup.

"That would be great," he replied, not noticing that she pulled out of his embrace. "Let me see if I can wake up Chance. I think the food will really help him." Jack turned back towards the kids and faced Faith. "Good morning, sweetheart," he said as he sat next to Chance.

Allie stared at him then managed a meek, "Good morning."

Mindy watched the exchange from the kitchen then turned back to the cup and filled it with coffee. She took the cup to Jack, setting it on the small table next to the couch.

"Thank you, darling." Jack smiled up at her.

He turned his attention back to Chance after giving Scruffy a few good scratches behind the ears. "Hey, buddy. Time to start trying to wake up." He shook the child lightly and then pulled the boy's small body next to him, cradling him against his chest.

The boy's eyes slowly opened. He blinked several times then his small fists came up to his face and rubbed in an obvious effort to wipe away the grogginess he clearly still felt.

"It's morning, and Mommy is making us a wonderful breakfast. You need to wake up so you can eat. Eating is going to make you feel a whole lot better."

The boy pushed his body up and sat up on his own. He looked all around, at first seeming confused, and then appearing to remember his short moment of being awake the night before. "Mommy?" he asked seeming confused again.

"That's right. There's a lot for me to explain to you. Do you feel good enough to stand up? We could take a little walk. Scruffy needs to go outside. Would you like to go with me to take him?"

Wide blue eyes turned to search Jack's face then shifted to the dog cuddled on the little girl who lay next to him on the bed. He nodded his head and began trying to push his body off the bed.

"Okay, take it easy, little guy. You might be a little bit wobbly at first," Jack warned as he watched the boy clambering to get off the bed. "Hope, honey, we're going to take Scruffy out for a minute. How soon before breakfast is ready?"

Mindy partially faced Jack then answered, "Ten minutes."

"Oh, perfect. We'll see my girls in just a few minutes."

Heath was now standing, while still rubbing at his eyes.

"Okay, I promised Faith pancakes so I'll mix those up real quick when we get back in. Come on, little man," Jack said while taking the boy's little hand and snapping his fingers for Scruffy to come with them. The wiry little dog happily bounced off of the bed and bounded up the stairs ahead of Jack and the child.

At the top of the stairs Jack unlocked the door. The deadbolt made a heavy clicking sound as the tumbler released from its hold. Then just as quickly, he locked the door behind him, sealing Mindy and Allie inside. Still holding the boy's hand, Jack led him through the house to the kitchen while on Scruffy's heels. At the back door Jack unlocked that too, and the dog immediately pushed through to get out into the sunlight. The morning was glorious with the sun already claiming the day.

"Let's take a little walk, and I'll do my best to explain everything to you. I know you're a little confused right now," Jack said leading the boy out into the daylight.

Following the dog, the boy walked with Jack through the woods along a half-beaten down path. Jack waited, allowing the sunlight and warmth of the day to provide some natural comfort before he began.

"First, let me start by telling you your real name. It's Chance, not whatever you've been called before. Also, I can finally tell you that I am your real father and Hope downstairs is your real mother. The little girl is your sister Faith. You see, when you were very young you were taken from us. I can't really explain why, but I'm sure people thought it was the best way to protect you. Now you're safe and back where you need to be. We're all safe now, here in this house."

The child stopped and looked up at Jack. His head tilted way back as he squinted against the sun that peeked through the trees. "Where's Mark?"

Jack hesitated for a minute then knelt down to eye level with the boy. "He is the one who brought you to me. You see, he was part of the whole plan—he and Maxine. The trip to California wasn't really a family vacation, but rather a plan to bring you back where you belong. They couldn't tell you because it wasn't safe to do so. There are still very bad people out there. Mark and Maxine love you very much, but had to keep secrets in order to get you back to me, your mother, and sister. Getting you home to us is all we've been dreaming of and what Mark and Maxine were required to do. It's their job as FBI agents to get kids back to their *real* parents," Jack emphasized *real*. "It's been a long time, and I couldn't be more proud of how brave you've been. I know there are times you've been alone and scared."

Jack stared into the boy's face. "Chance, we love you, and it has broken our hearts to be away from you for so long. But now… now we can really be a family, and no one can ever take you from us again."

Heath searched Jack's face and then suddenly was almost bowled over by Scruffy who eagerly jumped and licked at the child's face. Heath giggled and wiped at the wet kisses left on his cheeks. Jack laughed heartily with him, and soon they were both rolling around on the ground as the dog pounced on them.

Covered in leaves Jack stood up and pulled at the boy's hands, freeing him from the dog's continued tongue-lashing and lifting him onto his shoulders to give him a piggy back ride. "Are you hungry? I'm starving, and I bet that great breakfast Mommy is making is ready now."

Heath latched his arms around Jack's big shoulders. "Me too," he said still giggling.

"Come on, Scruffy. It's time for your breakfast too," Jack called out to the dog. Scruffy quickly turned hopping and jumping around and headed towards the house.

Chapter Twenty-Five

As soon as Mindy heard the door to the basement click locked, she went and sat next to Allie who remained on the couch absorbed in a cartoon on the TV. So far, Mindy was grateful that Allie seemed to have no recollection of meeting Jack. She was so young when Hope died and Jack hadn't really been around since having fallen apart following the accident.

"Allie, listen to me," the concerned mother said, making her small child look at her. "We are in danger here. You have been doing so good. In order to stay safe we're going to have to do whatever that man says. Do you understand?"

The little girl's blue eyes seemed dull compared to their normal bright and shiny glow that had always been filled with excitement and curiosity. She nodded her head, but said nothing.

"I know this is scary, but I hope someone will find us soon. In the meantime all you have to do is whatever that man says, okay? He won't hurt you as long as you play along. We can act like this is a game, okay? We'll pretend this is our real family."

Still staring up at her mother, Allie finally spoke, "Where's Daddy?"

Mindy choked back tears and forced a smile. "He's at home, and I'm sure he's looking for us every minute." Trying to keep her face from showing Allie her own concerns about her husband and other daughter's welfare, she pulled the little girl close to her, hugging her so tightly the child started to squirm.

"Mommy, you're hurting me."

177

"I'm sorry, honey," Mindy said letting her grip loose a little bit. "Now listen, the man will be back very soon. We have to play our game, okay?"

"Is that boy my brother?" Allie asked obviously confused.

"He is in the game. So just act like he is, okay?"

Mindy pulled back from the child and looked down at her again. The child's eyes stared up at her, and finally her little head nodded.

"Okay, now I have to make our family breakfast to make your pretend daddy happy." Mindy kissed her daughter on the head and then stood and returned to the makeshift kitchen. As she passed the bed she looked down at the frail old woman before continuing her duty of feeding the madman who had once been her sister's childhood friend and husband.

Chapter Twenty-Six

Max was exhausted. It had been twenty-four hours since Heath had been discovered as missing, and there was not a single sign of where he'd gone. They'd formed a search and rescue recovery room back at the LAPD headquarters, and she was suddenly surrounded by familiar faces from her days as a homicide detective on the force.

In addition, Mark had called in three of the FBI agents from the prior murder investigations from the Jack Tyler cases that had spanned across several states. She knew they had top talent and that they would not cease their efforts until Heath was found. She was struggling to keep her composure, and she could see the strain in Mark's face as well.

The task force already pinned up the details of what they knew, including photos of the open doors in the home. Crime scene investigators had searched Shauna's house from top to bottom, even crawl spaces and the attic, and found nothing.

They'd collected bits of evidence and fingerprinted every door frame and knob in the home, as well as taking prints from the entire family. It would take a few hours—maybe even a day, despite the chief's absolute demand that this had top priority—to get any prints that should not be in the home. Even then, those would need to be eliminated one by one as other friends of the family, repair people, or anyone that may have had access to the home for valid reasons.

Both Mark and Max gave their depiction over and over again of the events since their departure from their home in Virginia. They were repeatedly asked if there was anyone who may have shown a particular interest in Heath at the airports, on the plane, or at the beach.

Max began to feel chills run through her as she thought of her last conversation with Jack Tyler. He'd warned that he could be right near her, and she would never even know it. They knew he had changed his appearance by using a plastic surgeon's skills prior to killing the man and then vanished into thin air.

Wracking her brain she tried to picture anyone around them on the plane or sitting nearby in the airport that might have stood out or shown too much interest in them. She tried to remember every car at the beach, but she'd been so happy to be seeing her sister and nephew and to be watching Heath experience so many new things that she couldn't seem to conjure up any images that stood out. *Am I getting paranoid? Why would Jack take Heath?*

The white board had a timeline of events drawn out, a map of the area, photos of Heath, Jack Tyler, Hope, Faith, and of Mindy and Allie. As she sat and looked at the board she couldn't hold back her thoughts.

"It's a long shot, but we have to seriously consider that Jack Tyler has taken Heath and the Prescott's." She felt frantic and spoke cautiously, not wanting to inject her paranoia into the investigation. She'd already spoken this concern to Mark and the chief but now felt confident enough to speak it more broadly. She knew full well throwing ideas into the mix could cause long unnecessary distractions that could lead to delays in recovering Heath.

Her comments caused a lengthy discussion and no one really knew why Jack Tyler would take Heath. So far he had only been focused on what seemed to be the resurrection of his dead family. There was one question that everyone seemed equally concerned about and that was whether Tyler could have changed his focus to hurting Max. And why would he do that? They did all agree that there was no doubt he had focused on her during the prior investigation, calling her directly on more than one occasion.

Leaving the team to ponder the bomb she'd dropped, Max stood and stretched her legs and ran her hands through her thick hair. She felt like adrenaline was ramping through her veins. Anxiety was driving her every thought. She wanted Heath back and she wanted him right now, but had no way to just make that happen. Being out of control was maddening.

180

Mark and Cortez walked up to Max. Cortez handed her a cup of coffee. "It's not any better than it was when you worked here, but it's warm and there's caffeine in it." Cortez had a serious look on her face despite the subtle reminder of the terrible brew the LAPD was somewhat infamous for making. Her friend and former colleague almost always carried herself in strict professionalism on the job. Max knew her softer and funnier side from before she'd moved away because of the nights they had spent hanging out in Max's house drinking wine, talking smack about the guys in the LAPD house, and attempting to track Tyler's next move.

"Thanks, Cortez," Max said, accepting the Styrofoam cup and thinking to herself, *Oh great, more caffeine.*

"Do you have an update for us?" Mark asked.

"We don't have much. The Amber Alert has provided some tips, but nothing legitimate so far. There are techs on the phone, and we still have officers on the street re-canvassing the neighborhood and beach area."

Max nodded, noting the sadness in Mark's tone. Her heart tore as she remembered his story of the loss of his younger brother who was taken and killed by a neighborhood grocer when Mark was just a kid. She wasn't sure he could handle another loss like that, and she knew for certain he would feel responsible if something happened to Heath, just as he felt responsible for his younger brother Tommy's death.

"I know I'm close to this case, but my gut tells me Tyler is responsible for this," Max offered, knowing the implications of her words. So far no one Jack Tyler had taken had survived except for the little girl in Illinois, and even then he'd damaged her for life by cutting off her mouth and replacing it with that of another child he'd murdered. "We have nothing else, and while the Amber Alert is out we need to start focusing on Tyler. Have any of his known aliases been used in any way? We need to search everything, credit cards, prior bank accounts, passports—everything."

Mark nodded his head in agreement. Immediately taking charge and doing what he was best at, Mark seemed to shake off his own personal fears and stepped into his role of Special Agent in Charge. "We need to divide our efforts. Cortez, can we get the local team to focus on search and rescue efforts, while I align my agents around the Tyler theory? We'll get more done this way."

Cortez didn't even wait to answer. She turned and headed in the direction of the chief.

Mark looked down at Max before gazing at the white board and then called out to the team, "Jenkins, I want you working all past names Tyler has associated with. See if you can find anything. Everyone else, we need to focus our efforts on possible locations where Tyler might go, and we need someone to work on the possible names we have that Tyler might use next. Those are a long shot given we don't know where he might be, but if he truly is responsible for the abduction of the Prescott's, he's likely still on the west coast. That would put him in both Arizona and California in a very short period of time. Let's start our search in these two states then branch out from there."

Max jumped in. "I'll take the likely aliases. I have the file."

Without any more words, the small team went into action.

Chapter Twenty-Seven

Jack went into action when he returned to the basement and made the kids funny-faced pancakes adding them to the already fantastic breakfast Mindy had prepared. The dishes were washed and put away when Mindy asked Jack to go out and pick up some groceries, giving him a list of items she wanted. Jack was happy to oblige her request and didn't even realize that her motivation of the request was less about the need for any food items was and more about keeping him away from her and Allie. Even as he kissed her before leaving, he failed to notice the gasp she was unable to refrain from releasing.

Jack resisted the idea of taking Chance with him. As much as he desired having his son with him everywhere he went, he knew the boy was still settling in. After giving both kids a peck on their respective cheeks, he told them he would be home soon and then ascended the stairs out of the basement. Before departing the house he double checked all the locks.

The day was sunny and warm, causing him to smile at his good fortune. Everything was truly perfect now. Pulling the car out onto the street, Jack turned on the radio and tapped his fingers to the music as he drove. He arrived at the local grocery and parked the vehicle in the first available space before going inside.

Getting a cart, he started on the first aisle going through one by one collecting the items from his list. He rounded the corner of the fourth aisle and nearly stopped dead in his tracks when he saw Jimmy, Vivian's less than qualified former caregiver. Continuing down the row, he smiled when he got closer. "Jimmy, good to see you," he said insincerely while applying that natural charm that had always worked for him.

Jimmy looked up from the shelf he'd been focused on, a smile crossing his face. "Well, hello. How is Miss Vivian doing?"

"She's doing fine," he lied again, not wanting to disclose anything about the woman's condition. It took a lot of composure to maintain a pleasant look on his face when in reality he wanted to be anything but cordial.

"Well, good seeing you, man," Jimmy said smiling, and then returned to scanning the shelf where his attention had originally been.

"Yes, I'll be seeing you," Jack replied before continuing to gather the items on the shopping list. Walking through the aisles he could feel the sudden welling of darkness filling his entire being. His mind flashed to images of Reb laying on the cold stainless steel table, but even remembering his time with her wasn't helping his suddenly sullen mood.

Staring at spaghetti sauces, on every can and jar all he saw was Jimmy's face smeared with blood, the tomato pastes blending in with the images perfectly. Forcing himself to focus, he selected one of the sauces and placed it into the cart, then continued through the store getting all the items before checking out.

Placing his purchases into the back of the vehicle, Jack got in, closed the door, and sat in the parking lot for a moment trying to gather his thoughts and push back the dark feelings that overcame him after seeing Jimmy in the store. He mindlessly turned the key in the ignition, starting the vehicle's engine. A news story interrupted his thoughts. Reaching for the volume, he twisted the knob and listened carefully.

"The son of husband and wife FBI top serial profilers, Mark and Maxine Wells, has allegedly been abducted. The five year old went missing yesterday in the early hours. Local police and the FBI are working together, but at this time they reportedly do not have any solid leads. Because the Special Agents were the lead investigators in the case of 'Most Wanted' serial killer Jack Tyler, speculation is already swirling as to whether the serial murderer could be involved in the child's disappearance."

Jack was stunned at first, but then of course realized he'd known all along that the investigators would assume he was involved. He turned the rear view mirror towards him. He looked at his face, turned side to side, and smiled. No way would anyone recognize him. Feeling confident that he was safe from Maxine's clutches, temptation rose and an idea began to form.

Pulling out of the parking lot, he headed the car towards the Dollar General and pulled into one of the front row spaces. He exited the vehicle and clicked the remote to lock the groceries inside, and then walked into the store, making a left just past the register. Within a couple of minutes he had secured his item and stood waiting to check out.

Returning to the vehicle he looked around. He thought for a moment that he might be getting paranoid then shrugged it off, knowing full well that unlike what was depicted in the movies the police could not find someone by mere background noises on a phone call. Pulling his personal cell phone from his pocket, he first checked the video monitoring equipment and saw his family sitting together on the couch. Nothing seemed out of the ordinary. A perfect picture, so he felt confident he had more time.

He punched the button on his phone to bring up his contact list, and then reached inside the bag containing his purchase from inside the small convenience store. Quickly peeling off the packaging, he pulled out the disposable phone and went through the setup options. He punched in the numbers from the contact list in his personal cell phone and waited for the call to connect.

Soon his wish was granted. "Agent Wells," Max answered. The persistent ring jolted her away from the research she'd been focused on.

"I saw the news report, Maxine. It seems you have a new last name."

Snapping her fingers, Max stood. "Jack, so I do. What have you done with Heath?"

"Tsk, tsk. Why must you always go straight to business? You really should relax some."

Mark and the others quickly surrounded her, and Mark turned his own phone on next to hers in an effort to record the call. "Funny, Jack, but somehow my son being missing seems to have put a damper on my relaxation time. Now, why don't you tell me what you've done with him, and I can go back to vacationing?"

"Sorry, can't help you with that, but you know I must say that husband of yours really shouldn't leave such a beautiful woman

185

and child vulnerable like that. It's truly a terrible thing, someone coming in and taking a child right out from under your noses."

"How do you know he was taken from under our noses, Jack? Maybe because you were there? Why not tell me where he is?"

"It's not becoming of you, Agent, to sound so… desperate."

"Jack, come on. You know what it's like losing a child. If anyone would understand having the need to get a child back home, it's you."

"Nice try, Agent." Jack laughed at her efforts.

"How is your family holding up? I'm thinking your pieced-together family rotted away. Not quite what you hoped for. Was it? Is that why you took Mindy and her daughter? Did you need a fast replacement?"

"My family is just fine, Agent. Nice talking to you. Don't worry that pretty, red head of yours. All is well. I do hope things work out as they should for you, Agent. It's always nice talking with you."

Jack ended the call and tossed the phone in the plastic bag along with the packaging. Then he placed the car in reverse and backed out of the space, pointing his car towards home.

Chapter Twenty-Eight

Max stood staring at the phone. "Please, tell me you got it."

"Detective Cortez, we need a trace on Max's phone. Can you arrange that? This isn't the first time Tyler has contacted her, and he may do it again," Mark said immediately going into action.

Cortez took Max's phone, and with a nod, left the room.

"Agent Adams, please get this recording captured and do everything you can to pull out anything that might indicate where it may have come from. Run trace on Max's cell as soon as Cortez is done. Maybe he got careless, and the call will lead us somewhere."

Adams took Mark's phone and immediately went to work on it after sitting down at the table and plugging the phone into the USB port on his laptop.

Max watched as Mark got everyone in motion. The room seemed to swirl around her. She pictured the bodies of the children in Illinois with their limbs removed, and her heart raced as her mind placed Heath's face on each one of them. She could barely stand, her legs feeling weak under her. Trying to gain her composure, Max placed her hand on the back of the chair near the table she had previously been sitting in and stabilized herself. There was a glass of water on the table, and she reached for it and raised it to her lips, letting the cool water into her mouth.

Mark was suddenly near her side. "Are you okay? You don't look well."

"I'm scared, but I'm fine," she replied not making eye contact with him, knowing he would be able to read her.

Mark nodded. "We'll find him, Max. We have to find him."

"I know. We just need to focus. Come on, let's go over the call."

Mark pulled the chair out, allowing Max to sit down which immediately made her head feel better. He sat in the chair next to her and was joined by Agent Jenkins. "Okay, let's walk it through. The first part of the call I didn't get, so you have to tell us exactly what he said when the call originated."

Max sighed and ran her hands through her thick, red hair. She felt something that she hadn't noticed before now, something about her hair in the back. She ran her fingers through her hair again, and this time she was certain something was wrong. She worked her hands down the strands along the back left side of her head.

"Max, are you ready?" Mark asked, seeming confused by her silence.

"Mark, look at the back of my hair. It feels like it's been cut. There's a part that feels short compared to the rest." She turned her back to him, allowing him access to the back of her head.

Mark pulled her hair back into his own hands and followed her fingers along the strands. His strong, thick fingers struggled to feel with the same nimble movements, but Max's hand led his to the specific area of her concern. He bent his head down to look under the locks and could see the blunt cut across the back of her hair. There was a strand about two inches wide that was clearly two to three inches shorter. It was difficult to see as it was at the back and slightly under the outer most parts of her hair.

Max turned back to face Mark and asked, "Well?"

"It seems like there is a two or three inch square missing." Mark responded, concern covering his face.

"Tyler said something about my red hair. I assumed he was referring to photos he'd seen or from the television coverage during our investigation. I know he's seen me before, but I think he was taunting me. Mark, my hair is cut!"

"If he cut your hair, it certainly means he was in Shauna's home, and it means…," Mark's words trailed off, unable to complete the sentence that this would no doubt mean Tyler had taken Heath.

"Who else could have done this?"

Agent Jenkins lifted Max's hair again and snapped a few pictures with a camera on her cell phone, and then emailed them to each of the members on the team.

Mark held Max's eyes for a moment then spoke, "We have to focus. Walk me through the whole phone call."

Max looked at Mark and could see the pain in his eyes. She knew he was torn between concern for her and the thought that Jack Tyler had been close enough to cut her hair. She couldn't help but wonder if he was holding it while talking to her right now. He always demonstrated his smug attitude when he called. He clearly knew he had the upper hand. *Heath, focus on Heath. It's just hair.* "Okay let's do this," she said with a focused quick nod of her head.

"Okay," Mark nodded at her and glanced at Agent Jenkins. "What was the very first thing he said? We really need to get the first part of the conversation down."

***

About an hour later they had gone over the phone call several times and were now replaying a cleaned version of the recording Mark had made from holding his own cell phone up to Max's phone. Max's side of the conversation was very clear. Tyler was harder to hear, and it was nearly impossible to catch any background noises that potentially would indicate where Tyler was calling from.

Max listened to the recording several times and filled in any gaps. Tyler never actually admitted being in the house, but the reference to her hair and then the cutting clearly indicated that Tyler was, in fact, responsible for Heath's disappearance.

Agent Adams confirmed that Tyler used a disposable phone, and it was untraceable. Once again, they had nothing.

Mark stopped everyone. "We have to go back to what we were doing. There's a lead somewhere. We just have to find it. In five minutes I want an update on what ground everyone has covered."

Cortez returned to the room while they were going over Max's statement. "I know it is unlikely Tyler will call again. He's smart and knows we will attempt to trace any new calls, but if he does call, the trap is set and we'll get him.

Though Tyler had not admitted or said anything that could connect him to the abduction and disappearance of Mindy and her

189

daughter, he had them. Max was sure of it. She could only assume that something had gone wrong with the bodies he had so lovingly built. Her stomach suddenly rolled over at the thought of all the people that had died so he could make those pseudo replacements for his family. Now, he had moved forward to live replacements. She was certain of it. She could *feel* it.

"I believe he has Heath, Mindy, and Allie," she heard herself saying out loud.

"He's never kept hostages," Jenkins said, then nearly recoiled at the gravity of her words and what that would mean to her fellow FBI agents, specifically the boy's adoptive parents.

"Because he thought he couldn't. I don't mean not capable. I mean it never occurred to him. But Mindy and Allie, well, they're just too tempting, too much of a resemblance to Hope and Faith. My bet is those bodies, his little experiments, began to fail. He immediately needed to replace them. There were only two ways to do that: start over and hopefully perfect the process or find the very next best thing."

Mark nodded his head. "There's no doubt Mindy's a dead ringer for Hope." He turned to look at the white board and the assorted photos. The pictures of Hope and Mindy were remarkably close, as were the photos of Faith and Allie. "They both are actually very close, but how does Heath fit in?"

Max pushed her chair back and jumped up, grabbing a folder on the table opposite them, and then flipped through several pages. After several minutes she came and sat back down. "I can't find it, but I swear there was something Tyler said about a son. Maybe it's just my mind playing tricks on me, but something was said about him and Hope planning another child and how he wanted a son." She shook her head in frustration and concern that she might not be remembering something real.

Agent Jenkins spoke up, "We could ask the brother-in-law, Paul, if he knows whether Hope and Jack were planning another child. He may know. It's a start."

Mark added, "If we're right, I don't think he'll hurt them unless they try to get away or fight him in some way. Mindy knows he's a psychopath, so let's hope she's smart enough to keep him focused."

Max continued the thought, "She may be in more danger than the kids. If he believes she is his wife…" The idea hung in the air like a very thick cloud. Max knew if Jack thought Mindy was his wife Hope, there would be certain things he would expect from her, and if she couldn't deter him or comply with his demands she would be in eminent danger.

"What do we have so far?" Mark asked trying to get everyone back to tracking Jack, knowing it was the only way they would actually find him.

Jenkins spoke up first, "I've tracked most of the names against former bank accounts and social security numbers. Nothing pops. I'm working on credit report searches now. I should have each of those within the hour."

"Good," Mark said turning to Agent Adams. "What about you?"

"I've been triangulating off of the abductions sites and most recent activities while factoring in the time between the Prescott abduction and the time since Heath's abduction. He can only be in California, Arizona, Utah, or Nevada. He wouldn't have had enough time to drive into Oregon or New Mexico. I'm now trying to tie these out to the locations from the magazines Jack had as a child. We know so far he's stuck pretty close to those locations. Within a couple of hours I'll be able to state specifically where he is most likely located."

"We're going to have to narrow it down. That is massive geography," Max countered.

"I understand," Adams defended. "I'm working on it, trying to take the states within driving range since Heath's abduction and then narrowing in on the cities, which will narrow our search efforts."

Mark looked over at Max and could sense her frustration but continued to push, "Cortez, any luck with canvases?"

"Nothing has panned out. We've had several reported sightings from the Amber Alert, but all so far have been a bust. Additionally, we still have a foot patrol in the neighborhood conducting new and re-interviews as well as keeping a focus on the beach areas. Max's phone is set up to trace. If Tyler calls again, we'll trap him."

Max jumped in, "I've been working the potential names Tyler would choose next, based off the research Bobby gave us. I also have the history on prior names. The prior identities associate back to names of people that died as an infant. Those names were dormant with no social security information until Jack starting using them. " She nodded her head at Cortez, knowing she wouldn't have that information without her help. "The hardest part is narrowing the names down. The list is long for each. As soon as Adams has the cities narrowed, I can target those areas first. Then I can try to tie them back to a deceased infant of the same name."

"Okay, Adams. Pressure is on you." Mark directed, "Everyone focused."

With that direction they each went to their respective assignments. Everyone understood the gravity of the situation. Mark asked Cortez to get someone into an interview right away with Mindy's husband Paul. They needed to know anything and everything he might know about Jack's desire to have a son. All information Paul provided would be helpful in understanding what Jack might do next, or where he might take Mindy and the kids.

Max watched Mark make another call, after requesting Paul's interview, and petitioned another agent to be assigned to reassessing Paul and Mindy's home for any possible things that might have been overlooked in the original investigation. She knew it was a slim chance that anything new might be discovered, but realized Mark wasn't willing to take a chance on missing even the slightest detail that might provide a lead. Heath's safe return depended on every possible trace being carefully reviewed.

Max had to force her mind not to consider that Jack may have already killed the boy she had come to love dearly. If Jack was still creating people from the combined bodies of several victims, he may have wanted only certain parts of Heath. Her body shuddered at the thought and the images that came with it. Despite the terrifying feeling this gave her, she suddenly realized if this were the case there would likely be other kids missing too.

"Mark, we may be missing something. We need to focus on possible other missing kids. If Jack is creating a son rather than just taking one, there will be other kids. Let's face it; he killed people to restore his wife and daughter. So unless that process failed, he may follow it again." She swallowed heavily, realizing that she was suggesting that Heath may have been cut into parts to create the body of a potential son for Tyler's sick collection of bodies he considered to be his family. She winced slightly as she saw the look on Mark's face.

Mark's dark blue eyes flashed from torment to focus. "Okay, Jenkins, while you're waiting on the credit reports focus on possible other missing kids. Keep it specific to the areas Adams said are within scope. These would have to be very recent abductions. Keep the search narrowed, between the abduction of Mindy and her daughter and today. We can't know whether Heath would be the first child or not. Also, we should expect to see abductions, murders, or dumps of women or female children that match Faith's description. If his original creations have failed, he may have taken Mindy and Allie to start over."

Max's eyes met Mark's, and her heart tore. There was a sadness he couldn't hide. Cortez walked up and grabbed her by the arm. "Walk with me for a cup of coffee?" Max looked at her not wanting to waste any time, but she nodded and followed her friend and former partner to the break room.

"What's up?" Max asked, trying to hide her crumbling resolve.

"Just checking on you. How are you holding up? I'm worried."

Max shook her head. "I'm a wreck but trying to stay focused. Mark can barely look at me. I don't think I ever told you about his younger brother Tommy. Let's just say something happened to Tommy when they were young kids, and Mark feels responsible for his death. I know he feels responsible again. I'm not sure what happens to him if we don't get Heath back alive."

Max prepared a cup of coffee, and she could tell Cortez wanted to reassure her, but hesitated. She knew her hesitation was because the promises would be empty. Knowing Tyler the way she did, anything was possible. In fact, given Tyler's M.O. there was a really good chance that Heath was dead within hours of being taken.

"I appreciate it, Cortez. Let's just get Tyler and make this madness stop," Max said, balancing her coffee cup in her right hand.

"You got it. No getting away this time. Tyler is ours." Cortez patted Max on the shoulder as they headed back to the investigation room where the others were still working away.

Chapter Twenty-Nine

After hanging up the phone, Jack struggled to keep his composure. He replayed the call in his head and suddenly realized that he'd given Agent Maxine Wells a lot to think about. He smiled as he recognized that he never really confirmed anything about his involvement. The more he thought about the call, the more certain he became that there was no way the FBI agents would know how to track him. For a few moments, he felt good as he drove.

When he passed the grocery store he had been in earlier, he remembered Jimmy the surfer. He started thinking about the way that young man had treated Vivian, and the darkness seemed to close in again. He started thinking about his strong fingers wrapped around Jimmy's heart, and his mood lifted slightly.

Jack pulled into the driveway and navigated the vehicle up the curved path and then hit the button to open the garage door with the remote that was slipped over the visor. Inside with the door closed behind him, he retrieved his grocery bags and carried them through the garage and house to the basement door. Retrieving the key to the deadbolt from his pocket, he listened carefully for any movement while holding several bags in his other hand before he opened the door. Hearing nothing unusual he twisted the key in the lock, pulled the door open, and stepped through the doorway, closing the door behind him.

Descending the stairs he was pleased to see his family on the couch all cuddled together. Hope sat with Faith on her left and Chance on her right. Vivian lay nearby in her bed. It was a sight to behold. He could hardly believe his good fortune, his beautiful family enjoying the day together.

Chance saw him and immediately jumped up and ran to his side, as did Scruffy who had been lying near the couch on the floor. "What did you get?"

"Just some groceries, big guy, but I did get some donuts for a special treat, and some ice cream."

"Can I see what kind?"

"Sure, come over here and help me put the groceries away."

Heath hovered over Jack as he placed the items out on the small table and then slowly put them away. "Can we have pizza? I love pizza."

"Of course we can," Jack replied looking over at Mindy. "As long as your mommy says it's okay."

Mindy nodded. "Sure, we can. Maybe tonight for dinner."

Jack smiled at Hope. Her beauty always amazed him.

With the groceries put away, Jack grabbed the remaining bag that lay on the table and turned to Heath. "Chance, want to go with me to take Scruffy for a walk?"

The boy was bounding up the stairs with the small dog nearly as fast as the words came out of Jack's mouth. "Yes, can we walk in the woods again?"

"Sure, we can. I want to show you my playhouse from when I was a boy. You're going to love it. You know, that's where me and Mommy played all the time."

"Really?"

"Yes, really. Come on, I'll show you. Faith, do you want to come too?"

Allie pushed into Mindy and shook her head.

"She still seems a little tired. Maybe another day she'll feel a little better and want to go with you. You boys go and have fun. We'll be here when you get back," Mindy offered.

Jack smiled and nodded, not realizing Mindy's comments were intended to pacify his desire to have Allie go with him. He turned and followed Heath up the stairs. "Okay ready, Chance? It looks like it's just us boys."

"Ready!" Heath responded.

The man and boy slipped through the door behind the dog. Jack closed and locked the door then walked towards the back of the house. "Hold up, Chance. I need to get the shovel."

"What are you going to dig for?"

"I'll show you."

"Can I help?"

"Sure, buddy. Let me grab the shovel, and you can help." Jack smiled at his son, and his heart burst with pride. He retrieved the tool from the garage and returned to find Scruffy and Heath playing together by the back door. Scruffy immediately started hopping around anxious to go outside. "Hold on, Scruffy," Jack said laughing at the sight.

Jack pulled the back door open, and both the dog and the boy darted out into the sunlight. Heath quickly ran out into the woods and headed down the path. "Hold on, guys. Wait for me," Jack called out to them.

They wandered down the path, stepping over the brambles that seemed to try and wrap around their ankles. Heath ran ahead when he saw the small wooden building looming in the distance. "Is this the playhouse?" Heath shouted out with excitement in his voice.

"Yes, that's it. I spent a lot of time in there when I was a boy. Mommy lived down the road just a little. And she would ride over on her bike, and we would play out here for hours. The walls of that little house know everything there is to know about me."

Heath looked on at the building in amazement. "Can I go inside?"

"Of course you can. It's yours now. I hope you'll enjoy it as much as I did."

"I DO love it. It's perfect." Heath opened the door, the hinges complaining from lack of use over the years. He let the door close behind him and then stood and peeked back out at Jack through the small circular hole in the door. "Did you play games in here?" Heath asked standing on his tip toes to look through the opening in the door.

Jack considered this question, and his mind flashed to all the things he had done in that little building. "Well, why don't you come out here and maybe I'll start to show you some things I used to do. But first, we need to dig a hole. Still want to help?"

"Uh-huh." Heath came out of the building and anxiously stood next to Jack.

"Okay, let's pick a good spot."

"How do we know if it's a good spot?"

"Well, if you have something important enough to bury, then you better pick a spot that you can remember and that you are pretty sure no one else will ever find."

"What important thing are we burying?"

"We are burying a phone."

"Why are we burying a phone? Don't you need your phone?"

"This phone is a special phone, not my normal phone, and it's one I don't want anyone to ever know I had. Where do you think a good spot would be?"

Heath looked around. His eyes scanned the area. "Under the playhouse is a good spot."

Jack smiled. "You know, when I was your age I thought so too. I had some special things buried there, but someone found them, so I didn't find a good enough spot."

"Oh." Heath looked around some more. "What about under that tree?" He pointed to the east at a big oak tree that seemed to dominate the area.

Jack smiled. "Now that looks like a good spot. Let's do it."

They walked over to the base of the tree, and Jack dug the shovel deep into the soil, then handed the shovel over to Heath. Scruffy ran up and began digging with his paws, helping Heath out as the small boy struggled to manage the shovel covered in heavy amounts of soil. Jack's chest welled with pride as he watched Chance and the little dog digging away.

Seeing Chance getting tired, Jack stepped back in and helped finish the hole, giving it one last deep pitch. Then he lifted the bag containing the packaging and cell phone and dropped it onto the ground next to the tree. He pushed it into the hole with his shoe. He scooped a pile of dirt in on it, and then let Heath finish covering it up.

Jack stood back and looked at where they'd just finished and said, "Look at it, Chance. Will you remember it?"

"Yes," the boy answered.

"Will anyone else be able to find it?"

Heath looked around, and then his face fell. The mounds of dirt were uneven, and it was obvious the ground had been disturbed. The boy seemed sad when he realized that maybe he hadn't done a good job. "Yes."

"So what do we do about that?"

Heath looked around and then walked back to the tree and began putting leaves over the dirt. "Cover it up?"

"That's right, son. You got it. We have to cover it up so no one will see it."

Jack proceeded to help fill in the dirt with leaves and twigs. A few minutes later, he asked Heath the same question, only this time Heath stood looking up at him with a proud smile on his face.

With the phone properly buried and hidden, Heath ran off to explore in the playhouse again. Jack sat down on a fallen log nearby and watched as the boy and dog played. His eyes darted around the woods that he was so familiar with. He loved these woods, so many good memories here. A squirrel danced up and down on a nearby tree. Jack watched, his senses awakened by the twitching of the squirrel's tail.

Heath saw the rodent and pointed to it. "Look, Daddy."

"Yes, Chance, that's a squirrel. I used to play with those when I was a boy out here."

"You can catch them?"

"Well, I used to be able to. I would set up a little trap for it so I could catch it."

"Can we set a trap and catch it?"

Jack could see the excitement in the child's eyes. "Okay, but not today. We probably need to get back inside."

"Awww," Heath complained, but as Jack stood up he immediately followed him back to the house.

***

The day withered away. The kids watched some TV, and then Jack talked the whole family into playing a game together. Hope seemed to be more herself now, and he really enjoyed the time together. But as night started to set, he felt anxious, and it seemed as if his skinned crawled.

His blood felt hot inside his veins, and despite the happiness he felt, he couldn't seem to focus on his family. The darkness was starting to become demanding. Being in California was good; his family was good. But he was not practicing medicine, and without the outlet that he and Hope had designed for him to release the relentless desire, he couldn't fight the pressure that was clearly building. As dice lay on the table in front of him requiring his play, he could only see Jimmy's face. Each tiny dot appeared as a speck of blood calling him to action.

Struggling to maintain his composure, he wrapped up the game and then indicated to Hope that it was time for the kids to go to bed.

"Later I need to go out for a while," he explained to her, wondering what her reaction might be.

"Okay," Mindy replied.

Jack sighed with relief that she didn't challenge him on where he might be going. His mind flashed to the day in the playhouse when they'd vowed to work together to hold back the darkness. Today she seemed to understand and was not questioning him. He wasn't certain he understood her reaction, but was grateful nonetheless.

He began cleaning up the area and helped Heath get ready for bed. "Chance, I need to go to town and get you some more clothes and better things to sleep in. I'll do that tomorrow."

"Can I go with you?"

Jack pondered the child's innocent request. "Not this time, little buddy. We need to still be careful. I think we're safe now, but we have to be sure that all the bad guys are gone. I never want to be away from you again."

Disappointment filled the boy's eyes. "Okay," he said, accepting the explanation.

"I'll tell you what though, we can go out into the woods again. In fact, if you want to come out for a few minutes with me right now you can. I need to take Scruffy out." Jack hoped the compromise would help make the boy feel better.

Heath's eyes lit up at the offer. He was already heading to the stairs.

"Whoa, hold on, Chance. Let me finish helping your mother put our game away, and then we can go."

Mindy heard the comment. "You two go ahead."

"You sure?" Jack asked for confirmation. "I don't mind helping."

"It's okay. The dog needs to go out."

200

"Okay, thanks, babe." Jack leaned in and kissed Mindy on the cheek. "I love you, Hope."

"I know," Mindy replied as she continued to clean up the kitchen of glasses and dice.

Jack was so pleased with the opportunity to get out of the room that seemed overly stifling, that once again, he missed her subtle clues. A sliver of a shudder ran through her at his kiss, and there was a dull tone in her voice as she forced a response to his words of adoration.

"Come on, let's go," Heath said standing at the top of the stairs trying to open the door. Scruffy stood next to him with his paws on the top step, begging to get out.

"Okay, guys, I'm coming." Jack turned from Mindy and took the stairs two at a time.

Once out of the basement, Jack could almost immediately feel some of the weight removed from his body. The outside air cooled his skin and the night sounds helped calm the crawling feeling that had been racing through him for the last hour.

"Chance," he spoke. "It's important that you learn how to be safe in the darkness. Always listen to the night. It speaks to you."

"The night speaks? How?"

"Not in words, but in sounds. The sounds can tell you if there is danger or peace in the air."

Almost as if on key, a coyote bayed in the distance, followed by others in a near eerie frenzy as they chased their prey. Then as quickly as it started, the cries stopped in an abrupt and final, united scream.

"Those were coyotes. They're like wild dogs, and they're strong enough to kill a dog like Scruffy, or a deer, even a farmer's cow."

"Why?"

"They're just doing what comes naturally to them. Sometimes it's for food, and sometimes they do it because they just need to."

"Oh." Heath stood listening to the night. "Will they hurt Scruffy?"

"No, because we'll keep him safe. It's our job. Just like it's my job to keep you safe."

"How?"

"Any way we need to. When you're supposed to protect something, it's your job to do whatever it takes. I'll do anything to protect you, Mommy, and Faith."

Heath smiled up at him and slid his small hand into Jack's. "Are you really my daddy?"

"Jack stared down at the little boy. "Yes, son. I am."

Heath smiled. "I always wanted a real daddy."

Jack returned his smile and said, "Okay, enough exploring for tonight. It's time for you to get to bed. Come on, Scruffy." Jack called after the dog, which had stayed relatively nearby in the dark of the night. The little dog immediately responded and followed Jack back to the door.

An hour later with the kids fast asleep in bed, Mindy was sitting on the couch. Jack began, "Hope, honey. I need to go out for a while." He hesitated, hoping he wouldn't need to explain why he needed to go out, and was relieved once again when she didn't ask.

Before leaving he checked on Vivian, making sure her medication was set properly. He checked her bedding and made sure she was clean and dry, turning her slightly in hopes of keeping her comfortable and free of bed sores. Each day he seemed to be losing her more and more. This fueled the already burning fire inside. Once again the internal flame was itching in his veins.

Turning back to Hope he gave her a quick kiss on her cheek and left with a final message, "I'll be home soon."

***

When Jack left Hope, he was pleased. Pleased to have the time out of the dark basement. Pleased that he could take care of this annoying burning that had now flooded his senses, and pleased that Hope had not pressured him about where he was going or how long he'd be gone.

He was such a lucky man, having a wife that was so sensitive to his needs. He began to whistle as he locked his family safely in the basement. Grabbing a jacket from a hallway closet, he went out

202

to the van. He knew exactly where he was going. He had been there before.

Certain that he had the proper supplies in his doctor kit behind the seat of the van, he pulled the vehicle out of the garage. It was getting late–now after ten o'clock. For a small town like Ojai ten o'clock was button up time. The streets were nearly empty, and as he passed through the residential areas, the houses were cloaked in darkness. Street lamps gave the town the perfect glow. Jack loved the night time, the stillness that came with it and the fear most felt it held. Not him though, he felt empowered in the dark. Empowered and free.

He pulled the vehicle up in front of the house after paying close attention to the neighbors' homes. All were dark. Everyone had gone off to bed already. He killed his lights as soon as he turned onto the block, making certain not to disturb anyone.

He reached behind his seat to retrieve his gloves, booties, and a syringe. In the movies they always talked about the kill kit and showed all kinds of things. He smiled, guessing he was a simple man or maybe just a smarter one. These few items were all he needed.

Double checking that the dome light was turned off in the van, he removed the keys from the ignition, clicked the door open, and slipped out into the night. There was a light breeze in the air, and the neighborhood smelled of eucalyptus.

Approaching the house he followed the cobblestone pathway, avoiding the solar lighting that ran up the driveway. He noticed the moon was only a small crescent and was already considering what lighting source he might have inside. The challenge the total darkness presented did not deter him. In fact, it seemed to increase the adrenaline that was already pulsing into his muscles, senses, and breathing.

He pushed through two large Cannas, the leaves crackling against his body, and stood next to the fence separating the front and back yards. He could hear water running somewhere and decided there must be a koi pond in the back yard. Hearing nothing else, he depressed the latch with his gloved thumb, delivering a clicking noise that seemed to scream in the night. He paused and listened. Convinced the house was still, he continued through the gate and left it slightly ajar, not wanting to make the same noise again.

As he moved deeper into the yard, he peered through the first window along the side of the house. It was the kitchen. As he suspected the bedrooms were toward the back of the house.

He soon found the source of the running water noise, and as he expected there was a koi pond with a small waterfall running through it. In the middle it had a small island with a water-light. He would prefer it not be there, but it was dim enough that he continued on.

A window rose from the ground on either side of a sliding glass door that opened from the small patio that contained a glass-top table and cushioned chairs. The yard was covered in a multitude of flowers. Jimmy clearly had a green thumb, or he had a gardener that gave a lot of tender care to the numerous colorful plants that dotted the entire fence line.

Jack approached the window on the left of the patio door first and found it impossible to peer in. He moved over to the patio door and attempted to open it. Locked. He reached in his pants pocket and disappointment started to fill him as he realized that he had forgotten his trusty and reliable Swiss Army knife. He calmed himself and accepted that he would have to get in another way.

Next he went to the remaining window and peered through. The blinds were pulled open about two inches, enough to be able to see there was a bed and dresser. It seemed someone was rolled up in the blankets, and he could tell there was another door in the room, which believing it to be a bathroom caused him to draw the conclusion that this was the master bedroom and room where he would find the means to relief from the darkness that had nearly consumed him.

Returning to the second window, he gave it a gentle push and felt it give slightly. Not wanting to make any noise while trying to force it, he went back to the master room window and peered in again. He noticed the lump in the bed was still in the same position. He continued on around the corner of the house and found a door that had eight rectangular square windows in it.

He could see into the garage. Turning the knob, the door opened and granted him access to the inside. There was a workbench with several tools on it and several containers of surfboard wax. The wall on one side had three different surf boards, each a slightly different shape. Saw horses filled the main part of the garage floor. This was Jimmy's apparent workshop for his surfing hobby.

Jack could barely see inside the garage, but the adrenaline seemed to be enhancing his vision just enough that he could see a door. Watching his step, he moved cautiously towards it, and reaching out, he took the knob in his gloved hand and twisted. His breath held as he anticipated it to be locked. He had to resist laughing out loud when the door opened, and he realized he wouldn't need to use his trusty and missing Swiss Army knife after all.

Pushing the door inward slowly, he listened carefully to both the inside of the home and the hinges of the door, hoping neither would betray him. The door squeaked almost immediately, which forced him to pause. He turned around and looked closely at the workbench, and then after squinting in the darkness, he saw a shelving unit on the opposite wall that seemed to contain paints and sprays.

Once again carefully watching his steps, he approached the shelf and scanned the items on it. On the second to the bottom shelf he found what he was looking for–WD40. Lifting the blue and yellow can, he carried it back to the door and depressed the small red button two times on each of the hinges. Setting the can down on the workbench, he pushed slightly on the door and relaxed as the door opened quietly inward.

He stood inside, just left of the kitchen, in a small laundry room. The home had subtle lighting by the illumination from the clock on the stove, microwave, and DVD player. The subtle lighting was all he needed. He passed through the kitchen, glancing only for a moment at the living room until he found a hallway.

Controlling his breathing, he took gentle steps down the carpeted hallway and approached the bedroom to his left. He was very certain the room was the master and where he needed to go, but he had been unable to assess the other room and wanted to be sure his assumption that it was unoccupied was accurate. The door stood open. He stepped in and looked closely at the bed. It was an obvious guest room, and tonight there were no guests.

Turning, he crossed the hallway. He heard something and froze. There was movement inside the bedroom. Then he heard a flushing sound. Jimmy was awake. He would wait until his prey settled down again, recessing back into the safety of the empty guest room. A glow came from under the master bedroom door. At first, he worried a light had come on, but then he recognized that it was the soft glow of a phone.

For several minutes the light remained on. It went off, and the room went quiet again. It seemed Jimmy was texting or using the Internet and now had returned to bed. Jack silently exhaled, forcing himself to wait a few more moments. He needed Jimmy to be nearly asleep. He couldn't afford a repeat of the situation he had with Reb. She had surprised him, and one thing for sure was he learned from his mistakes.

He also knew Jimmy was an avid surfer and would therefore have superior upper body strength to Reb. The burning sensation of the darkness that was raging inside made him feel irritable. While he waited he considered his approach in the room. Tilting his head slightly, he could hear a low buzz. He was unable to determine what the source was, but he was certain it was some sort of small appliance. Focusing harder, he heard slow breaths, the kind that comes with the first stages of sleep. It was time.

Chapter Thirty

The hallway had a slight, fading blue hue that was cast from the lights, illuminating the time on the stove in the kitchen. To anyone else it might have seemed ominous, the glow casting odd shapes that seemed to bounce back off the doors that lined the narrow path leading to the source of Jack's obsession.

Jack stepped out of the dark room and into the blue cast, allowing it to devour him. He silently moved toward the bedroom door where he could hear the rise and fall of sleep-filled breath that grew louder with each step forward. *REM sleep, the best time to approach.*

He paced his own breath to match that of his sleeping prey. Stopping in the doorway, he allowed his eyes to adjust to the subtle lighting of the bedroom before moving closer to the bed. A clock on the nightstand glowed 11:18 in huge lime green digital blocks. His eyes shifted back to the bed. There was a large bundle that faced the opposite wall. As he inched closer to the bed, his shoes silently stepped on the medium napped carpet pile.

As he stood over the sleeping bundle, he reached his gloved hand into his pocket, pulled the syringe and rag out, and instinctively inhaled before pressing the plunger to squirt the toxic sedative into the rag, ensuring he didn't inadvertently inhale any of the fumes. He leaned in, and in a quick movement forced the rag over the face of the sleeping man. Then just as quickly, he pressed his right knee into the man's back as he wrapped his left arm around the man's neck. There was a short struggle before the man went limp in his arms.

"Good boy, Jimmy," he said as he shoved the rag and syringe back into his pocket, careful to not allow the needle to come in contact with his skin. "Time for us to have some fun."

Jack got Jimmy prepped for the ride back to the house. He wrapped him in the blanket from the bed so he wouldn't need to carry him more than necessary. He dragged the bedding to the floor and grabbed two ends of the blanket containing the unconscious man and pulled, dragging him down the hall and back out through the living room. He looked around until he found Jimmy's keys. He continued through the house, letting the blue glow direct his way and his senses guide him back to the garage.

Jimmy clearly parked outside. Assessing the garage he decided there was room to open the garage and pull his van in. There was plenty of room, all he needed to do was move the saw horses out of the main part of the floor to clear the way for his vehicle. He looked around and found a small step stool and opened it just under the garage door opener. Stepping up, he was careful to not allow his booty-covered feet to slip as he reached above his head and turned the light bulb out far enough that the light would not come on when the garage door opened.

Returning the stool to its rightful place, he pushed the button on the wall and watched as the overhead door curled open. The sound of the small chain-fed motor seemed deafening in the silence of the night, and his pulse quickened.

He quickly walked out into the night and down the driveway past Jimmy's vehicle and to his own van sitting under a tree at the curb. Climbing in, he started the engine as he pulled the door closed with a gentle click. He nudged into the garage without turning on his headlights and squeezed in between the saw horses and surf boards. After shoving the gearshift into park, he climbed out and quickly hit the button on the overhead door, locking himself back into the safety of the home.

Jack took a moment to calm his breathing before heading back into the house to collect his prize. As he was about to begin dragging Jimmy the rest of the way through the house, there was a knock at the front door. His heart rate immediately increased. He slid his back up against the wall and considered just ignoring the loud rapping at the door. Thinking better of it, he went to the door and opened it slightly while keeping his hands from sight, knowing the gloves would raise concern.

"Hello," was all he could think of offering to the skinny man that stood before him. Jack sized him up quickly. His clothes were disheveled, hair slightly askew, he had a stubbly beard and looked to be in his sixties, but Jack guessed he was much younger.

"Oh, hey, I was looking for Jimmy," the man said rubbing nervously at his beard, seeming surprised to find Jack at the door.

"He's not home, went on a nursing gig. I'm watching the place for him for a couple of days," he lied.

"Huh," the man grunted out as he looked out at the car in the driveway, the grey whiskers on his chin jutting out.

Realizing the car was a problem, Jack quickly offered an explanation, "Some kind of special thing, two of them had to go. His co-worker wanted to drive. I think the patient was a big guy with some special needs. Jimmy said it would take two of them to lift him. I dropped him off at his co-workers house then came on up here."

The guy grimaced a little at the description of the supposed patient. "Oh, okay. Well, I saw the garage open, and Jimmy has never opened it to pull in so I got a little worried."

Great, nosey neighbor. "Well, he should be home in a couple of days. Can I leave a message for him?" Jack threw on his most gregarious smile and continued, "I'm sorry, I didn't even ask your name."

"No. No message. Name is Ron. I was just checking to see that everything was okay."

"Sure, I understand. You can't be too careful these days."

"How is it that you know Jimmy?"

Jack thought quickly before answering. "We surf together." He stopped short of trying to explain where they would catch waves together as he didn't want to take a chance on getting it wrong since he was not sure if nosey Ron would know Jimmy's favorite spots.

Ron rubbed his grey chin hair with spindle like fingers and dirty nails stained with nicotine. "Well, glad everything's okay." He turned to walk away then turned back. "What'd you say your name was?"

"I don't believe I did, but it's Sam," he lied again, not wanting to give out his real name.

"Well, nice to meet you, Sam. I live just over there." He pointed to the house directly across the street. "If you need anything, just let me know."

"Ya know, I just picked up some beer, want to come in and have one?" Jack asked following an impulse. He was taking a chance, but temptation overcame him.

Ron had already started to walk away but turned back. His eyes assessed Jack, and his tongue darted out of his mouth, flicking quickly across his lips. "Oh, what the hell. Why not?" He smiled as he stepped forward. Jack gambled on the origin of the man's ruddy complexion, obvious heavy smoking habit and thin frame. Ron clearly liked alcohol as much, if not more, as he liked being the nosey neighbor.

This was going to be good. *Two in one night?* Jack could feel an unprecedented excitement begin to run through him. This was going to be almost as good as cutting Maxine's hair, he thought as he stepped back from the door and opened it just far enough for Ron to enter.

Pushing the door closed, he snaked his gloved hand around Ron's neck and locked Ron's arms down in a tight squeeze with his other. With his arm bent at the elbow, Jack applied pressure against the man's carotid arteries. From his medical training he knew this would cause cerebral ischemia, or loss of blood flow to the brain, and the lack of oxygen to the brain would quickly drop Ron into unconsciousness.

The neighbor's fingers reached up to Jack's arms, and he swore through his teeth in his initial surprise. It took only moments before he started to lose the battle against the much stronger, fit man who held him tightly in a grip that certainly must have felt like death was eminent. Ron fell limp on the floor.

Jack knew this condition was only temporary and turned to the garage where he could retrieve the duct tape he carried in his bag. At the passenger side of the van, he reached across the back seat and dug his hand in the bag, curling his strong gloved fingers around the tape before re-entering the house.

Thirty-five minutes later Jack was pulling back into his own garage with a double bounty. He felt almost intoxicated. He'd never had two guests at one time. Even when working in the emergency room in his early days as a resident doctor, he always focused on one patient at a time during surgery. Sometimes it was back to back, for sure, but never in the same operating room at the same time.

Jack got out of the van once the garage door closed fully behind him and walked around to the back, opening the compartment where the two men laid side by side. Jimmy was still unconscious and rolled inside the bed cover, while Ron was awake again but unable to do little more than struggle against the tape that bound his legs, arms, and mouth. Seeing Jack, Ron began to struggle more, as if his anger would somehow help free him.

"Hello, Ron. Sorry about the tape, but you see, you really shouldn't spend so much time spying on your neighbors. In fact, it really is bad manners. Don't worry though. We'll get you out of that tape soon enough. Just sit tight for a minute." Jack did not wait for Ron to answer. He knew full well that not only he couldn't answer, but also that whatever he would say, even if he could, would be just spewing of rage and unreasonable pleas.

Jack pulled at the rolled bedding and got Jimmy to the end of the van before yanking him down onto the floor of the garage. He went and opened the door to the house before tugging Jimmy up the two steps and towards the kitchen. Jimmy's head bounced inside the blanket as he went up each of the steps, causing the man to moan slightly. Jack watched him closely for a moment before dragging him through the house to the door near the basement entrance. Certain that Jimmy was still out of it, he left him lying there and returned for Ron.

Again, the man reacted to Jack's presence, kicking his bent knees. Jack laughed at him as he saw sweat covering the man's brow, knowing that sweat was the tell sign that Ron was afraid. Jack couldn't help but enjoy the feeling he got in knowing he held the man's fate in his hands. Ron had, after all, nearly caused him major issues tonight.

Pulling Ron toward him by the ankles, the skinny man kicked at his hands. Jack decided he wouldn't take any chances and went to the side of the van, opened the door, and retrieved his medical bag. He opened it and reached inside taking a moment to collect what he was looking for.

With a syringe in his hand, he pulled Ron closer and injected the clear fluid into the man's boney arm. Moments later Ron relaxed, and while he was wide awake he was unable to respond any more to Jack's touch. Ron no longer could flinch at Jack's approach or kick as he tried to carry him away. Jack slid him from the van and lifted him onto his shoulder. The man was monumentally lighter than Jimmy and was no challenge for Jack's strong body.

At the basement stairs, Jack dug with one hand to get the keys out of his pants pocket so he could open the basement door. Fumbling with the small key, he slid it into the lock and lifted the bar away while balancing Ron against the wall. Pulling the door open, he rebalanced his load and headed into the nearly dark basement.

The kids were sleeping, and he looked for Hope. He saw her slender frame in the bed. He stood at the bottom of the stairs for a moment, hesitating and thinking about the door being open at the top of the stairs. After deciding everyone was asleep, he went quickly to the surgical room.

He struggled with the keys again. He picked the smaller one and again fumbled a bit with the lock until the key engaged. With the door to the surgical room open, he went in and dropped Ron onto the steel table before turning to head back up the stairs to retrieve Jimmy.

Jack glanced again at the kids and Hope; no one had moved. After a quick check on Vivian he went back up the stairs. Jimmy was just starting to show signs of consciousness, so he knew he needed to hurry. Sliding the bedding down the first few steps until it cleared the landing, he closed the door and locked it, depositing the keys back into his pocket with a double check of the door to ensure it was locked securely.

He stepped over the bedding roll and pulled the heavy lump down the remainder of the stairs to the bottom and across the floor. The roll banged against the couch, causing a thumping noise until it finally cleared the tight space. Jimmy groaned again. Jack was sweating, his brow damp, and his body filled with heat, yet he felt chilled on the outside from the cool night air.

Jack was faced with making a decision. For the first time ever he had two house guests, and with both inside the surgical room he tried to decide what he wanted to do first. He had been thinking about Jimmy for a while. However, Ron had really tried to ruin things for him, and that deserved punishment. Then an image of Vivian not being properly cared for crossed his mind, and he knew what he must do.

Jack left the men in place and went back to the stairs, trying to be quiet while taking the stairs two at a time. He retrieved a small chair from the main kitchen upstairs and brought it to the basement. He locked the door again and hoisted the chair up over the couch as he passed. Taking the chair into the surgical room, he put it in the corner facing the table, then lifted Ron up off of the table to place the man in the seat. Ron reacted in the only way he could–his eyes wide and darting all around.

Jack took a roll of duct tape from the shelf and secured Ron's hands and feet to the chair, ensuring he couldn't fall to the floor. With Ron in the perfect viewing position, Jack pulled the blanket away from Jimmy, and then lifted him off the floor, struggling at first with the younger man's weight. Finally, Jimmy's body position was just right so he could pivot him up onto the table.

Jimmy was really starting to come around now, and Jack realized he needed to secure him fast. He cut Jimmy's clothes away from his body and rolled him from side to side to pull the clothes free. With the clothes removed, Jack secured the surfer's hands and feet to the table with white zip ties.

Looking over at Ron, Jack smiled as he saw the gaunt man staring on. He felt a prickly chill cover his skin. The sweat was slick, and his tongue darted out, sliding over his lips. They tasted of salt. He slipped out of his own clothes and pulled on a set of scrubs, a hair net, and gloves. Just as he was ready to begin his procedure, he heard a noise and turned to see Chance staring at him. In his rush to get Jimmy secured before he became fully alert, he had forgotten to close and lock the door.

213

Chapter Thirty-One

Mindy watched as Jack left. She waited a while before deciding she really needed to take a chance and see if there was any possible way of getting out. She knew Jack had the room rigged with cameras, but she had a feeling he was going out to perform the crazy things for which he was wanted by the FBI. She was starting to feel desperate and not sure how much longer she could keep up the façade of a loving wife. It was risky, for sure. If she happened to get caught, it could be the moment that she caused two innocent children to be killed. She was banking on the fact that he was focused on wherever he was going or whoever he was going after, and it was now or never.

She went up the stairs and listened closely at the door. The house seemed silent, and the floorboards were quiet. Usually she could hear him walking across the floor overhead and depended on her deep memory from her childhood to tell her which room in the house he was in. Her mind would follow him from the kitchen to the living room or garage, her mind's eye tracing his steps with each creaking board.

For now it was quiet. She assessed the door and saw the locks on the inside and knew he was carrying those keys with him at all times. She pushed against the door; it didn't give at all. This obviously was not going to be a good solution for escape, and her spirits dampened. Retreating back down the stairs she realized that she needed to assess the other areas of the basement. Moving to the back part of the basement, she knew there was another room, but since she had been afraid to leave the confines of the area that Jack had defined as their living quarters, she had no idea what was there.

215

Slipping past the couch where the kids slept, she moved her hands along the wall, struggling through the room lit only by the television glow. She felt a door and wrapped her hand around the knob. Holding her breath, she slowly gave the metal handle a twist. Nothing. The door was locked. She shook the knob again. Even though her mind knew there was no use, she pushed then pulled. "Damn it!" she swore under her breath.

Continuing to feel along the wall, she found nothing else, and then wondered what she could use as a weapon. Maybe when Jack returned she could attack him, maybe when he was sleeping. *I could kill him in his sleep. I just need a tool to do it,* she thought to herself.

Searching a piece of furniture that appeared to be an old laundry table that sat at the end of the narrow nook past the door, she squinted to assess the items on the table, including a small wrench. It wasn't much, but it might work. She took it and continued the rest of her search. There was nothing else she could use. She thought about the items in the kitchen. Nothing would work. Jack had provided all plastic utensils.

Inside the bathroom she looked around and saw the toothbrush. She'd seen on TV how you could make a knife out of it by melting the end and shaping it into a point. She wondered if she could do this without Jack noticing that it was gone.

Moving from the bathroom to the bedroom, she slid the wrench deep in between the mattress and box spring, then stood there wondering if he would find it. She looked around the room, trying to consider a better hiding place, but found nothing. For a minute she considered hiding it in Vivian's bed, but knowing Jack checked her bedding regularly, she reconsidered. For now the bed seemed the best solution.

Her eyes traveled along all the walls and then the ceiling. There seemed to be nothing in terms of a way to get out. Then she noticed a gap in one of the ceiling tiles and wondered if there was some way to get up there and force her way out through the floorboards.

Considering the time, she decided she better not push her luck tonight. Jack might be back soon or decide to observe the video and see what she was doing. She couldn't take any more chances, not tonight. But before she gave up she noticed a pair of Jack's pants on the chair. He had tossed them there when he had gotten ready for bed the night before. She walked over to them and hesitantly lifted the pants from the chair, reaching into the pockets.

Her hand recoiled when she felt something strange. Overcoming her apprehension she reached in again and pulled out the soft silky item from inside. She choked back a scream when she realized that she was holding a lock of auburn red hair. Unable to contain her repulsion, she shoved it back in the pocket. There was something else in that pocket—a Swiss Army knife. She wanted desperately to take it but resisted, certain Jack would know it was missing. Despite a trembling that had consumed her, shaking her to the core, she reached in each of the other pockets but found nothing else.

Unable to fight the churning in her stomach she returned to the bathroom and wretched in the toilet until she thought her guts would come out. When the waves finally subsided, she washed her face and brushed her teeth and got ready for bed while still considering how she could make a weapon. One thing she did resolve to do was pretend to be asleep when Jack came home.

Terror filled her as she lay there with the covers pulled tightly around her neck. She wondered if he had seen her looking around and, if so, what he might do to her. Or worse, to the kids. A new terror flooded her as she started to wonder if he would try to wake her, and she silently prayed he would simply never come back at all.

She dozed, drifting in and out of sleep, trying desperately to stay awake, wanting to be aware of what was going on around her. But sleep pulled her in. Her mind flitted through images of severed bodies, the horror of Jack on her, kissing and pawing. Sorrow filled her as her dream crossed over to images of Paul's dead body ripped apart in the living room of the loving home they had shared.

She woke with a start just as she was nearly pulled into a torturous vision of her beautiful eldest daughter…The door opened at the top of the stairs, and she froze. Trying not to hold her breath, certain she would soon hyperventilate, she waited.

There was a thumping noise as Jack came down the stairs, and she had to resist the temptation to turn and see what that noise was. She could hear Jack's breathing, almost a grunt, as if he were struggling. She had heard that noise before. *When was it? Was it when she was drugged, and he brought Vivian's bed downstairs? Yes, that was it.*

He was bringing something down the stairs. She was sure of it. *But what would he be bringing down here in the middle of the night?* Instinct told her it wouldn't be good, and she prayed the kids wouldn't wake up. Whatever he was doing she was certain would terrify them. Remaining still, she continued to listen with her eyes squeezed shut and her hands clutching the pillow in tight fists.

She heard the door at the back of the basement being opened. The very door that she herself had tried to open earlier. She began wishing she could see in there. *Maybe there's a window.* He returned up the stairs, locking them in again. *Damn.* Subconsciously she wished he would forget.

Her mind drifted to the wrench that lay just beneath her. Could she hit him when he came to bed? Her heart rate climbed again, and she had to mentally focus on not allowing her breathing to accelerate. A tear fell from her eye onto her pillow as the fear started to overcome her. *Focus, Mindy!*

She could hear shuffling noises and then a door close. She expected Jack to come out and head towards the bed, but instead it was quiet. Then she heard strange noises, groans followed by a man's voice that said something. "Dude?" she thought she heard from the forbidden room. There was a clanging sound, then mild laughter–Jack's laughter. *Oh God, he has a man in there!*

For several moments she wished Jack had just kept her sedated. But then she remembered the kids. They needed her to help get them out of here alive. Allie was barely herself, and Heath seemed to like it here. He believed Jack's story and was easily being tricked into believing that Jack was his father.

Swallowing hard, she tried to focus again. It seemed to be quieter now. She wondered if Jack had killed the man, and she felt almost certain he probably had. Her mind returned to the idea of the wrench under the mattress.

Chapter Thirty-Two

Max sighed, pushing back from the table and computer that had occupied her time for the past two or three hours. She stretched and pulled her long red hair back from her face, wrapping her thin fingers tightly around the thick tresses. Her fingers paused for a brief moment on the shortened strands.

Mark walked up behind her. "Cortez has something to share. She thinks she might have a lead."

Max didn't need to hear more. She was on her feet and moving to the table across the room in front of a projection screen that was already being lowered. Cortez was standing next to it, and as she saw her former partner her chin dipped towards her chest in a silent nod. Max knew this meant she was onto something and was about to show the first hint of a lead they had so far. Everyone gathered around the table and waited for Cortez to begin.

"Jack Tyler was born and raised in Ojai Valley, California. He lived there until he went to college but never returned. We believe he was a very abused boy, the perpetrator his own mother. A week ago this woman," a photo flashed up on the projector screen, "Rebecca Tillman, went missing. There has been no sign of her since. Her car was found around the corner from her house in an unusual place. Her dog is also missing. The pet was her companion, and at first family members thought maybe she had gone on a trip, taking the animal with her, but now she's been gone too long and with no contact. Her employer says she never called in when she was supposed to report to work. This is totally out of character for her."

Max stood looking at the photo. This woman looked nothing like Hope. The only link so far was that she disappeared from Ojai.

Not getting the connection, she started to object, but before she could do so, Cortez continued.

"Rebecca went to Ojai Valley High School with Hope and Jack. In fact, until their junior year Hope and Rebecca were close friends. I talked on the phone with Rebecca's ex-husband. He and Rebecca married shortly after high school after dating all through school. He claims that Rebecca warned Hope to stay away from Jack, that there was something off about him, and after that Hope wouldn't speak to her anymore."

Max shook her head. "Why would he go back to Ojai? He wanted to get away from there. He and Hope basically bolted as soon as they could and never looked back."

"That's a flaw in the theory, but it's pretty ironic that Jack is on the run. We think he's in California or Arizona, and now a friend of Hope's from high school has vanished. A friend of Hope's that betrayed Jack."

Max took it all in. "I need to see her house." Her eyes moved to Mark.

"Cortez, you and Max go to Ojai, check out the house, and interview neighbors. Agent Jenkins, check for any other missing persons in or around Ojai—male, female, and children."

Jenkins looked up. "Sir, I have something to report too. The credit reports have just come back on all of Tyler's prior aliases. There's a single hit. He ran a people search on intellicus.com, must have forgotten that his account was established under the name he used in Illinois."

"Who was the people search for?" Wells asked.

"I'm trying to get that information but had to request a warrant. They wouldn't release it without it. I'll have that in the hour."

"Let me know the minute you know who he was looking for. Is there any way to trace where the transaction came from?"

"We're searching the IP address, but so far have not been able to trace it. Although, the last known address associated with the credit card was in Illinois. We'll know a lot more as soon as we can get the information on the account."

"We need that information now!" Mark barked, and then tried to catch himself by resuming the control he normally possessed in his tone. "Agent, push them. We need to move."

"Yes, sir." Agent Jenkins went back to the table she had been working at and immediately starting punching numbers into the cell phone.

"We may be onto something, and I need a full team. Agent Adams, go to the hotel and get rest. I need you back in four hours fresh."

"With all due respect, sir, I'd rather stay."

"I appreciate that, but I need to keep this team going twenty-four seven, and I can't do that if no one rests."

Adams nodded his head, though the disappointment at the order was clear on his face. He wouldn't argue. Wells was a good and well trusted leader. He began packing his laptop and stood to leave.

Cortez walked over to Max. "I'll have a car in ten minutes out front."

Max merely nodded as she returned to the table and began collecting her things. Leaving her files behind for the others, she made eye contact with Mark, who stood across the room giving a few additional instructions to the team. He finished the conversation and walked towards her, taking her by the elbow and leading her out into the hallway as the others tried not to watch.

They stood just looking at each other for a few moments, neither willing to say anything. Max broke the silence. "I have to see for myself if anything looks like his work."

"I know. I also know no one will recognize it better than you. But…"

Before he could finish she filled in his words. "I'll be careful. It's not like Jack is going to be waiting for me in her home."

"I know."

"If he has Heath, and he's near his old stomping grounds, I'll know." Max leaned in and kissed Mark on the lips, ignoring protocol. Right now she only cared about finding Tyler and saving Heath. "If that bastard has our son…," the words trailed off as Max controlled herself from letting the rest of the words trickle off her tongue. "I'll call you later as soon as I can. Let me know if anything else pops on the trace that Jenkins has going."

"Max…no heroics."

She tilted her head in an agreeable nod, causing her thick hair to topple to one side, and then turned and walked out the door.

Chapter Thirty-Three

"Daddy, what are you doing?"

Jack turned around, facing the small boy and kneeling to eye level. "Hey, buddy. What are you doing awake right now?" Realizing how frightened Chance could be, he quickly decided to address what the boy was seeing. "You know Daddy is a doctor, right?"

The boy rubbed at his sleepy eyes and nodded his head.

"Well, I got called for an emergency. That's why I had to go out late, and now these men need my help. Come on now, I need you to go back to sleep so Daddy can work real fast."

Heath's eyes were wide as Jack turned him out of the room and pulled the door closed behind him, blocking the child's view. Leading the boy back to the bed, he lifted him up and tucked him back in.

"I'm sorry if that scared you. Surgery can be very scary, but it has to be done. Now, can you be a big boy and go back to sleep?"

Heath nodded, in the low lighting his blue eyes took on the color of the dark sky as he stared back into Jack's eyes.

"Good boy. Don't go in there again, okay?"

Heath nodded once more.

Jack sat next to the boy a little longer, pulling the covers up to his chin. Jack's hand brushed the locks of hair away from the boy's eyes, and he leaned in to kiss the small soft forehead. In a few moments Heath's eyes began to close. "I love you, little man," Jack said before rising to return to the surgical room.

Inside the room again, Jack turned the lock in the door, securing himself and his captives inside. *No more interruptions.* His skin seemed to sing with anticipation. This was truly a new and exciting event. He couldn't wait to watch Ron witness the true beauty of his work. He thought for a moment how, at first, he had truly been annoyed with Ron for knocking on the door, and now how thrilled he was to have him sitting here in the room with him.

A tray hung suspended over the table like an arm baring a platter of shiny offerings. Jack lifted the #5 scalpel and turned it over in his hand, the glint of the metal casting a reflection against the tray.

He paused briefly considering how he would handle Jimmy first then Ron. He certainly liked having a guest for longer than a few hours, and with two of them he had options. With his mind made up, he turned to Jimmy. The surfer was finally awake, *perfect timing.*

"It's about time you woke up," Jack said with a sinister sneer under his face mask.

"Dude!" Jimmy shouted out.

"Quiet now. My family is sleeping. If you can't settle down I'll have to silence you a different way."

"What do you want, man? You're nuts."

"Nuts? Maybe. It's all relative, don't you think?"

"Whatever, dude. Let me outta here."

"Let's talk about that, ole' Jimmy boy. Let's talk about how you treated Vivian. How about this… I ask you a question, you tell me the truth the *first* time," he applied pressure on the word *first*, "and maybe I will consider some leniency."

Jimmy squirmed against the ties but suddenly stopped. "What? What do you want to know?"

"Okay, question number one. Did you ever leave Vivian in her soiled bed longer than should be expected?"

"What the f…?"

"Jimmy, answer the question now or I'll…," Jack swiped the scalpel across Jimmy's chest in a sweeping motion indicating the cut he would make.

"Okay, okay, dude. Yes."

"Yes. What?"

"Yes, I left her too long," Jimmy seemed defeated, his voice shaking now.

"Tsk, tsk. I knew it. Question number two. Did you ever ignore her ringing bell when she clearly needed your assistance?"

Jimmy began to squirm again. "Fuck you!"

"Such foul language, Jimmy. That might be question number three if you don't hurry up and answer me now."

"Yes. Alright, sometimes I waited. Now let me go." Jimmy was attempting to flail now, the fog from the drug really starting to dissipate from his mind.

"Good boy, Jimmy. For telling me the truth, I'll show you some mercy. I think I'll let you die tonight rather than keeping you around for a few days. After all, I still have ole' Ron here for that."

Jimmy's eyes followed Jack's gaze, his head turning to the far side of the room. Seeing his neighbor, Jimmy arched his back and hissed in anger, "You son of a…"

Jack laid the scalpel down and snapped up the duct tape in one quick sweep and slammed a wide strip across Jimmy's mouth. "I'm sorry, but you are really starting to annoy me, Jimmy. First, you mistreat a poor defenseless old woman. Then you rudely attempt to wake my family up." Anger bubbled up inside Jack at the thought of how Jimmy had treated Vivian. He'd known it all along, but now he knew for sure. Jimmy was about to pay dearly.

He took another long strand of tape and wrapped it over Jimmy's forehead then around the table to secure his head in place. A final strip was wrapped in the same fashion completely around the table to cover Jimmy's mouth. The struggling surfer was immediately silenced to no more than grunts and groans. His hands were bound in tight fists, and his feet wobbled back and forth as if they were waving for someone to assist.

"I'm actually a bit surprised at your reaction to seeing ole' Ronnie boy over there. I'd think you would be glad to be rid of the nosey ole' fool."

Jack took a look around and laid the tape back on the tray and retrieved the scalpel he had laid down so abruptly. He took a deep calming breath and said, "Now, where was I?" With that, he made a long incision right down the middle of Jimmy's torso.

As the blood began to spill out of the wound, Jack looked up and locked stares with Ron, whose eyes popped in his paralyzed body. "It is lovely, isn't it, Ron?" Jack asked as he watched the silver table take on a new crimson shine. "Oh, and I've just begun. The best parts are coming. Just wait, you'll see."

With those comments hanging in the air, Jack continued. He took the ribs spreader and pushed it down into the opening, pushing the bones apart and exposing the organs that were the focus of his quest. His hands entered through the new opening, and he had to consciously remember to include Ron in the process. He looked over at his guest and smiled, noted only by the pinching at the corner of his eyes.

"See, it's beautiful in here. I'd let you feel for yourself, but well, I hate to share." Jimmy pitched and pushed against the obvious pain brought on by no anesthetic during the massive invasion into his chest cavity.

Jack could feel the cool of his gloves quickly turn to silky warmth. A coppery smell began to fill the air. He breathed in the thick fragrance and held it inside. The air of the room seemed to immediately calm the nerves that had been jangling inside him all day. Finally, he was beginning to get some relief from within.

His fingers felt past the ribs and in between the lungs until his strong fingers looped around the muscly heart. Thump, thump, thump…thump……..thump, the beats faded as he squeezed. He pulled back, relaxing the pressure. Thump, thump, thump…thump………thump, he squeezed again and again until the beats came much less frequently, and then finally stopped.

Jack took a few moments to explore some of the other vital yet less fascinating organs. Replacing the scalpel on the tray, he left a bloody stain and picked up the small scissors. Reaching back inside the lifeless body, he snipped away at the atria and ventricles, and then the fibrous value flaps until he cleared everything to hold the delicate muscle in place. He tilted and turned the muscle until he lifted if from the chest cavity. He stared at the magnificence of the organ. Carrying it around the end of the table past Jimmy's head, he approached Ron.

Holding the organ gently in his hands, he displayed it in front of the terrified man's face. "I told you it was beautiful. Would you like to hold it?" He stared at Ron's face, the eyes bugging out of the skinny, weathered face. "No? Hmmm…too bad. You're missing out on something incredibly marvelous, but your choice, I suppose."

Returning to the other side of the table again, Jack laid the muscle back down in the middle of Jimmy's gaping chest. He studied the man for a moment. "Well now, I bet you wish you'd been a bit nicer to Vivian, don't you?"

With that he began the process of cleaning up the bloody mess. He clipped away at the duct tape and zip ties until Jimmy's body was free from the stainless steel table. Jack rolled the body onto the blanket on the floor. Jimmy's head met the cement through the blanket with a thick thud. "Oh, that would have hurt. See, I did you another favor."

Ron's eyes dropped to the body on the floor, and he watched as Jack rolled his neighbor into the blanket then carefully secured the ends with duct tape. Opening the surgical room's locked door, Jack lifted a long roll of heavy duty clear plastic from the shelf next to the door and stepped out into the main room to roll out a long strip. He sliced the plastic free from the roll with a scalpel from the tray then stepped back in the room. He then lifted the blanket and placed it into the middle of the plastic sheeting. He rolled the blanket up inside the plastic sheeting and duct taped the ends. Now the blood was secured inside the plastic cocoon.

Leaving the bundle in its place, Jack stepped back into the room and locked the door again behind him. For the next hour Jack worked furiously to clean the room, including the floors and walls, and the surgical tools, as well as his own body, putting everything back to their glimmering state. When he was satisfied he dressed then turned and looked at Ron. "Tomorrow will be your turn."

He lifted the seemingly frozen man and laid him out on the table, cutting away his clothing. After securing him tightly to the table with zip ties, he left the room for the last time that night, leaving Ron in the dark with the visions of Jimmy's brutal death dancing through his mind.

***

Mindy lay frozen in place. She could hear the muffled terror from the room at the back of the basement, and she knew what Jack was doing. She'd heard him come in and saw him carrying in the bundle and then a man over his shoulder. She had to resist all temptation to get up when Chance had gotten out of bed. Her desire

227

to protect the boy from seeing what he would likely see was overwrought with the fear of what the kids would do if he killed her. She knew she needed a plan—and soon.

As she lay in the semi-dark room with her eyes pinched closed, her mind raced trying to consider what Hope would do. Clearly her sister had married this madman, and she knew deep inside that Hope would never allow him to just kill random people. Her sister had been loving and kind, not the wife of a crazy killer. Obviously, Hope had somehow managed to keep him from doing these horrible things. *But how?*

Chapter Thirty-Four

Max slid into the passenger seat of the police issued vehicle that Cortez checked out for their hour and thirty minute trip to Ojai. Max felt like she could breathe for the first time in hours. The cool, fresh early morning air felt great, and suddenly she felt alive and ... *what was that feeling? Hope?* Yes, she felt hopeful.

"What do we have?" She jumped right into working the case doing exactly what she did best–catching bad guys. It felt good to be back in L.A. and riding with Cortez. She loved the FBI, but this was familiar and familiar seemed incredibly important right now.

"Photos from the house and lab reports," Cortez said handing a file that sat in the middle of the seat.

Max took the file and began flipping through the pages. After a few minutes of silence, Cortez waited just letting her take it all in, and Max finally spoke, "What are the chances of him returning to Ojai?"

Cortez seemed to be really contemplating the question before answering. "What is there to return for?"

"Exactly. Why go back, for what? What is there for him? His family is dead, and the memories are all painful." She paused to think. "Except those of Hope."

"Right and those kids ran from that place as fast as they could. So, why go back?"

"I don't know," Max admitted. "I hope we're not chasing a red herring. Heath doesn't have time for us to just be running around looking for Tyler in some place. I won't forgive myself if I've allowed Tyler to get me so focused on him that I lose sight of Heath."

"I'm with you, Max. It doesn't make sense, but then what does Tyler do that makes sense?"

Max flipped through the file again. She looked at a couple of photos from the high school year book. Jack, Hope, and Rebecca were all in one picture together. The caption under the photo read, "Friends for Life." There was some irony in the caption. She tried to read Jack's face in the photo. It seemed a mixture of love and distain. Oh yeah, he hated Rebecca. She could see it, almost feel it from the photo in her hand.

The wheels turned under the car, and palm trees were replaced by the dry hills of Calabasas. Max watched out the window, her mind processing all of the information. Heath had been gone for nearly four days now, and they really had nothing. Internally, she cringed at the reality of the time that had passed. She couldn't stop her mind from thinking about the children in Illinois; Jack didn't keep his victims four days. With the kids, he had killed them almost immediately.

New palm trees started to come into focus as they approached Thousand Oaks. She found a small amount of hope in remembering beautiful little Jessie—the little girl that Jack had actually shown compassion by allowing her to live. He had severely injured her before leaving her at the emergency room entrance. She hoped if he had Heath that in some way he would connect with the boy, and she could find him before Jack had time to hurt him.

The pair descended the smooth snake-like Conejo Grade, a steep seven percent drop that would deliver them into the Oxnard Plain and the Camarillo Valley. The 101 Freeway was skirted with a runaway truck lane to help big rig drivers avoid certain death should their brakes fail to handle the push of the inertia from the combination of the speed, grade, and weight of the eighteen wheeled vehicle. Max stared at the strange necessity that had always intrigued her.

She loved the natural beauty of California and rode silently in awe of the sparkling lights that lay out below her. The sun was just starting to rise, and both women remained quiet until they were climbing again, this time into the Ojai Valley. It was unusual for the two women to ride without talking. But then nothing was usual right now. Normally they would have picked the possibilities apart, tearing down Jack Tyler's thinking bit by bit, but each stayed inside her own head for the majority of the drive.

Cortez broke the silence as they slid past Oakview, a sleepy little town of four-thousand, that sat between Ventura and Ojai. "How do you want to play this?"

"Who's meeting us?"

"The Ventura County Sheriff's department, Ojai sub-station."

"So, we get Barney Fife?" Max sneered, referring to the overreacting blowhard from the American classic *The Andy Griffith Show*.

"I hope not," Cortez offered, not sounding too certain. Looking down at the folder that Max had placed back on the seat between them, she said, "Captain Kennard."

"We're meeting him at the house or the station?"

"The station, but he knows we want to go right over to the house. He wants to go over all the interviews. Neighbors, you know."

"Right, Barney Fife," Max rolled her eyes.

Cortez burst into laughter and Max joined her. It felt good to laugh. She hadn't let out any emotion other than stress and fear for days now.

Their laughter fell off as they pulled into the quaint, beautiful town of Ojai. The town typically known for its shopping, majestic, mountain views, spa treatments, and great food suddenly took on an ominous feel. The car grew quiet again as Cortez navigated down the main street towards the police sub-station.

Cortez pulled the cruiser into the first available space in front of the adobe style sub-station and looked over at Max. "Ready?" Cortez studied her former partner's face, the stress obvious in the deep lines around her eyes that were not normally present.

"Yeah, let's do this," Max replied pulling on the door handle and stepping out of the car into the morning sunlight. The air was still brisk, typical of California mornings. The air was refreshing to the strain that Max had felt throughout the entire drive. She took a moment to allow the cool morning to settle the feeling that had covered her since shortly after getting into the car. Taking a deep breath, she headed towards the building with Cortez on her heels.

Inside the building they were greeted by a desk sergeant who, immediately upon introduction and request to see Captain Kennard, picked up a handset on the old-style phone that sat next to him on the desk and spoke briefly. Hanging up, he offered a quick nod and said, "He'll be right up." He motioned that they could take a seat in the chairs that lined the hallway. Both remained standing, enjoying the stretch of their legs from the long drive and also demonstrating their sense of urgency.

Moments later, Captain Kennard presented himself. Shaking hands with both women, he asked them to follow him back to his office. He was in his mid-forties and sported a thick, dark mustache that matched his thick hair and served as a cap to his full lips and broad smile that exposed excessively white teeth.

Max wondered if those teeth were caps or dentures, thinking they were inconsistent with his age. There was an obvious strength in his stance. His tall frame was supported by broad shoulders, coupled with a serious look in his grey eyes that helped dispel the earlier concerns of meeting up with Barney Fife that she'd so freely joked about in the car.

After closing the door, he led the women over to a conference table that sat at a ninety degree angle to his desk, which was directly ahead inside the room. The conference table was surrounded by six executive style chairs, and the table was lined with a number of photos and documents. Without offering a seat, he began explaining what they were looking at.

"Rebecca," he started then corrected himself of an obvious familiarity with the missing woman. "Ms. Tillman has been missing now for going on ten days. She has been a member of this community her entire life." As if justifying his earlier use of her first name he explained, "This is a small town, and everyone knows each other if you're around for any time at all. I actually graduated just a few years before her and was friends with her ex-husband."

Max's eyes narrowed in on some of the photos, the rumpled bed sheets, the vehicle parked along the street, and the yearbooks opened to expose some photos of Rebecca throughout school. Her eyes stopped on photos of Jack and Hope Tyler.

"Did you also know the Tyler's?"

"I did. They were all freshmen when I was a senior. Jack was a pretty good football player and got to dress for varsity, which was

232

fairly unusual for a freshman." Kennard tapped a captioned photo of Jack catching a football. The caption underneath read *"Freshman-Tyler goes long for a 43 yard touchdown against Buena Bulldogs."*

Max looked at Kennard, locking his grey eyes in her gaze. "What did you think of Jack Tyler?"

Kennard seemed to consider his words before answering. "He was a bit unusual, I guess. He didn't really seem to have a crowd that he fit in with. He and Hope were somewhat isolated, and I think that got worse as they got closer to their senior year. Jack was very focused on getting into medical school, and I think most of us chalked up his isolation to that drive. Hope clearly supported him a hundred percent. They were very close, really inseparable."

"What can you say about how Ms. Tillman fit into Jack and Hope's relationship?"

"Every indication was that Hope and Rebecca really parted ways in the middle of their sophomore year. I was a senior, but the rumor mill had it that Reb stepped over the line voicing her opinion about Jack to Hope. You know making comments like, he isn't right for you. The kind of statement that immediately caused Hope to severe the friendship. I guess back then everyone just saw it as your typical high school girl drama."

Max nodded then continued to look at the photos, picking up one of the bedroom in Rebecca Tillman's home. "What about forensics? Any fibers, DNA, or blood left in the house or car?"

"Nothing, both are clean. We've run prints on all doors and windows, the nightstand, door jambs, and we pulled fibers from the bed, floor, and car. So far everything matches clothing and prints of Ms. Tillman, her ex-husband or family members."

Max lifted another photo. "Broken window?"

"Yes, everything would indicate that she left on her own, except for that."

"Debris?"

"None."

"How soon can we go over to the home?" Something about these photos was bugging Max.

"We can go now. I'll drive you over."

Max turned and was already half way out the door. Cortez immediately turned as well, causing Kennard to react quickly and obviously surprised by the sudden departure.

233

When she got outside, Max stopped to wait for Kennard to catch up and then followed him to his police cruiser. He led the way around to the side of the building and pointed, indicating which vehicle they were going to. Max climbed in the back to allow Cortez to take the front seat since she stood a good four inches taller. Really she just wanted to think, and being isolated to the back made her feel like she could do that.

The trip over to the house took no more than five minutes, travelling just a few blocks across Main Street and up onto the hill. Max assessed the house as they pulled up. Nothing stood out specifically about this home versus any other. There was nothing specifically lavish that might attract it more than others on the block for a robbery that might have gone bad. It did sit on the corner, which could isolate it a bit more, making it a little more desirable, but the landscaping of the house two homes down would indicate to a robber the possibility of more valuables inside. *If I were going to rob one of these homes, that is the one I'd pick.*

All three officers exited the vehicle and walked up the small pathway to the front door. There was still crime scene tape around the entry. Max stopped Kennard before he ducked under the tape. "Show me the window first," she requested.

Max followed the captain around to the side of the house to the window that was broken out. She reached in her vest pocket, pulled out gloves, and slid her hands inside. Cortez and Kennard followed her lead. Looking around the ground, her eyes landed on a medium sized rock that lay off to the side. Her gaze travelled to the window, and she stepped forward, mentally accessing her height to the window. She reached up to the window and determined she could hoist herself through it if she really wanted to, despite the fact that it was at eye level to her.

Turning to Kennard, she asked, "How tall are you, Captain?"

He looked at her and responded, "Six-two."

Comparing him to Tyler she asked, "Do you think you could easily hoist yourself through that window?"

Kennard stepped forward. "Easily."

Max bent and looked at the wall below the window. There were no obvious scuff marks or abrasions indicting that someone had recently climbed through this window. She took a closer look at the

234

ground and then asked the captain to retrieve the rock in an evidence bag.

Satisfied that she'd seen everything she needed to out here she said, "Okay, let's go inside now."

Cortez stayed behind for a moment longer looking over the ground more closely. The ground was very dry, and even their footprints did not make imprints where they had just stood. Turning away, she followed Max and the captain back around to the front of the house.

After dipping under the tape Kennard opened the door with a key he retrieved from his pocket. An eerie silence filled the rooms inside. The door closed behind them adding to the strange aura as the morning light was blocked out.

Max stood still, her eyes scanning the room. She looked at pictures on the walls and book shelves. The house was homey and yet somewhat sterile too. In the kitchen there was a set of small dog dishes, one about half full of dog kibble and the other water. "Any sign of the dog?"

"No, that's been a bit of the mystery. It's as if they both disappeared off the face of the earth."

"Would she leave the dog behind if she left on her own free will?"

"According to her ex-husband, no, she took the dog with her everywhere."

"What do we know about him? Is he a possible?" Cortez asked, suggesting that he might be a suspect in his ex-wife's disappearance.

"He has an alibi for several days around the time she went missing. He was actually out of state on a business trip in New York, was seen in several meetings and during evening functions, making it unlikely that he was involved. The timeline wouldn't allow him to fly back from New York and get back to meetings by morning. We checked flights in between the two cities, and there was nothing with him on the passenger list except for his flights to and from the meetings on his original itinerary."

"She was first reported missing by her employer?"

"Yes, I know him. As I said, this is a small town. He called worried and asked if we would just check it out. When we got no answer at the house, we called the ex and other family members. No one had talked to her in a few days, but that was not reported as unusual. The main concern was the no call, no show to work. At first we just assumed it was a scheduling misunderstanding, but after a couple more days of no contact we started a more in-depth investigation. We gained access to the home and found the broken window and what appeared to be a quick exit from the bedroom." Waving his hand around the room, "She was pretty tidy, so the mess of a bed seems out of character."

"What about her purse, keys, and cell phone?"

"All missing, cell phone goes straight to voicemail as if the phone is turned off or dead."

Cortez jumped in, "When did you make that first attempt?"

Kennard stood thinking for a moment. "She'd been gone for a few days."

Following Cortez's thoughts Max questioned, "So the phone could have lost its charge by the time you made the first attempt?"

"Yes, but her boss tried to reach her before that and got the same result."

Max continued to slowly walk through the home, following her instincts to the area where the window was broken. She stood facing the broken window. Based on the size of the window, it seemed unlikely the woman, Rebecca Tillman, would leave it broken. The nights were certainly cool, and it would be impossible to ignore it or have it go unnoticed.

Without approaching, her eyes scanned the wall and then the floor. There were no scuff marks on the wall and no apparent glass on the floor, but she noticed something else. The carpet seemed to be vacuumed in a pattern inconsistent with the rest of the house. She turned to look behind her and followed the pattern up the hallway and into the living room. In every place but under that window the vacuum tracks moved north to south. In this area they were east to west, as if someone had vacuumed only that area.

"Cortez, we need to find the vacuum."

Cortez's eyes followed Max's. "I see it. Foot prints in the middle are probably from the crime team, but there's a definite vacuum pattern."

Kennard stood behind Max and followed her eyes. "We didn't catch that," he said in obvious disappointment.

Cortez left the room, and from somewhere else in the house called out, "Got it!"

Max took a step back, forcing Kennard to back away so she could leave the room. Following the sound of Cortez's voice, Max found her standing in front of a closet where she lifted a Eureka vacuum out and stood looking at it. The cord was neatly wrapped around the handle. No one had wildly put the unit away. Max knelt down and popped open the canister lock and pulled the cylinder out. She held it up to look through the clear hard plastic. "It's empty."

Opening the lid, she looked deep inside. There was the typical dust residue but no visible glass. "We need this checked for prints and glass fragments. If there are fragments or residue, we need to see if there's a match to the window. Let's see if there was an intruder that tidied up. At least we'll narrow this down to her leaving on her own or potentially foul play," Max said handing the canister to Kennard.

"I'll put a rush on it."

"Have the rock analyzed too for any glass fragments while we're at it," Cortez said.

Kennard pulled his cell phone out of the holster on his belt and punched in some numbers. He gave some pretty direct yet basic instructions before hanging up and snapping the phone back into its case. "I'll have someone here in less than ten minutes to take this to the lab. We can get a preliminary report by the end of the day."

Knowing the typical delays in getting forensics, Max contained her reaction to the end of the day. It would be lucky if that really happened, and although she knew that, it was difficult to wait. She wanted those results immediately so she could know if there was truly foul play, though her instincts already told her the answer.

Proceeding on through the house, the team continued their journey down the narrow hallway. Max pushed open the door to the first room on the right and found what appeared to be a guest room. A quick scan of the room told her it hadn't been disturbed any time recently. The bed was perfectly made, there was nothing out of place, and a light layer of dust lay on the nightstands. The carpet was perfectly brushed in the same consistent pattern with the rest of the house, except for the spot under the broken window.

The room on the left was a bathroom. It was nicely appointed. Max looked at the items on the sink, and it appeared this was not the bathroom primarily used by Rebecca. She continued on, and at the end of the hall found the master bedroom.

The door stood open. Max stepped in the doorway scanning the room. Like everything else in the house the room was tidy, except for the bed. The bed covers were very disheveled. Not just rumpled, but pulled way back and hung half off the bed. Either Rebecca Tillman had a very restless night, or something had disturbed her and a struggle had occurred.

Moving into the room, Max walked over to the closet and opened the door. She stood facing a good sized walk-in closet. Stepping inside she studied the contents, considering the clothes on the hangers and shoes on the floor. Her eyes scanned a few small boxes and then landed on the luggage in the corner. Her eyes narrowed in on the tag on the handle. She walked over, careful to not touch anything else, and read the tag. It was from a recent trip out of state. *You didn't leave here on your own did you, Rebecca? You would have taken your luggage.*

Cortez went deeper into the master bathroom, and as Max closed the closet door she said, "Toothbrush, brush, blow dryer, tooth paste, hair spray, and make up right here. And…there's a small travel bag with travel toiletries in the bottom drawer."

"Luggage in the closet recently used. This lady didn't go anywhere on her own. She was taken."

"I agree," Cortez confirmed.

"Look at the bedding too. If I'm getting out of bed, I throw the covers back, away from me. These are dragged off the bed."

"She could have had a lover in there with her," Cortez countered.

Max nodded, accepting the idea as an alternative solution and began talking it through, "She brings him home, things get frisky, and it goes south. They struggle, he knocks her out." She continued the theory, this time shaking her head, "But no blood, hair, fibers." Turning back looking for Kennard, who had stepped away from the room, Max called out, "Hey, Captain? Did the forensics team check the sheets for fluids?"

Kennard returned to the doorway. He nodded. "Yep, nothing but a little sweat."

Max thought for a minute. "Could have used a condom?" Could be her sweat, early menopause?" She asked sharing possible reasons for the lack of any fluids and justification for the sweat.

Cortez shrugged her shoulders and nodded her head, accepting either possibility.

Max returned to the bathroom and looked in the small waste can next to the toilet. Empty. "Did crime scene collect the trash?"

"I don't think so," Kennard answered.

Cortez was already in motion. "Kitchen," she called out over her shoulder.

Max and Kennard followed her and watched as she opened the cabinet under the kitchen sink and removed the waste can that sat nestled in under one side of the sink. Inside there were a few items, a couple of envelopes from the mail, a sales flyer for Walmart and an orange peel. "No condom, no glass."

"Let's check outside. Has the trash been picked up?"

Kennard replied, "I'm not sure. It comes on Tuesdays and Fridays to this street, but unless Rebecca had it out at the curb it would still be there."

The three went outside and looked inside the trash can. There was one bag, and after a careful look through the bag it didn't appear to contain anything out of the ordinary. So far nothing hinted of a boyfriend or a spontaneous lover.

The more they looked around the more Max was convinced the woman had been abducted. The person was clever and thorough, leaving nothing behind. That smelled of experience. The kind of experience like Jack Tyler had, but so far she had nothing to tie him to this case and no reason to believe he would come back to this town. In fact, everything she knew about Tyler led her to believe that he wouldn't come back here ever.

"Okay, I think we've seen enough here," Max advised. "We need that forensic work back as quickly as possible to see if we can prove there was a disturbance. Until that comes in we've got no more than we had before. But from what I see, she didn't plan on going anywhere."

"I'll lean on them and get you the report the minute it comes in." Kennard offered referring to the lab work Max was demanding.

Kennard had that stern look in his eyes again as he spoke, and Max got the feeling that he was able to get results when he wanted to. She was glad about that and felt a little more comfortable thinking he might just be able to get them back tonight.

The return ride to the police sub-station was quiet, and when they arrived Max thanked Kennard for his help. She provided him with her business card and asked him to contact her immediately with the results or if any new information came in. They all shook hands before the two women returned to their car.

Max turned to Cortez, "Drive by Vivian's house. Let's make a house call."

Cortez looked at her. "You think he'd go back to that house?" Cortez continued before Max could answer. "Besides, she would recognize him. Even with the plastic surgery. Surely she'd call us the minute he left."

"No, I don't really think he'd go back there. But if he did, he'd want to look around. Maybe there's something there that he'd want to retrieve. Who knows? I agree, she'd recognize him, but we never told her what he'd done. We only told her that we were worried about him. She might not realize how dangerous he is." Max thought for a few seconds then finished off with, "It's a long shot, but it's all we got."

Cortez shrugged in agreement. "Well, I could use some of that fresh squeezed lemonade."

Max smiled at her, remembering the woman's sweet demeanor and hospitality when they had visited her during a previous attempt to find Jack Tyler.

Cortez backed the car out of the space and turned in the direction of the Jack's childhood home. According to Vivian she moved into the home that Tyler inherited and then sold because he had no interest in returning to the house. By then he was living in Los Angeles with a thriving medical business.

The streets were lined with bougainvillea and jacaranda trees, creating a beautiful blooming tapestry. Despite the heavy mood from their earlier time inside Rebecca Tillman's home, the natural beauty that filled the town helped to calm the anxiety in Max that seemed to be rising with each passing hour.

Cortez navigated the cruiser into the curved driveway. The home was as beautiful as Max recalled. Pulling in front of the walkway to the front door, Cortez stopped the car. They stepped out of the vehicle, again being embraced by the cool breeze and the

240

warmth of the sunshine. As they walked up the sidewalk, something stood out to Max. The lavish foliage showed obvious signs of poor care. Nodding her head at it for Cortez to notice, she approached the door and rang the bell.

Chapter Thirty-Five

"Agent Wells," Jenkins approached with a report in her hand. "You're going to want to see this."

"What do we have?" Mark asked turning towards his fellow agent. Jenkins was a highly competent agent. She'd passed the FBI Academy with high marks in her class about five years previous.

Her creamy, dark skin and high cheek bones outlined serious eyes. "I got the report back from the credit card. Jack Tyler performed an Internet background check using intelius.com." She paused, an obvious hesitation in her voice. "Sir, the Internet search was on Rebecca Tillman."

Mark took the report from her hands, his eyes scanning the details on the page. A serious look covered his face, obvious by the deep furrow that sat like a canyon between dark brows hooding his tired blue eyes. Looking up at Jenkins he offered a mere, "Thank you," before reaching for his cell phone.

Dialing Max's number, he grew frustrated when it went straight to voicemail. It wasn't like Max to turn her phone off. Knowing Ojai was located in a valley nestled into the mountains, he wondered if she was having reception issues. *Or could it be something else?*

"Agent Jenkins, please brief the team on your findings. I'll try Cortez's line." Wells was already dialing. Once again the call went straight to voicemail. *It must be a reception issue.* Now in motion, Wells left the room and made a left in the hall, then followed the marbled tunnel to the chief's office.

Following the sound of the barking loud voice, Wells found Chief Harding standing in the middle of the room shouting into a phone. It was obvious he was chewing on someone about a press related issue.

Seeing Wells approach, Harding ended the call abruptly. "Agent Wells, is everything okay?" His solid jaw jutted out to the left, obvious concern covered his face. "Do we have something?"

"We do. Jack Tyler conducted a background check on Rebecca Tillman–the missing woman from Ojai. Cortez and my wife went to investigate the woman's home. Neither is answering her phone. Do you have the name of the contact from the Ventura Sheriff's Department?"

"One moment," Harding turned away and in a brisk walk carried his large frame over to a desk across the room. He returned immediately with a folder in his hand. Wells could see Tillman written in a scrawl across the tab.

Flipping the file open, the chief scanned the page, his thick finger sliding over the paper. "Captain Kennard. Number's right here."

Wells punched the numbers in his cell phone as Chief Harding rattled off the area code followed by the seven digits. Two rings later an electronic phone system answered, and Wells listened and made the proper choices that would guide him to the desk sergeant. Within a minute he was connected to Captain Kennard.

Skipping the formalities, Wells was very direct. "This is Special Agent in Charge Mark Wells of the FBI. Earlier today you were to meet with Agent Maxine Wells and Detective Lorraine Cortez. Are they still with you?"

Kennard hesitated briefly, "Agent Wells, yes. They were here, but they left over two hours ago."

"Did they indicate where they were headed?"

"Not specifically, but I assumed back to L.A."

"Was there anything specific identified during their time with you?"

"Yes, a few things. We collected a few more items. The canister of the vacuum was already empty when we found it, but Agent Wells wanted me to have it checked for glass fragments to see if there was a match to the broken window."

"Have you received those results?"

"Not yet. They won't likely come in until later today. I've got a rush on them, but it's not easy to get any forensics on a same day turnaround."

"I understand," Wells acknowledged. "We're going to need your help. We now have information showing that Jack Tyler did, in fact, have an interest in Rebecca Tillman."

"Certainly, what can I do?" Kennard responded, sucking in his breath.

"I'm going to get a flyer faxed over to you. It is a likeness of what we believe Tyler may look like today, given recent plastic surgery. We need to get it circulated to stores, likely places where Tyler would have to shop if he were staying somewhere in Ojai. My team and I will be there as soon as we can."

"You got it," Kennard answered, and before he could say any more the line went dead.

"Thank you, Chief," Mark said turning back the Harding. "We're going to have to get to Ojai as quickly as possible. Tyler may have Tillman there, and knowing Max, if she figured any of that out she may be following that lead on her own."

"I'll send two of my team to assist. One of my detectives is in this too." Harding turned, and Wells began the walk towards the investigation room. He could hear Harding barking out orders.

The trip to Ojai was clearly the longest drive of Mark's entire life. As they passed through Ventura, he watched the waves slapping angrily at the sand, seemingly peeling it away much in the same way Tyler peeled opened his victims. He turned his head, changing his gaze to the opposite side of the freeway. His eyes soaked in the mountainside that was speckled with expensive homes, packed tightly together like pushpins set into the hills.

His gaze fixed on a tall cross that stood high above the city like a beacon protecting everything below. The cross gave him an eerie foreboding feeling as if it were specifically warning him. He punched Max's name on his cell phone again, hopeful she'd pick up, but unfortunately, he got the same response—direct to voicemail.

Chapter Thirty-Six

Jack buried Jimmy's torn and ragged body deep in the woods near the creek, close to where Reb was laid to rest. After showering and obsessively bleaching and scrubbing his body clean he fell into bed next to Mindy. He didn't even realize she was actually awake when he leaned over and kissed her cheek before dropping into a blissful sleep.

Morning came quickly since his late night escapades kept him up most of the night. He was rattled awake by Mindy preparing breakfast and rolled over to watch her in the makeshift kitchen. For a moment his head was a fog of mixed visions floating between Jimmy and Ron, then of Heath coming into the surgical room. He turned over to look at the couch. The kids were still asleep. He flipped back over to Mindy. *Oh, Hope, you are so beautiful.* The sight of her in the kitchen–her blonde hair cascading down her back, thin legs, and tight buttocks– made his heart tug in his chest. It was so good having her back with him.

As he watched he heard the rustling of the sheets from the couch, and a moment later Heath stood staring down at him. "Good morning, Chance."

"Hi, Daddy," the boy said rubbing at his sleepy eyes.

Jack pulled back the covers and pulled the boy under the blankets, snuggling with him. "You cold?"

"No," Heath said, nestling into the man he believed to be his father.

Mindy looked over at Jack and the boy. Jack smiled at her. *Life is perfect.*

"Did you fix the sick man?" Heath innocently asked.

Jack studied the boy closely. "No, buddy, I wasn't able to this time. He was a very sick man, and sometimes when people are too sick, they just can't be saved."

Before the boy could ask more questions Scruffy jumped at the side of the bed, bouncing like a pogo stick in an attempt to get up on it. "Oh, look who needs to go outside. Want to come with me?" Jack asked.

"Okay," Heath answered, immediately climbing out of the bed.

"Okay, okay, buddy. I hear ya," Jack said to the dancing dog as he swung his feet over the bed and started to pull on the pants he dropped next to the bed after his nighttime hike into the woods. They had some dirt on them, so he carried them over and dropped them into a laundry basket near the bathroom. Then he retrieved another pair from the back of the chair. As he lifted the pants, his pocket knife fell and spun on the floor. He quickly retrieved it and dipped it into the front right pocket. As he did so his fingers were enveloped by silky threads, and he smiled as he remembered clipping hair from Agent Maxine Wells's auburn head.

Pulling the strands out of his pocket, Jack stood staring at the rich ginger locks, his fingers sliding over the silky hair. Realizing he was being watched he looked up. Mindy was staring at him. He shoved the hair back in his pocket and flashed a warm reassuring smile at his lovely wife.

After he finished dressing, Jack helped Heath pull on play clothes and shoes, and then he let Hope know they'd be back in a while. He crossed the room to be by Hope's side and looped his arms around her waist. "Do you know how much I love you?" Not waiting for an answer, he spun her to face him and leaned to kiss her. "I love you, Hope," he said before placing his mouth on hers and slipping his tongue between her lips.

Feeling a tug at his shirt, he pulled away. "Daddy, let's go."

He leaned in and kissed Mindy again. "Okay, okay, buddy," he said to the anxious child. "We'll be right back," he said to Mindy with a smile before releasing her and following the running boy and dog up the stairs. He didn't see her wipe the back of her hand across her mouth in an effort to clean away his kiss.

With the door to the basement secured, the man, boy, and dog took their usual wander through the thick underbrush. New paths were starting to form from the recent visits out into the woods.

Holding Jack's hand as they walked Heath asked, "How do you become a doctor?"

Jack stopped and turned to look down at the boy. If he had any doubt that this boy was truly his son it vanished in that single question. Kneeling down he was subjected to wet slaps from Scruffy's tongue, but Jack laughed and patted the little dog. Focusing back on the inquisitive boy, he responded to the child's question, "Well, it takes a lot of work. For me, it was something I had to do. I need it even more than I like it."

"Can you teach me? I want to be a doctor." The little boy's eyes searched Jack's face with a sparkle that reflected hopeful excitement.

Jack stood looking at Heath, his mind filled with delight. His boy wanted to be just like his father; pride filled every ounce of him.

"I practiced a lot when I was a boy. I was about your age and a lot like you." Leading the boy around to the side garage door, Jack pulled from his pocket the keys he carried with him and unlocked the door. With Heath following closely behind, he went inside the garage and spent a few minutes gathering the necessary items to take back outside.

"Okay, if you're really going to be a doctor you first have to learn all about the anatomy of living beings. The anatomy is the things that are on the inside, like the heart that makes your blood pump and the lungs that help move the air through the body so it can breathe. You have to know how all those things work. Then once you know that, you can learn about how to fix those things if they get broken."

Heath listened intently and followed Jack back out into the woods. "What are we going to do?"

"We're going to build a trap."

"How?"

"I'm going to show you, but first the most important part of a good trap is a good location. You have to find a spot that will allow you to catch something quickly. Jack began walking around and started explaining how to identify the right spot. He talked about

249

animal droppings and showed Heath how to determine if the droppings were from small or large animals.

A few minutes later Jack selected a spot and began compiling the items he retrieved from the garage into a makeshift trap. He was surprised at how quickly it came back to him.

Jack showed Heath the importance of making sure the hinge functioned properly, or the animal could easily get away. He explained how to choose the bait for the trap. For this trap he used dog food.

"Make sure you place the food way at the back. The animal will usually set off the trap when they try to get the food. It will climb in to get the food, and when they do they will bump the prop and the top will fall, catching them inside the trap." Jack demonstrated using his hand knocking the prop over and causing the trap to drop to the ground, leaving his hand still inside and with the cage over his wrist.

Pulling his hand back out, he reset the trap. It was ready and set to spring. Jack promised to make a better one if Heath actually liked learning about the animals. "Okay, we've been gone for a while. We better go back inside. We don't want Mommy to get mad at us for being late for breakfast."

Before going back to the house, Jack leaned down with his hands on his knees. "Son, there are two more things you must know. Not everyone will understand why you need to do these things. Not everyone wants to be a doctor, so there is no way they could know what it feels like to want that. The other thing you have to remember is that you never use your family pet for your studies. Do you understand?"

Heath nodded. "Will it take a long time?" the boy asked with excitement filling his voice, glancing back at the trap.

"It depends, but we can come back out later and check it."

***

The morning was spent not only eating the breakfast Mindy prepared but also watching morning cartoons. The whole family piled on the couch with Heath sitting on Jack's lap.

Mindy watched closely at how gentle Jack was with the boy and felt a wave of relief in that, but she wondered how she was going to get the children away from him before something terrible happened. She knew he had killed a man last night, and she feared the little boy had seen it. He seemed fine today, and that scared her almost as much as Jack scared her.

Her thoughts often moved to the weapon under the mattress, but she couldn't figure out how to use it without putting the kids in jeopardy. If she attacked him and somehow he over-powered her she'd be dead, and then the kids would be left alone with him. She couldn't take that risk. And Vivian, the poor woman, she nearly gasped at the thought of Vivian. She sucked in her breath as an obvious sigh to mask the gagging she felt in her throat.

Allie sat tucked tightly under her arm in a protective snug. Mindy was worried about her. Her darling little girl hadn't spoken in days. A subtle nod when spoken to was about all she offered. The thought of the trauma her daughter was enduring made her stomach lurch. She struggled to not allow the fear to pull her into absolute despair.

While Jack was doing whatever awful things in that room, she had laid in bed and had prayed her daughter would not wake up to hear the atrocities. Through the darkness Mindy had seen Jack carry a bundle up the stairs, and she could hear the crinkling of plastic. As he had approached the top of the stairs and the door opened, letting light in from the second floor, Mindy had dared to look, and her eyes had burned with tears as she saw Jack lugging the long, rolled bundle on his shoulder through the door.

She had known what he had done, and her mind raced—a collage of images of escape, killing him, vivid images of her demise, the torture he would certainly level against the children one day, and a search for how Hope had managed his needs for so many years. She racked her brain through their childhood and remembered the intense focus Hope had suddenly pushed on Jack to become a doctor. She searched through the memories of the years past and finally determined that had begun sometime around seventh grade.

She decided to take a chance. If she could just get him to stop killing it would buy her time and stop the kids from more exposure to his insanity.

"Jack." She jumped, startled at the sound of her own voice. "I think you should try to get on at the hospital."

Jack turned, his eyes searching hers. "I'm so enjoying our time together though, darling. I wasn't there for you once, and I won't make that mistake again."

Mindy tried to think how to respond. "I know you worry about us, but I need you to be strong. You know, like we always planned. People need you, and you need them. You're such a skilled doctor." She took a chance, silently praying that her hunch was right. She held her breath, and her eyes dropped, expecting a rage to flow from the devil that sat near her on the couch.

Jack watched her. She could feel his eyes on her. "Okay, you're right, Hope. You're right, you've always been right. Tomorrow, I'll call tomorrow and see if there are services I can offer."

Mindy let her breath out. She found herself waiting and then words began to flow naturally out of her mouth, driven purely on instinct. "I think it's best—for us, for the kids."

***

Jack didn't like disappointing Hope. She was right, but he feared that if he wasn't with them he would be unable to protect them. He knew that she didn't like the way he handled his darkness when he wasn't working. Whenever he was working and able to perform surgeries, he was able to keep the darkness at bay. It was, after all, how they had lived for so many years. *Before*…He couldn't finish the thought. The accident was no longer part of their reality. They'd beaten it and had his family back, and even more now he had a wonderful son who he knew was going to make him proud. *Yes, he had a son.*

He had some unfinished business though. Ron was in the surgical room, and tonight he would allow the darkness to take him one last time before returning to a respectable profession. He knew allowing the darkness to drive him was dangerous and felt torn between protecting his family from danger and placing himself in danger. His thoughts tormented him, and he felt restless.

Getting up, he went over to Vivian and pulled a chair beside the bed. He talked to her, check her, and held her hand, taking great care to make her comfortable. Unfortunately, even tending to her didn't temper his restless feeling.

"Come on, Chance. Let's take Scruffy outside," Jack said standing and patting his leg to get the dog to follow him.

Both the dog and boy hopped off the couch and were right at Jack's side. The dog jumped around like a bouncing ball, his pink tongue flopping from one side of his mouth, hopping up the stairs as his furry little legs drove him towards the door.

After they were out of the basement and out of earshot of Hope and Allie, Jack said to Heath, "What do you think, Chance? Will there be anything in our trap?"

The boy was practically running towards the door. "Let's go see, Daddy."

Outside of the house Heath pulled on Jack's hand as he ran to the place in the woods just a few feet from the trunk of a large oak tree. The very oak tree that Jack and Hope had carved their initials into the day she'd caught him with an animal in his hands and covered in blood. The sun peeked through the canopy of trees, creating a patchwork of sparkling leaves and shadows.

Jack pulled back on the boy's hand to slow him down. "Hold on, buddy. We have to go slow. No need to scare our prey."

Approaching more slowly now, Scruffy suddenly stopped, and wiry hair rose on the middle of his spine. He began to growl and bark, pouncing side to side around the small trap.

"Scruffy!" Jack barked out commanding the little dog to back down.

Jack approached, still holding Heath's hand. Inside the makeshift trap a small rabbit sat frozen in fear. The terrified animal breathed rapidly, and its eyes were wide and unblinking. "It looks like we got something."

"A bunny," Heath said with a wide smile on his innocent little face.

"Yes, a bunny."

"Can I pet it?"

"Of course, but hold on though. We don't want it to get away."

Jack knelt down next to the trap with his knee resting on the ground, and with one hand he lifted the trap door and slowly reached in to capture the rabbit by the scruff of the neck. The rabbit kicked its back feet wildly at the air as it was lifted off the ground. Dropping the trap door, Jack wrapped the rabbit in his arms, securing its feet and calming it down. Within a couple of seconds it settled in his embrace, unassumingly trusting.

Heath reached over and placed a small hand with plump little fingers in the soft fur. A big grin covered his face.

"Okay, ready to practice?" Jack asked. "Do you want me to show you how I practiced being a doctor when I was a little boy?"

Heath's eyes took on an almost sparkling green hue in the midday sun. There was naïve innocence in his nodded response.

Standing up, Jack carried the rabbit with Heath and Scruffy following behind. The small dog hopped up and down trying to get a good smell of the furry creature.

Jack walked across the yard to the small playhouse and stepped onto the platform while still holding the animal by the loose fur around its neck. He balanced the rabbit in one hand and pulled the door open with the other, then stooped in through the small door and let Heath inside with him, shutting Scruffy outside, much to the dog's disappointment.

Dust rose from the wooden floor and danced in the air in the stripes of sunlight that peeked through the small cracks in the slats of the wood. Jack kneeled down on the playhouse floor while maintaining his grip on the scrap of the rabbit's neck, setting the animal down.

Heath watched intently. Jack reached his free hand into his pocket and pulled out the Swiss Army Knife then plucked the largest blade open with his thumb. A peak of sun glinted off the shiny metal as he looked at Heath.

"This isn't the best, but it's all we have right now. Ready?"

Ten minutes later the boy sat staring down at the matted fur of the beautiful animal. Tears streaked his face. Crimson blood had already begun to dry on his small hands, making them feel papery and stiff. "Why did it die, Daddy?"

Jack looked at the boy and saw the disappointment in the death of the animal. "I know it's hard to understand, but if you want to experience life as closely as we just did, sometimes your patient will die. But if you practice long enough, you'll learn how all those parts inside work together, and then you'll be able to learn how to fix those parts when they become broken."

Jack stood up slightly hunched over in the small playhouse. He lifted the dead animal. "Come on, we need to bury it and then go clean up."

Heath followed Jack as he went to get the small shovel, and then walked with the man, stuffing his small bloody hand into Jack's as they trudged a little way into the woods. Heath stood watching as Jack dug a small hole, laid the animal inside, and then covered it back up.

Silently they went back towards the house. Jack called Scruffy away from the grave of the rabbit, where the little dog sniffed and pawed at the ground. After putting the shovel away, they went back into the main kitchen. Jack pulled a chair over to the sink and stood Heath on it, and then turned on warm water. He tested the temperature and helped Heath rinse the blood from his little fingers and watched as the water rushed down the drain—first red, then quickly replaced with clear bubbles from the soap he applied. Jack then washed his own hands until all the crimson blood was gone.

When both had dry hands, he lifted Heath off of the chair and held the boy in his arms for a moment. "You will make a wonderful doctor one day. Daddy's proud of you. You did really good today."

The boy smiled slightly, a hint of confusion and pleasure in his eyes. He wrapped his tiny arms around Jack's neck and laid his head on the muscular shoulder. Scruffy whimpered at their feet.

***

Allie didn't speak the entire time Jack and Chance were gone. She sat on the couch and stared at the TV, but Mindy couldn't tell if she was really watching any of it. Chance, she wasn't even sure if that was his real name or some crazy idea Jack had concocted. It was the only name she knew him by and couldn't just think of him as just a boy.

Mindy took a chance and went to the room at the back of the basement—the room where Jack had taken that bundle. Despite her fear, she tried to open the door. Her heart pounded so loudly in her ears that she had to force back a scream. The rattle of the door handle made her jump, confusing the noise she had made with what she thought was Jack returning too quickly. She stifled a chuckle at her fear then tapped on the door. *Jesus, I'm going crazy.*

She thought she heard something inside, so she placed her ear against the door and called out, "Hello?"

She listened carefully, and was sure she could hear a muffled groaning. *Oh, God, there is another person in there.* Stepping away from the door, she walked over to the bed and slid her hand in between the mattress and box spring. Her fingers wrapped around the wrench. *It's still there.*

She stood when she heard footsteps overhead. He was coming back. Her eyes darted to Allie on the couch, and she could see her daughter's fingers rapidly fidgeting with the fringe of the blanket. She had been calm until now. Her heart wrenched inside her as she watched her daughter's terror manifest in repetitive motions.

Food, it's time for food again. She heard water running above, and she quickly moved to the kitchen, opened the small refrigerator, and pulled out some chicken and vegetables.

Mindy couldn't help but notice there was something strange about the boy's behavior after he and Jack returned with the dog. He was sullen and quieter than normal. He seemed slightly withdrawn from Jack, too. He joined Allie on the couch and quietly watched TV.

After they ate, to her relief, Jack left the basement for quite a while. While he was gone she sat near the kids and placed her arms around each, trying to offer them assurance that she herself didn't feel. Heath soaked into her side, but Allie seemed completely withdrawn.

When Jack returned he was showered and had on fresh clothes. He went to Heath and suggested the boy take a bath. He lifted the child from the couch and out of Mindy's arms and carried him off to the shower. Soon the boy was freshly dressed and smelled of shampoo. Mindy wondered where the fresh clothes came from.

She assumed based on the tags that Jack had shopped for them during one of his outings.

The day wasted away. Her thoughts were like a ping pong ball dancing across the table trying to find a way to escape the certain slamming of the paddle. No matter how hard she tried, she couldn't find a way to escape from the hold Jack had on her. With each passing moment fear rose in her, and she felt like she was slipping away.

***

Jack waited for the children to fall asleep then encouraged Hope to go to bed. He explained that he had something to finish up before attempting to start work again. He didn't explain any further knowing full well she wouldn't approve. There was nothing he could do to stop this anyway. He certainly couldn't just let Ron go. The man had seen far too much.

Flipping off the lights and leaving only a slight glow in the room from the subtle lights of the kitchen appliances, he walked around the couch into the darker corner of the basement and unlocked the surgical room door. Inside the room with the door closed and locked behind him, he flipped on the lights, shedding a brilliant glow over the secured, naked man on the table.

The paralyzing drug had worn away, and Ron was now fully alert. The presence of his captor sent him into a violent flutter like a bird with broken wings.

"Calm down, Ronnie boy. You wouldn't want to hurt yourself, now would you?"

A hissing sound escaped from Ron's nose as he attempted to breathe through the tape that held his mouth closed and head tight to the table. Bloody tears around his wrists and ankles indicated that he'd obviously been working at the zip ties.

"It's not worth your struggles. No one can hear you and you can't get away. But I think you know that already, don't you? Let me ask you, Ron. How was it watching me work on Jimmy? Did you enjoy it as much as I did? It is truly amazing. Life, I mean."

Jack leaned over close to Ron's face. He talked slowly and watched Ron's eyes grow large; the pupils dilated from fear. His head shook in a mild tremor. Jack briefly wondered if he was cold, but ultimately decided it didn't matter.

As much as Jack wanted to spend days with Ron, like he had with Benz in Oklahoma and Reb here just days before, he had made a promise to Hope, and he planned on keeping it. There was nothing, including his darkness that would get in the way of making Hope happy. He would return to the days of managing the darkness through his surgical skills, making his explorations specific only to moments in the effort of trying to save people. That was the arrangement he and Hope made all those years ago.

Jack pulled on a full set of scrubs and inhaled deeply, and then lifted the scalpel from the tray. He ignored Ron's thrashing and bouncing against the zip ties and pain as he took his time ripping through the man's body, exploring all the slippery organs and toying with the heart as he worked it to the edge of death then pulsed it into a throbbing beat between his fingers. It finally failed after several minutes of the torment and lay stalled in his hand.

Wiping sweat from his brow, he realized he had lost complete track of time. Peeling his hands out of the center of Ron's chest, he went through the cleaning ritual he'd so perfectly mastered over the years. He hosed everything down including his own body that was now striped of the scrubs. Once he was satisfied that the room had been restored to its pristine state, he packaged the man for a plastic-encased wooded burial.

The morning was greeted by a sparkling sunrise and a light breeze. Jack got up early to go upstairs and shower. Today he would keep his promise to Hope and call the hospital to see if there was some way he could assist with emergency or surgical procedures. He knew his ability to control the demanding urges could only be tempered with rightful opportunities to get inside the patients' bodies. He also knew he would try to keep his promise to Hope. He wanted to make her happy. All he ever wanted was to make her happy.

Deciding the best approach was to go to the hospital in person, Jack dressed appropriately, gathered the documents to support his latest identity, including his medical license, and with everything in a folder he set off to talk to the hospital director.

Two hours later Jack returned to the house. He had secured an agreement to work on-call for any major emergencies. Then he had stopped by the grocery to pick up a few items and was excited to get home to Hope to tell her the good news.

As he started to pull into the driveway he saw a car pull in ahead of him. Something told him to not follow it. He passed the house slowly and watched as the car stopped. Two women got out. One of the women was Agent Maxine Wells, the other her attractive former Hispanic partner. He'd seen them both before in Oklahoma when he'd hidden in the back room posing as Thomas the nail salon employee.

Blood pounded in his ears as he considered his options. Parking his van on the street, Jack reached behind his seat and grabbed his medical bag. He slipped out of the van and quietly closed the door with a slight click of the latch and worked his way along the driveway through the trees. Rounding the corner of the house he heard the door bell ringing.

He slipped inside the house through the back door and went directly to the front door. Punching the button on the intercom he asked, "Yes?" in a very low voice, staying behind the door almost entirely.

"Hello, is Vivian home?"

"She's not doing well these days. She's resting."

"We certainly understand, but it is very important that we speak with her," Max said while holding her badge in front of the camera eye.

"FBI, oh my," Jack said maintaining his low voice and trying to sound overtly surprised.

"May I ask who you are?" Max asked.

"I'm Vivian's caregiver, Jimmy. Vivian has cancer," Jack lied.

"Well, we really do need to see her," Max continued to prod.

"If you can give me a few moments I can see if she is feeling up to guests."

"That would be great," Max said glancing back at Cortez.

Jack clicked off the intercom and returned to the garage. He wrapped his fingers around the hammer in the tool box that sat just inside the door and retrieved two syringes from inside his medical bag before opening the front door, intentionally staying behind and out of view.

Max stepped through the doorway first followed by Cortez. Jack swung the hammer down on Cortez's skull. There was a loud crack, and she slipped to the floor. Max started to swing around and reach for her weapon, but Jack dropped the hammer and swept his arm around her neck. His other hand plunged the needle of the syringe into her neck.

Max pulled with all her strength at the arm that coiled around her, but was rapidly taken by a haze of quick flashes of Cortez lying like a crumpled rag on the floor with a crimson halo surrounding her head.

Chapter Thirty-Seven

The cruiser finally pulled into the town of Ojai, and though Wells continued trying to reach both Max and Cortez, neither phone answered. Each attempt went directly to voicemail. Wells was becoming increasingly concerned that something was wrong. It wasn't like Max to not check in or keep him updated with the status of her findings.

He gave instructions to the remaining team back at the Los Angeles precinct to continue working their plausible theories, and he brought Agent Jenkins and two detectives with him. He was beginning to wonder whether he had made the right choice or if he should have brought even more agents with him. He had a feeling he was going to need them.

By the time they arrived at the sub-station where Captain Kennard told them to meet him, it was late afternoon. The sunny day was beginning to show signs of ending as the sun was slowly setting behind the mountains they had passed through. It would soon be dipping into the salty ocean, the waves lapping away the last signs of light.

Wells knew that nightfall would make their search more difficult, and he unconsciously prayed for Max to call and explain that they had been out of cell coverage. He looked down at his own cell phone as he exited the car and saw that he had three bars. His brow furrowed with deeper concern.

Kennard met them inside. Apparently, he had been waiting for them to arrive. After brief introductions Kennard asked, "Any word from Agent Wells or Detective Cortez?"

Wells shook his head. "Have we received any leads from the distribution of the photo?"

"Nothing so far," Kennard replied. "It's being circulated. We've gotten it out to nearly every store. If the likeness is right and he's in this town, someone will see him. It's just a matter of time."

"I'm afraid we don't have time."

Wells's phone rang, and he reached to retrieve it, hoping it was Max returning his numerous calls. Disappointment filled him when he saw the call was coming in from Agent Adams.

"Wells," he answered abruptly.

On the other end Agent Adams began speaking, "Sir, I think we may have something. I've been researching the names that the L.A. analyst, Bobby, gave us as probable aliases Tyler might use. With the focus on Ojai, I decided to narrow in on that city, and one of the aliases recently purchased a home in Ojai. Sir, it happens to be the home that Jack Tyler grew up in." Adams stopped, waiting for further direction.

Wells listened carefully. "Adams, good work. Send me the address."

Hanging up the phone, he turned to the others. "We've got something. Tyler may have returned to his childhood home. Captain, are you familiar with the house?"

Chapter Thirty-Eight

Max couldn't feel her body. She could see everything that was happening, but was unable to move, speak, or feel anything. She watched in horror as Jack carried Cortez away. She lay on the floor and could see a tremendous amount of blood. A cloying coopery smell filled the room. She tried to shake the fog from her brain and out of her limbs, demanding that her body respond to her commands. *Nothing!*

Trying to force her brain to function again, she worked through what had happened. A man had come to the door and let them in; she didn't see his face. A loud crack, and when she turned to see what it was, it was too late. Cortez was on the floor, and *oh God, all that blood!*

He said something to her. *What was it?* Her mind was a clutter like a child's closet. *"Well, hello, Agent Maxine...Wells, is it now?"*

Jack! That son of a bitch hit Cortez with something. Her eyes darted around, and she looked far to her left past the blood. On the floor next to where Cortez had been just a few moments before was a large claw hammer.

Her eyes slammed shut. *Think, Max. Damn it, think!* She felt despair starting to creep in. The lack of mobility and control of even her own body weighed on her. She had imagined this day over and over—literally hundreds of times over the past year and a half—but never had it ended with her on the floor like a shell with eyes. *How could you have been so stupid? Why didn't I call Mark and tell him where we were going?* Her muddled mind was a flurry of questions, ridicule, and accusations. None of which was going to help her or Cortez now.

She heard a noise. A door opening, keys rattling. She wanted to scream out. Maybe Vivian was here and would hear. She could hear shoes walking towards her, heavy shoes—shoes of a man. Then she saw them and pants, then hands reaching for her. Suddenly, she was being dragged up from the floor.

"Agent, how are you feeling? I think your pretty detective is feeling a little bit like Humpty Dumpty right now. Hmmm, I guess we'll see if I can put her back together again. How would you like to watch?"

Jack reached into Max's pockets and retrieved her cell phone. He slid his thumb across the screen while balancing her under his arm and her hand draped around his shoulder. She could see him scrolling through the phone.

"Well, good, you've made no recent phone calls or sent any text messages. This should mean we have some quality time together. It does appear someone has been desperately trying to reach you though. Oh, well they'll just have to keep trying. You know I've been looking forward to officially meeting you. Though your lock of hair is certainly nice, it's not nearly as lovely as you are in person." He stared into her eyes, pure evil piercing her.

Lock of hair? He had taken my hair. That means...Heath!

She tried to move her arm again, but little more than a twitch of her fingers came out. *But they did move. Didn't they?* She wasn't quite sure. Suddenly, she was being dragged again, and then carried.

She watched as Jack powered off her phone and opened a door. She heard keys again, and then it felt like she was falling, and then level again. She was in a room; it was darker and smelled damp. She could hear a TV, cartoons playing, the sound of another door opening and shutting, bright lights, and then, *OH, GOD, NO!*

Cortez was lying on a metal table. She had a huge cut on her head, and her hair had a dark matted stain. She wasn't moving. Fear filled Max—fear of Cortez being dead, fear of not being able to save Heath if he was still alive, fear of dying and never seeing Mark again.

She was slammed down into a chair. Her head rolled back and hit something hard. She knew it should hurt, but it didn't. She watched as Jack used duct tape to attach her arms to the chair.

"Well, Agent, what shall we do now?" Jack asked her with a mild laugh in his tone. "It would appear the lovely detective is in a bit of trouble here, wouldn't you say?"

"I just bet that you've wondered over and over again, what it's like to be me. You know, there are no words that could describe it. You really just have to experience it. So, why don't we do this together, huh? What better way for you to get to know me?"

With that Jack turned away from Max and began removing Cortez's clothes, snipping them away with scissors. He rolled her to the side, causing her head to flop at an odd angle with her body.

Max closed her eyes. She refused to watch this. She would not give Jack the satisfaction of making her witness his madness. Suddenly, he slapped her, but she didn't feel it. Her eyes flew back open, and her head jerked with the movement.

"Agent, you must stay with me. I really do want you to participate. Now don't close your eyes again. Or…well, let's just say, you won't like it."

A few moments later Max could feel tingling in her hands, feet, and head. The effects of the drug were beginning to wear off. She wanted to wiggle her fingers and toes but resisted the temptation, not wanting him to know that the feeling was coming back into her body.

"Now, where were we?" Jack asked as he finished removing Cortez's clothing. Next, he pulled on scrubs and gloves. He maneuvered closer to him a tray that seemed to dangle in space over Cortez's body and lifted up a knife with a curve at the end.

"Do you like this one?"

Shaking his head, he put it back down. "Not my favorite one either, though quite handy for the right circumstances." He lifted another smaller knife that looked like a scalpel to Max's untrained eyes.

"Do you prefer this one?" He stared at her, waiting as if she could actually respond to him.

"Yes, a good choice indeed, one of my favorites. It's a #5 scalpel, quite ideal for this sort of procedure. You are catching on so quickly, Agent."

With that, he took the scalpel and made a long incision down the middle of Cortez's abdomen. Max choked back a scream. Her throat seemed to close off and nearly take her breath away. Her mind wanted to kick and writhe and fight against her bindings as she wanted to lash out at him, protect Cortez, and kill him, but her body did not respond.

All of a sudden there was a loud noise. The door slammed open, and in a flurry of motions, Jack swung around as a woman– *Mindy!–*attacked him and hit him with some sort of a tool. *A wrench she hit him with a wrench.*

Max watched in horror as she saw Jack sprawl to the floor. The scalpel went flying, and the two bodies intertwined in a frenzied wrestling match on the floor. Jack rolled over, holding his head as a gaping wound became visible above his brow.

His arms swirled around the woman. "Hope! What are you doing?" His body crushed down on top of Mindy's small frame.

Mindy was screaming, kicking, and clawing. "I'm not Hope! She's dead. She's been dead for almost two years now!"

Jack clambered to his feet and yanked Mindy off the floor by her arm, then pulled her against his muscular chest.

Max watched as Jack held the woman tightly against his body. He spun her with him, her arms still grabbing at him and her legs swinging in efforts to kick away. Opening the small refrigerator, Jack reached in, but Max couldn't see what he retrieved before he dragged the struggling woman out of the room.

Forcing herself forward, she began trying to rock the chair. Her body was still struggling to follow basic commands, and her efforts were fruitless. She could hear grunts and kicks from the room outside, then a child's scream of, "Mommy!" followed by a few more sounds of an obvious scuffle.

"How could you betray me, Hope? I've always loved you. Everything I've ever done was for you and our family."

Max listened as she heard deep guttural sobbing–the kind only experienced through deep loss or death. As she tried to rock the chair over again by compelling her body to lean forward, she heard what sounded like furniture moving. *What the hell are you doing, Jack?*

Max wanted to scream out to him to distract him away from Mindy and the child, but her voice wouldn't work. Her mouth barely moved at her demand. She assumed the child was Mindy's daughter. It sounded like a girl. *Right?* Could it have been Heath's voice? She felt like she was going crazy, her mind playing tricks on her. Had she heard a child scream at all?

Suddenly, it was eerily quiet. Jack's heavy sobbing stopped, and there was no movement at all. Max listened intently, but all she could hear was her own heavy breathing and a hammering of her pulse in her ears. Her eyes drifted momentarily to the table where Cortez lay. She tried to see a rise and fall of breath. Uncertain, she took her eyes away. She was not able to accept the amount of blood that had pooled around her friend's body. *Come on, Cortez. Stay with me*, she silently pleaded. She leaned forward again, fueled by the desire to get Cortez out alive. *I'm going to kill that son of a bitch and get you out of here!*

Chapter Thirty-Nine

A police officer approached and spoke quietly with Captain Kennard as Wells stood impatiently waiting for an answer to his question.

Kennard turned to Wells. "Yes, I'm familiar with the Tyler home." Before Wells could say anything else Kennard continued, "We also have a hit on the photo we're circulating. A clerk at the Radio Shack said the man in the photo bought a bunch of monitoring equipment for his home. My officer interviewed him. Kid was very specific, said he remembered it well because it was his biggest sale all month."

"We need to get to the Tyler home immediately. Can your officers assist?" Wells asked.

"Certainly, Agent, but sir, there's more." Kennard continued not waiting for the go ahead, "My officer showed a picture of Rebecca Tillman to the clerk, and he said she was in the store right behind Tyler, bought a package of batteries."

"We need to go. Captain, please have your team meet outside in five minutes." Wells was already turning to his team to give the orders.

Outside the air was cool and night had fully settled in now. Wells gave the instruction on how they would approach the Tyler home. He and Agent Jenkins would approach from the front. Captain Kennard and two officers would cover the other exits. They would go in with no sirens and lights out. There was no way to predict what Tyler would do if he knew the police were surrounding the home.

With the instructions clear, everyone loaded into the police cruisers and headed towards Jack Tyler's boyhood home. Wells, usually calm and cool, could feel his heart racing. He feared his wife and son were both dead or even possibly would never be found. He squeezed his eyes closed, preparing for what they would find when they arrived at Jack Tyler's house.

The police cars lined the street rather than pulling into the drive. Wells pointed towards the van that sat on the street and asked Kennard to radio it in to see who it was registered to. Within moments they had the answer; it was the same alias that had bought the home. Tyler's vehicle was sitting on the street.

They began making their approach. The police cruiser that Cortez had checked out of the motor pool that morning was sitting in front of the house, driving Wells's heart to race even faster. He gave the hand signal for the teams to move around to the back of the house. He hesitated just long enough to give everyone time to get into position before approaching the front of the house with Agent Jenkins behind him.

At the front door Wells noticed the intercom and the camera that would allow anyone inside to see who was at the door. He reached out and turned the knob. To his surprise the door opened. Using a flashlight, he scanned the area in front of him and saw a large pool of blood on the floor just inside. A hammer lay just off to the side.

Signaling to Jenkins, they moved forward and silently cleared the room they were in. They continued forward by passing through a dining area and into a kitchen. A back door was visible. Wells clicked open the door to allow Captain Kennard and his officers in. He motioned towards the front of the house to the stairs that led to the second floor.

Wells pointed to another door and swung it open. It led to the garage. They cleared this room as well while two more officers filed into the home. They worked room by room. Just as Wells was beginning to think Tyler had taken Max and Cortez somewhere else, the beam of his light flashed over a door that seemed to have something mounted on it. Moving forward with his Glock pointed and ready, he saw the door had a mount for a bar to secure it closed.

The bar was leaning next to the door against the wall. Motioning again to Agent Jenkins, they stood on opposite sides of the door as Wells pulled it open. His light flashed onto a set of steps that descended into a dimly lit room below.

Taking the first step, Wells began the descent into the basement, cautiously expecting to be attacked from below. Near the bottom step, he saw Max lying on the floor with a shiny object in her hand. Resisting the desire to race towards her, he knew he needed to secure Tyler before he could provide her any assistance.

Scanning the rest of the room, he saw a small kitchen table at the back. He felt himself gag as he saw the macabre picture of what seemed the perfect family seated for dinner, except for the body of a white haired elderly woman showing obvious signs of rigor and the way the small girl's head sat oddly to one side—a younger version of the woman sitting next to her with her mouth agape. And the way the small boy, *his boy,* sat slumped forward with his arms dangling at his sides.

For a moment he felt like he was a boy all over again with that familiar feeling of failure overwhelming him. He had failed Tommy all those years ago, and now he had failed Heath. He stood frozen in the spot, and from somewhere in the room he heard Agent Jenkins calling for medical support. At the head of the table sat Jack Tyler. His head cocked sideways, and his eyes plumped open. A strange grimace splayed over his face as if he were laughing.

Wells pushed forward, approaching the strange dinner party. He went first to Tyler, his training forcing him to ignore his desire to go to his son. With his Glock trained on the source of their year-long manhunt, he placed his fingers on the man's neck. He felt nothing. "He's dead," he called out to the others that were now filling the room.

Fear covered him as he turned to Heath and reached forward to feel for a pulse. His knees almost buckled as he felt a beat. Fearing he imagined the *thump...thump,* he kept two fingers against the child's neck. After being certain he turned to Jenkins. "He's alive. We need medics right now!"

Kennard appeared from nowhere and was already confirming that the other child was alive as Wells turned to Mindy Prescott. "The kids and mother are alive!"

Wells finally turned to Max and found an officer already talking to her. Her eyes were open, and the officer was trying to remove a blood-covered scalpel from her hand.

As he kneeled down to Max she whispered, "Cortez."

***

Moments later the entire room was filled with light, as medical personnel began working on each person. Max was lifted onto a gurney, and as she was taken from the room her eyes found the grotesque picture at the dining room table. Jack Tyler's gaze seemed to be taunting her. She could hear in her head the words he had once said to her, *"You and I are so much alike."*

Chapter Forty

Max and Heath had been rushed off to the hospital. Both were confirmed to be in stable condition, so Mark was torn between going with them since Rebecca Tillman was still missing.

The team continued to search every inch of the home and room by room the reports came back as cleared. Wells walked outside and stood in the dark night and listened to the rustle of the trees. His instincts told him that the wooded area behind the house held many answers. As he was waiting on the cadaver dogs to arrive and help search the property Captain Kennard approached, "Agent Wells, we have another problem."

Mark turned to face Kennard. "What is it?" A grave look fell over his face.

"Two more people are missing. A local caregiver and his neighbor both have not been seen or heard from in two days."

"Do we have reason to believe it's connected?"

Kennard nodded. "Apparently the caregiver, a man named James "Jimmy" Noland," Kennard said looking at a small notepad, "was Vivian's caregiver for nearly six months."

"When will the dogs be here?" Mark asked.

"Should be here within five minutes," Kennard answered.

Headlights lit the trees and flashed across the house before stopping in the driveway amidst all the other police and medical vehicles. The driver exited the car followed by a passenger, both dressed in full police gear. The two moved to the back of the vehicle, and the driver opened the hatch to allow two large German Sheppard dogs out.

Wells and the team surrounded the handlers, and within minutes Wells split the officers and agents into teams. The back of the property was the obvious area to search first, so after spreading out the two assigned teams began their search.

Flashlights waved in the dark, and the underbrush crunched beneath the feet of the officers. Mark was working with the team on the west side of the property, and about half way into the thicket the dog began to report, barking wildly at the base of a tree.

A forensics team was standing by for recovery efforts if there were to be any and immediately approached the barking dog.

After carefully securing the area around the tree and setting up flood lights, the crime scene analyst took a number of photos before beginning the removal of the loose soil that showed signs of having been recently disturbed.

The removal of the soil didn't take long before a small animal was lifted from the makeshift grave. Laying the animal out on a sheet of plastic, it was obvious the creature had been killed recently. A close assessment disclosed that it was a rabbit and that it had been essentially gutted. Its internal organs hung through the hole in its abdomen.

The analyst spoke first, "Looks like it was slit open with a sharp implement. No jagged edges. Precision."

Mark turned back to the handler. "Keep looking." He stood there for a moment staring at the mess on the plastic sheet and wondering why Tyler would have resorted to killing animals again.

Agent Jenkins spoke, "It doesn't make sense, does it?"

"No, it doesn't, unless he thought he could temporarily temper his urges."

Agent Jenkins nodded, her dark skin accented in the flood lights.

The two agents turned back into the dark thicket to follow the rest of the team that had resumed the search. A few moments later Mark could hear water trickling and realized there must be a stream or creek just ahead.

The dog began to report again, and then another dog baying could be heard off to the east and back closer to the house. "Agent, please go to the other team and radio me with what they've got. I'll stay here."

Two hours later there were flood lights illuminating two more areas on the property. Four bodies had been recovered near the creek–three males and a female. It would take some time for positive identification, but Wells assumed that Rebecca Tillman and the two local men would be identified. The additional man was unknown.

Under the child's playhouse were two more bodies. It was the same playhouse Max and Cortez had reported finding animal bones and the magazines that had been instrumental in tracking Jack Tyler to Tulsa, Oklahoma over a year earlier.

This grisly discovery was the obvious first attempt Tyler had made at restoring his family, and in actuality they were several bodies combined. He had murdered people, and using the body parts, put together replications of his wife and daughter. The process he had used to preserve the bodies had obviously failed, and it was then that he abducted Mindy and Allie to start the process all over again with the closest representation of his wife and daughter he could find.

Mark stood with the other agents around him as they watched the careful recovery of the bodies. By morning the team was tearing down flood lights and bodies had been moved to the morgue for autopsies and identification.

Two days later fingerprints confirmed the female to be Rebecca Tillman and two of the men as James "Jimmy" Noland, Vivian's caregiver, and Ronald Camp, Jimmy's neighbor. Based on the preliminary time of death it appeared they had been killed within hours of each other. The other body was identified as a missing person from Ventura, a jogger that had gone missing from the beach weeks earlier.

Lots of forensic evidence was gathered, including a small bag containing glass fragments from Tyler's own trash. Mark was certain these glass fragments would match the glass from Rebecca Tillman's window. There was no disputing Tyler's skill at being able to elude police and cover up his crimes.

Mark couldn't find any solace in Tyler's death because he knew there were many more killers out there working right now who were just as clever as Tyler. In fact, he already knew there was a case that was going to be handed to him and the team almost immediately upon return to Virginia.

Chapter Forty-One

It had been two weeks since Lorraine Cortez's funeral. Max was released from the hospital the day after they had entered Jack Tyler's home. She'd gone to see Cortez's mother to express her sincere condolences. She left there feeling like she had handed over an empty bag of words. Nothing could bring Lorraine back to her mother, and nothing she could say could change that fact.

Most days she just felt guilty for keeping Cortez involved. She had left to go to the FBI. She could have left Cortez out of the entire thing, but she had continued to involve her, sharing her theories and asking for assistance.

Mark had filled her in on the discoveries out at the Tyler house. He'd brought her the files to read, shared the photos with her knowing full well she wouldn't rest until she could understand all of the events that had taken place while she was in the hospital. Her eyes had carefully studied every photo, each numbered in the order in which they had been discovered.

Mark continued to tell her that Lorraine wouldn't have had it any other way. The final report indicated that the continued focus and professional tracking had left Jack Tyler nowhere else to run, and in the end Max and Cortez together had helped drive Jack Tyler to commit suicide by giving himself a very lethal dose of anesthesia.

Max took pleasure in knowing Tyler's death would save the government a ton of money by not keeping a madman on death row, eliminating the endless appeals that no doubt died with him. But she felt like in the end he had won.

He had prevented her from getting into his head, asking all of the questions she'd wanted to ask, gaining the answers she desperately needed. He had stopped her from the pleasure of taking his life, killing him and having the satisfaction of knowing that she'd prevented him from killing any more innocent people. Taking his own life had stolen from her the ending she'd pictured so many times and stolen her friend… her *best* friend.

Though Tyler had administered a potentially lethal dose of Rohypnol, Mindy and Allie had been discovered soon enough, and the doctors had been able to reverse the intended effects. They were released after spending a couple of days in the hospital and had returned to Arizona to put their lives back together. Max had met with Mindy once and learned that Allie still hadn't spoken since their rescue. In the hospital Mindy had been reunited with her husband and daughter, and Mindy and Paul were beginning therapy to help Allie overcome the trauma from the time spent in that basement.

The autopsy on Vivian indicated that she had been dead for over a week. It turned out that she was actually Jack's biological mother, Janice *Vivian* Tyler. Jack's father apparently knew his wife wasn't capable of managing the house, and with Jack's older sister Suzanne dead, his father had left the real estate to Jack. The elder Tyler must have assumed Jack would care for the home and his aging mother, but instead Jack had left his mother and the home behind. She had remained in the home and remarried shortly after Jack had moved away. Vivian married a man named Donald Wilson soon after the senior Tyler died, and Vivian's new husband later purchased the house from Jack.

Max felt nothing but anger at the thought that she had missed the important detail of Vivian's name. They'd never run a background check or any other research on Vivian or Jack's parents, and as a result never made the connection that Vivian was the very same Janice Tyler the old woman had so openly spoken of during their visit with her over a year earlier. Unfortunately, less than five years later Vivian's new husband passed away, once again leaving Vivian alone to care for the home on her own.

When Max and Cortez had first gone to visit Vivian while trying to find Jack, the pleasant old woman who Max now knew was suffering from dementia had entered a place in her life where the illness had changed her. It had changed her for the better, and there was nothing suspicious in her story or in her demeanor that raised concern, but even still Max could take no comfort in the thought that the connection could have changed the course of the investigation and Cortez would be alive today.

Further research into Vivian's background uncovered a history of schizophrenia and long periods of her being on and off of medication. They had come to the conclusion that when off of the medication she would perform horrible acts on little Jack Tyler, but in her elder years she was a kind woman who politely offered even unexpected guests lemonade and openly shared stories of other's transgressions, seemingly unaware she was speaking about herself and her own family.

The theory in the FBI's official report indicated that Jack was unable to cope properly with the abuse he had endured at his mother's hand as a child, had fragmented, and had begun killing animals at a small age. With Hope's love and guidance he had been able to keep it together, but after her death he had fragmented again and had fallen into a murderous abyss.

Why he returned to the home was anyone's guess, but they assumed like so many abused children, he seemed to forgive Vivian for the things she had done to him. He was a boy that was unable to accept that his own mother could hurt him the way she had for all those years.

Heath surprisingly seemed to be doing pretty well. He also had been released from the hospital after spending just a couple of days. He'd asked about the little dog that had been found lying next to Jack Tyler's feet. It was taken to animal services and after discussions with Rebecca Tillman's family, who had admitted they did not want the animal, Mark had requested to adopt the little dog and surprised Heath when he'd gotten out of the hospital. Max hoped it would help the boy's recovery.

And after returning home, they immediately got him into therapy. Max knew it was going to take time to get him to understand all the things that had happened to him. They knew Tyler had told him lies about being his real father, what his name was, so many lies, and Max worried about him not knowing who to trust.

The situation brought her and Mark even closer together. He had obviously been able to put away some of the childhood demons that had plagued him his whole life. Mark had been able to save Heath unlike his brother Tommy, and there was a noticeable calm over him. The close reality that Max could have died in that basement along with Cortez drove an even richer appreciation for the time they had together and the future they would share.

They were committed to giving Heath the love and support he would need. She just hoped in time he would be okay and wondered what the long term effects would be of those days in the basement with Jack Tyler.

Max sat on their back porch sipping coffee in the morning sun while Scruffy laid quietly at her feet. She felt grateful that she would return to work tomorrow. The idleness of being at home seemed to feed the guilty feelings that would swell over her like the tide on a jetty during a hurricane. Her mind replayed those final hours over and over.

Going back to see Vivian had been her idea. Cortez hadn't seen the point in it. Yet it was there that the yearlong hunt for Jack Tyler had ended, and there where Cortez would sustain injuries too severe to recover.

A single tear slid from her eye as she recalled Mark telling her that as Lorraine took her final breath in the ambulance, she whispered to the medic a final request to, "Tell Max we got him."

Max brushed away the tear. The sun shined on her auburn waves as her finger twisted at the strands of hair that remained a couple of inches shorter than the rest, and a small smile crossed her lips as she whispered into the wind, "Yes we did."

Epilogue

Max watched Heath playing under the trees towards the back of the yard. He seemed good as he bounced around in between the sunshine and shade. It was really amazing how resilient he was.

The little boy certainly had been through more than any person, much less a child, should ever have to endure. She felt grateful and a sense of pride at his strength.

A sudden eerie feeling came over her as she watched him crouch down and stare in fascination at a small squirrel. There was something strange in his ability to stay so incredibly still, a focus not natural to a boy his age. He began to creep towards the small animal as if ready to pounce. When he got too close, the snap of a twig scared the squirrel, and it scampered away. Its tail twitched as it leapt onto the tree and scurried up to a limb safely out of the boy's grasp.

Heath remained crouched down. His head turned to peer up into the tree while he continued to watch the animal for several more seconds. The squirrel clicked at him in a teasing manner.

Heath turned around and saw Max watching him. Did she imagine it, or was there something different, something dark in his eyes? He gave her a crooked little grin and wiggled his chubby little fingers at her. Her mind flashed to a picture from the files. Photo # 1 showed a dead rabbit lying on a sheet of plastic with a gaping hole down its center and its internal organs hanging out. A chill ran down her spine.

The End

About the Author

Valerie Knupp lives on seven acres outside the Tulsa area near Inola, Oklahoma. She loves to travel and is an avid reader of anything with a grisly plot. When not doing one of these things, she enjoys spending time around the house with her partner and two adopted children. This is her 3rd book in the Jack Tyler Series.

If you find any errors while taking any Jack Tyler journey, want to provide feedback and comments or just want to stay up to date on what the author is working on please visit:

www.thrillersbyknupp.com

Acknowledgements

Hollie Zunun, my editor, you are the very best!!! Without you I am not sure I would have ever gotten all three books on paper. Your input has been invaluable!!!

Shout out to Mom for giving me honest feedback throughout each of the Jack Tyler stories.

My "work world" colleague Patrick Plunkett for the shameless plugs he throws out for my writing efforts every chance he gets.

Chris Snidow for the final touches after Hollie and I have exhausted every chance to get it right! Your keen eye is very appreciated!

My family, I love you!

www.ingramcontent.com/pod-product-compliance
Lightning Source LLC
Chambersburg PA
CBHW061545170626
46811CB00001B/94